Praise for

THE KILLINGS OF STAN

"**Unexpectedly elegant**. It's **a masterful sto**
humor and slightly intimidating with its sha
lends **poignant** immediacy to Ketchel's life and persona, elevating his scrappy determination to near-mythic proportions without sacrificing the passionate human being at the center of the story. . . . This book would be hard for anyone to put down. Its playful sensuousness and stoic determination are **impossible to resist**."

—*Rocky Mountain News* (A Favorite Book of the Year Selection)

"Expansive. . . . This **wonderfully written adventure** is part biography, part American picaresque novel, part crime story—episodic but **compelling, humorous, exciting**, and ultimately tragic."

—Otto Penzler, *New York Sun*

"*The Killings of Stanley Ketchel* presents us with an America at its most raw. . . . **A daring book** where deft writing brings an era to full-blooded life. . . . **Unforgettable.**"

—*Edmonton Journal*

"**James Carlos Blake is a master** at using history to tell a fictional tale, and he's at it again with *The Killings of Stanley Ketchel.*"

—*Denver Post*

"**Packs a literary wallop** . . . and brims with violence, sex, and humor."

—*Tucson Citizen*

"The novel **resurrects Stanley Ketchel**, maybe as good a boxer pound for pound as any. . . . Blake captures Ketchel's life . . . in prose so graceful readers may forget it packs the strength of a master. . . . ***Killings* moves with grace, hits with power**."

—*Salt Lake City Tribune* (A Best Western Book of the Year Selection)

"Not only the story of a **remarkable** life but also a paean to the vitality—and brutality—of turn-of-the-century America. [*The Killings of Stanley Ketchel*] **resonates long after the last page is turned**."

—*Fort Worth Star-Telegram*

JUN -- 2014

"**Terrific.** . . . Reflects the country as it was then: flawed and brutal but dazzling with possibilities for anyone brave enough to reach for their dreams."

—*Arizona Republic*

"**Blake's prose is as finely chiseled as sculpture.** . . . [A] master of the taut and tough tale of amoral outsiders. . . . An earthy, **often funny** novel."

—*Montana Standard*

"**A fine work** of historical fiction. . . . James Carlos Blake's **deftly crafted** new novel . . . paces the narrative adroitly . . . and it's suitably delivered in his characteristically muscular style."

—*Tucson Weekly*

"Ketchel fits the mold of a James Carlos Blake protagonist. He lives on the edge. He is fearless, violent, attractive to women, [and] imbued with the outlaw spirit. . . . Mr. Blake's prose is deft and hard-boiled, [and] the book **packs a wallop**."

—*Dallas Morning News*

"**[*Ketchel*] comes out slugging.** . . . A vivid mix of history, myth and fantasy; its language consists of **hard-boiled** dialogue, period diction and florid description. . . . Readers who like their action raw and history bloody should find **plenty to cheer** in *The Killings of Stanley Ketchel.*"

—*Columbus Dispatch*

"Hard-bitten, yet surprisingly **moving.**"

—*Kirkus Reviews*

"**Action-packed.** . . . **A fascinating tale.**"

—*Publishers Weekly*

About the Author

The Killings of Stanley Ketchel is JAMES CARLOS BLAKE's ninth novel and tenth book of fiction. Among his many literary honors are the Los Angeles Times Book Prize, the Southwest Book Award, the Quarterly West Novella Prize, and the Chautauqua South Book Award. He lives in Arizona.

OTHER WORKS BY JAMES CARLOS BLAKE

Handsome Harry

Under the Skin

A World of Thieves

Wildwood Boys

Borderlands

Red Grass River

In the Rogue Blood

The Friends of Pancho Villa

The Pistoleer

JAMES CARLOS BLAKE

The Killings of STANLEY KETCHEL

HARPER PERENNIAL

NEW YORK • LONDON • TORONTO • SYDNEY

WILLIAMSBURG REGIONAL LIBRARY
7770 CROAKER ROAD
WILLIAMSBURG, VA 23188

FOR

the Sisters of the Holy Ghost
at the old Saint Joseph's Academy
in Brownsville, Texas,
who taught me the language.

HARPER PERENNIAL

This book is a work of fiction. References real people, events, establishments, organizations, or locales are intended only to provide a sense of authenticity, and are used fictitiously. All other characters, and all incidents and dialogue, are drawn from the author's imagination and are not to be construed as real.

A hardcover edition of this book was published in 2005 by William Morrow, an imprint of HarperCollins Publishers.

THE KILLINGS OF STANLEY KETCHEL. Copyright © 2005 by James Carlos Blake. All rights reserved. Printed in the United States of America. No part of this book may be used or reproduced in any manner whatsoever without written permission except in the case of brief quotations embodied in critical articles and reviews. For information address HarperCollins Publishers, 10 East 53rd Street, New York, NY 10022.

HarperCollins books may be purchased for educational, business, or sales promotional use. For information please write: Special Markets Department, HarperCollins Publishers, 10 East 53rd Street, New York, NY 10022.

First Harper Perennial edition published 2006.

Designed by Chris Welch

The Library of Congress has catalogued the hardcover edition as follows:

Blake, James Carlos.
The killings of Stanley Ketchel : a novel / James Carlos Blake.—1st ed.
p. cm.
ISBN 0-06-055436-3 (alk. paper)
1. Boxers (Sports)—Fiction. 2. Tramps—Fiction. I. Title.

PS3552.L3483K55 2005
813'.54—dc22

2004059205

ISBN-10: 0-06-055437-1 (pbk.)
ISBN-13: 978-0-06-055437-8 (pbk.)

13 14 15 ❖/RRD 10 9 8 7

And the wild regrets, and the bloody sweats,
None knew so well as I:
For he who lives more lives than one
More deaths than one must die.

—Oscar Wilde, *The Ballad of Reading Gaol*

I can entertain the proposition that life is a metaphor for boxing—for one of those bouts that go on and on, round following round, jabs, missed punches, clinches, nothing determined, again the bell and again and you and your opponent so evenly matched it's impossible not to see that your opponent *is* you. . . .

—Joyce Carol Oates, *On Boxing*

The Golden Smile

Ketchel's manager, Willus Britt, lays it out plain and simple. "We put in the contract that if there's no knockout the fight's a draw. All Stevie and Jack have to do is make it look good from start to finish. The white hope middleweight against the Negro heavyweight. Like David and Goliath, only better. And only it's a draw. I'm telling you, the whole country'll go crazy. They'll be screaming for a rematch. And that's when we make a *real* killing."

Across the table, George Little, who manages Johnson, smiles and nods.

It is late summer of 1909. They are in a secluded booth next to a window in a San Francisco hilltop restaurant. The fog banking in from the bay is blue in the city's early evening light. Even from this vantage it is difficult to believe that a little more than three years ago the town had been charred rubble.

"Not that we won't do plenty good on this one," Britt says. "Hell, we'll pack Sunny Jim's to the top rows. *Plus*, the odds'll be so heavy on Jack, we'll rake in even more with side bets on the draw."

"We'd have to spread them bets around so's not to raise suspicion," George Little says.

It's the remark of a man who's decided he's in, and Britt smiles. "Naturally. We'll use fronts to lay the bets."

George Little nods.

Britt leans farther over the table toward him. "Christ almighty, man, they'll pour in for the rematch like the Johnstown flood. We'll charge even more for tickets and *still* need a place double the size of Sunny Jim's to hold them all. I'm telling you, we'll need a goddamn freight train to carry off the gate money."

He sits back and fingers his red bow tie to ensure its proper lay. A spare man whose perpetual half-smile and sleepy aspect can fool people into thinking he lacks astuteness.

George Little leans back too, smiling small, eyes narrow.

Beside him Jack Johnson grins. His gold teeth gleam in the lamp glow and his shaven head shines like polished ebony. Arthur John Johnson is thirty-one years old and the heavyweight boxing champion of the world. At 210 pounds and just shy of six feet two, he is by far the largest man at the table. The stickpin of his cravat is also of gold, the fob chain looping from his vest pocket, the head of his walking stick. He wears a diamond on his pinky. His suit is custom-tailored. His shoes are of crocodile hide.

Sitting next to Britt, Ketchel smiles too, and thinks how grand it would feel to knock out those gold teeth.

On Johnson's other side is a slender strawberry blonde with cool green eyes, her cheeks and nose powdered with freckles fine as cinnamon. She'd been introduced as Sheila. Although Ketchel is appalled that a white woman would keep company with a Negro, especially a woman as pretty as this one, and especially in public, he affects indifference. Yet he is intensely aware of her, of the push of her breasts against her shirtwaist. He would bet they were freckled too.

Johnson catches Ketchel's appraising glance at her. "She a pulchritudious eyeful, ain't she, Mr. Stanley? Lady from Australia. Say something in Australian for the man, honey." He has a fondness for polysyllabic words, especially of his own concoction, and is prone to the malaprop.

"We speak English in Australia, Jack, as you bloody well know."

"Spake," Johnson says. "Aus-*try*-lya. Bl*ooo*dy well. Man, I loves that lingo."

She rolls her eyes and looks out the window at the encroaching fog. Johnson puts his hand under the table and she smiles and gives him a sidelong glance.

"What say we stick to business, Jack?" George Little says. He is clearly uncomfortable with the woman's presence, has repeatedly admonished Johnson to be more discreet about the white ones.

Ketchel smiles to mask his indignation. The dinge pawing her in a public place with three white men looking on and the bitch barely shows a blush.

"So?" Britt says. "We got a deal?"

George Little turns to Johnson. "What say, Jack?"

Everybody knows what his answer will be. His share of the purse when he won the title was a pittance, and he hasn't been able to get a big-money fight in the ten months since. He needs the cash. He's a high-roller. He likes the night life, flashy clothes, the horses, the dice. Bold white women. A fight with Ketchel means a payday too big to turn down.

"I say fine," Johnson says. "Make me feel kinda lowdown to mix it up with a little fella, even if it ain't for real, but sometimes you got to take what you can get."

"Gosh, Jack, that's sad," Ketchel says. He'll be damned if he'll let the coon nettle him with that "little fella" crack. He is the world middleweight champ, and at five feet nine inches and 160 pounds is larger than the average man of his day. In more than fifty official fights he has knocked out nearly all of his opponents, more than a dozen of whom outweighed him by at least twenty pounds.

"Then again, everybody say you the little man with the big punch," Johnson says. "Middleweight who hits like a heavy, I hear tell."

"I hear tell you got a pretty good punch yourself, Jack."

"What you gonna scale for me, Mr. Stanley, one sixty-five, one-seventy?"

Ketchel shrugs.

"Tommy Burns was one-seventy and I got to tell you, I been hit harder by some women."

The redhead snickers. Johnson winks at her.

"Maybe you should fight smaller women," Ketchel says.

Johnson laughs and slaps the table. "Ooo-*eee*, little man got him a counterpunch. You a mirthaful man, Mr. Stanley."

"What's it matter what he weighs?" Britt says. "It's gonna be a draw."

"That's right, makes no difference *this* time," George Little says cheerfully. "Now, come the *re*-match, well . . ."

"We'll worry about that when the time comes," Britt says.

"*You'll* worry about it," George Little says. "Not me. Not Jack. Won't play out like no David and Goliath."

"The thing is," Johnson says to Ketchel, "Tommy Burns had no business being heavyweight champeen. He hardly bigger than you. He no more a heavyweight than I'm the pope a England."

"The thing is," Ketchel says, "I ain't Tommy Burns."

"Well now, you right about that," Johnson says. "You beseeked *me*. I had to chase that man all over the world for two years before he quit the dodge."

Ketchel knows all about it. Everybody does. Most white boxers of the time refused to fight Negroes on the widely understood ground that it was demeaning, but there had been growing suspicion that Tommy Burns's true reason for avoiding the much larger Johnson was fear. An indignant Burns had finally said he'd stoop to defend his title against the so-called "Galveston Giant" anytime the dinge agreed to let him have 85 percent of the purse. He was stunned when Johnson accepted the terms.

They fought in Sydney, Australia, on the day after Christmas, and the outcome was apparent from the opening round. Both men had reputations for taunting their opponents during a match, but after the first minute or so of the fight Burns had little to say. Johnson talked constantly and made jokes and hit Burns at will, provoking the white crowd to a yowling frenzy. He'd tell Burns to watch out for the jab and then snap his head back with it. He'd warn him to guard his flanks and then stagger him into the ropes with a hook to the ribs. Johnson cakewalked to his corner at the end of every round. His cornermen implored him to quit the shuck before somebody shot him. He basked in the crowd's execrations. He could have made shorter work of Burns but was enjoying himself too much. After each knockdown he'd lean on the ropes like a loitering thug, laughing as Burns struggled to his feet and the throng urged him up, pleaded with him to kill the big nigger, kill him. So it went, Johnson larking and japing, humiliating Burns, ruining him by slow degree. By the fourteenth round Burns's ears looked like small bunches of grapes and his eyes were swollen to slits. He was lurching almost blindly, clutching at Johnson like a drunken lover. At which point a squadron of police swarmed into the ring and put an end to the proceedings. Both parties had been warned during contract negotiations that the police would stop the fight the moment it seemed there might be serious injury to either boxer, and the fighters had agreed that in such an event the referee would decide the winner. The referee was Hugh McIntosh, promoter of the bout. It broke his heart to raise the Negro's hand, but only with a baseball bat could Johnson have beaten Burns more obviously. The spectators grasped a straw of solace by telling each other that Tommy had by God been game to the end and at least not been knocked out.

Among the reporters present at that match was the celebrated author Jack London, who remonstrated in print with undefeated champ James Jeffries to come out of retirement "and remove the golden smile from Johnson's face." Now Jeffries is reported to be in serious training, laboriously shedding the excess weight he's gained in more than five years since relinquishing the title. Newspapers across the republic hail him as the Great White Hope. Few whites would complain, however, if Stanley Ketchel should trump Jeffries and take Johnson down first. Indeed, Ketchel being the smaller man, his victory over the Negro would be all the sweeter.

"So we're agreed," Britt says. "The sixteenth of October at Sunny Jim Coffroth's arena in Colma. Twenty rounds. We split the gate down the middle and use fronts to lay our bets on the draw. Like the man said, boys, we're going to do jim-dandy."

"Then we sign for the rematch," says George Little, "and we make a *real* killing."

"You said it," Britt says.

"No, *you* did," George Little says. "We'll need a damn freight train!"

They close the deal with handshakes all around. Ketchel's grip feels to Johnson like a large rock, Johnson's to Ketchel like something on a leash.

"Let's us absquatulate on back to the hotel, my cherry amoor," Johnson says to the redhead. "Papa Jack got him a bad itch needs scratching."

She doesn't blush at that, either. Ketchel wants to slap her.

With his derby cocked over one eye and his gold teeth glinting, the redhead on his arm and George Little trailing behind, Jack Johnson twirls his walking stick and makes his easy way to the front door, turning every head in the room as he goes.

Ketchel watches them leave. "I can take him, Willie."

"Christ, kid, that's what I been telling *you*. Come the rematch, you'll prove it to the whole damn world."

"I can't wait," Ketchel says.

Circumstance and Mean Luck

His mother was Julia Oblinski, born of Polish immigrants, an intelligent and variously talented woman with a gift for the piano and a special fondness for Chopin. But circumstance and mean luck wed her to Thomas Kaicel at the age of fifteen.

Kaicel was an immigrant Russian of Polish ancestry, a large man of rough ways and rash temper. Dark rumor clung to him like an alien odor. It was said he had killed a man in Russia and fled to London and from there shipped to America. He had lived for a time in New York and toiled as a street cleaner, gravedigger, ferryman. He'd been with a red labor union, they said, had battled in the streets of Pittsburgh and Cleveland, had acquired the scar over his eye in Chicago. It was anyone's guess why he moved to western Michigan or how he had come by the means to buy a dairy farm.

Whatever the case, he knew about milk cows, and the dairy turned steady if not bountiful profits. Over time he gained a passing acquaintance with some of his neighbors, but he was not one for socializing. He lived quietly and minded his business, kept his own counsel and the nightly company of whiskey.

He'd been in the region a year when one Saturday in town he ran into Fredrick Oblinski, whose wagon he had once helped to extricate from a mudhole, and was introduced to his wife and daughter. It was early winter. Their breath formed plumes in the air. Kaicel had for some time been in want of a wife, and the moment he set eyes on young Julia he determined that she was the one.

Two weeks later he asked for her hand. In that rural past, farm girls married early and brides of fifteen were no rarity. Nor was it of great social import that Kaicel was the girl's senior by at least twenty years, his age but one more thing about him no one knew for certain. Julia's parents were aware of the frightful rumors that attached to Thomas Kaicel, yet they respected him as a hardworking man of property and were in favor of the marriage. When the girl declined his proposal with the explanation that she thought herself too young to become a mother, Kaicel dismissed her objection as irrelevant and appealed to the parents to set her straight. The Oblinskis sympathized with him, but they had been in America long enough to have assumed much of its social attitude. If their daughter did not want to marry right away, well, give her a little time, they told him, she was barely more than a child but she was smart and practical, keep wooing her, she'd come around. The mother whispered that the girl was not one to admit it but was probably just fearful of the marriage bed.

What could he do but as they advised? He called on her each of the next three Saturday afternoons, hat in hand, black beard trimmed and hair heavy with pomade, footwear scraped of cow dung. His forefinger tugged at the unfamiliar clinch of necktie. They sat in the parlor over a tray of tea and cookies set out by the mother and made small talk punctuated by periods of silence during which the girl seemed well at ease while he sweat prodigiously in the heat of the fire and badly craved a drink. Young Julia was polite, if somewhat distant. She owned a poise beyond her years that slightly unnerved him. Nevertheless, every visit made him more determined in his suit.

For her part, his calls were an ordeal to be endured in the name of etiquette. He did not speak English very well and never would, and it required effort to hide her amusement at his accent and maladroit diction, which in truth afforded the only fun she found in his company. His most recent visit had so bored her that she offered to entertain him at the piano in order to entertain herself. She asked what he would like to hear but did not know the Russian folk tunes he named, so she performed bits of Beethoven, Bach, Mozart, asking with each segue if he knew the music. He shook his head repeatedly, feeling his ignorance hoisting into display like a red banner. Then she began the "Marche Funèbre" and he said "Yes, I know!" She asked him to name it, or its composer, and his jubilation fell like a swatted bee. Her smile was mocking and she left off the march for a polonaise. He sensed her perception of him as an uncultured peasant and felt an angry ache in his chest. When he got home that night he uncorked a new bottle and next morning awoke on the floor.

OVER THE NEXT days he grew fretful that Julia Oblinski would never deign to marry him, and the looming doubt was unbearable. Late one evening, sitting before an untouched bowl of congealing stew and a nearly depleted bottle, he determined to resolve the issue without further delay. He drained his glass and snatched up his hat and coat and went out to saddle his horse. He rehearsed with the animal his apology to the Oblinskis for calling at this hour, but he was certain they would understand his need of a definite answer. He rode into a night of cold wind and rushing clouds. The snowless ground was dappled under the radiance of a gibbous moon. But it was even later than he thought, and when he came in view of the house not a window showed lamplight. He reined up under the trees beside the front gate and reconsidered. The wind had grown stronger, jostling the heavy shadows of the pines. He had sobered appreciably.

Fool, he thought. I am a damned fool.

He was about to rein the horse around when the moon came clear of the clouds and he saw her creep out of her second-floor window. She moved in a crouch to the end of the eave, and as she shinned down the drainpipe the wind raised her skirt and he glimpsed long pale legs. She dropped the last few feet to the ground and hurried away into the darkness, bearing for the vague shape of the barn.

He dismounted and hitched the horse and set out after her, a hand clamped to his hat against the wind. Not until he was almost to the barn did he see the dim glow at the side window. He sidled up to it and peeked within. The animals were placid in their stalls in the light of a lantern hung on a post at the rear of the barn, where she and a burly young man stood embraced and kissing. The young man's hand was under her shirt. She pushed off his hat and Kaicel saw that the boy was perhaps sixteen or seventeen years old. He shed his jacket and said something and she laughed, though Kaicel could not hear them. They kissed again and unbuttoned each other's shirts and lowered out of Kaicel's sight behind the partition of an empty stall.

He found the boy's horse tethered behind the barn. The saddle scabbard held a Winchester carbine. He slid the rifle out and levered the magazine empty of cartridges, then put the weapon back in its sheath. Then returned to the door and opened it just wide enough to slip inside, trying to be noiseless. But an inrush of wind blew straw the length of the barn and twirled the flame in the lantern, shaking the shadows on the wall. He heard her urgent whisper: *"Father."*

There was a hasty rustling. The boy rose and peered over the stall at Kaicel, then stepped out shirtless, buckling his belt, and said, "Who the hell are *you*?"

Kaicel stood smirking through his beard, his thumbs hooked in his pockets. The boy was not as large as he'd thought. Now the girl peeked from behind the stall, holding her removed blouse to her breasts.

"Oh God," she said, "Mr. Kaicel."

"The Russki?" the boy said. She nodded and the boy's face clenched. "What're you sneaking around here for, mister?"

Kaicel took off his coat and draped it over a wheelbarrow, hung his hat on a rope hook, began rolling up his sleeves.

The boy could fight but was no match for a brawler of Kaicel's size and seasoning. He cut the Russian's lower lip and welted a cheek, but Kaicel bloodied his nose and blacked both eyes and broke two of his ribs, then finished him with a knee to the crotch. The boy lay helpless, holding himself and rocking in pain. The girl looked on with her fist at her mouth and tears coursing. Kaicel ordered her to bring the rest of the boy's clothes, then pulled him to his feet and half-dragged him out to the horse. He jammed the boy's hat on his head and heaved him up into the saddle and stuffed his shirt and coat under the cantle. He put the reins in his hands and told him never to come back. Then slapped the horse on the rump and it loped away in the windblown night.

The girl was still crying as she followed him back into the barn. She begged him not tell her parents. She swore it was the first time she had ever met with the boy, swore they had done nothing but kiss and touch. She had put her shirt on but it remained unbuttoned and he could see the inner swells of her breasts. He could not tell if she were being truthful but thought it unlikely that one so callow could lie with such conviction. He perceived an advantage in saying he did not believe her. She wept harder and made to button the shirt but he pushed her hands away.

"If I too, then I cannot tell to nobody and you stay the secret. Yes? Be the clever girl."

She was in a state. If she had another choice she didn't know what it was. He took her silence for consent and snatched her into the stall, her single small cry less of pain than dismay, and anyway lost to the wind.

IN TRUTH SHE had been meeting with the boy about once a week for more than two months. They had known each other since childhood and attended the same school, though he was several grades ahead of her. It wasn't until the most recent summer, following his graduation and her sudden womanly bloom, that their friendship progressed to something more and the barn assignations began. Although he was her first such experience, she was scarcely his, and she knew it. He was too easy about it all, too apparently practiced. Yet the knowledge in no way diminished her delight in their sport, and she anyhow believed herself in love. He guided her from first timid kisses and tentative touches to kissing in the fabled French mode and caressing in thrillingly wicked ways, and as the last of her reserve fell like an apple from a shaken tree, the lovers clove in the most intimate embrace of all.

She knew nothing of the boy's difficulty with a girl just the year before, a difficulty that threatened public accusations and cumbersome legalities until his father's generous allocation of cash settled the matter to the satisfaction of all parties. His father, a widower, could well afford such a solution, having prospered hugely in the timber business and being even richer than his neighbors supposed. But he was not used to being put over a barrel. He had himself been no model of deportment in his younger days and had traded his share of bruises. His name was Jerome but everyone addressed him as Captain Jerry. When he beheld his son's battered aspect at the dinner table the day after the boy's encounter with Kaicel and asked what happened, the boy, who would not lie to him, related the particulars. The father sighed deeply at the girl's age and the possible necessity of another payoff. Only the remembered follies of his own youth checked his impulse to take a belt to the seat of his son's pants and never mind that the boy was almost seventeen. As for the Russian dairyman, there was a time Captain Jerry would have taken a pick handle to him as encouragement to mend his bullying ways, but such days were past. He was tired, the father, weary of combat in all forms and venues from saloon fights to courtroom confrontations. He hankered after a tranquil dotage. For some years now he had been wanting to take permanent leave of Michigan and its protracted winters, and when business had taken him to the Missouri Ozarks a year ago for the first time, he found the region so lovely and amenable in climate that he bought a house in Springfield in anticipation of relocating there for good.

His son's fight with Kaicel and the reason for it decided him that it was as good a time as any to make the move. The next day Captain Jerry put his Michigan properties on the market and that evening departed with his son on the train for St. Louis.

THE FOLLOWING DAY the postman delivered the boy's hastily scribbled note of farewell. Julia read it and burned it and wept in her life's single instance of self-pity.

On the subsequent Saturday, just a few days after the episode in the barn, Thomas Kaicel called again. To her parents he explained the bruises on his face as the result of a clumsy fall from a wagon while repairing a seat brace. Julia's only surprise at his call was at her lack of surprise. Of course he would come, she thought. Only such a one as he would persist in a suit for such as she. So enwebbed was she in despair, in a sense of ruination that could never be made right, in fear of what might become of such a worthless fool as herself, that when he once again tendered his proposal of marriage, she accepted. On the single condition that she could take her piano with her. He agreed and felt victorious. Her parents were delighted at the news of their betrothal and said to Kaicel that they had told him so.

Three weeks later they were wed in Grand Rapids. None of the ceremony's attendees could recall a less-animated bride, though none was so unkind as to say so. The first true smile of her marriage came at the birth of her child, a blond and hazel-eyed son, who arrived a month earlier than expected and was christened Stanislaus, after a favored uncle of hers who had died young. Everyone beamed on the mother and remarked on the boy's likeness to her. That the child's features showed no ready resemblance to the father was not uncommon in newborns, they said to Kaicel.

When the child matured, they said, the similarities would emerge. But he sensed their effort in his presence to hold down eyebrows and suppress knowing smiles. And as the boy grew from infant to toddler to grammar school student, Thomas Kaicel more and more knew the same bitter taste that had always jumped to his tongue when the carnival sharps turned up the correct one of the three cards, the shell that hid the pea.

The Getaway

The years passed and the distance widened between Thomas Kaicel and his family. Evenings found him on the porch with his whiskey and whittling knife, muttering to himself in the gathering gloom until full dark and time for bed. Julia never called him by any name but Kaicel, even when speaking of him to her two sons, the younger one, John, born ten months after Stanislaus.

The brothers called him "sir" until the summer day when Kaicel cuffed Stanislaus harder than usual for some alleged failing and the boy rushed at him with fists swinging. From the first of his school days Stanislaus had discovered his natural bent for fighting, the exhilaration of trading punches. He had not yet heard of adrenaline but well knew its effect, the small trembling that came whenever he was about to fight but which had nothing to do with fear, only with his body's readiness to inflict and absorb pain. By the time he was twelve, even some of the older boys kept their distance. He had not completed the eighth grade when he was permanently expelled for fighting, and he had since spent his days laboring on the dairy farm.

However, at 135 pounds and a few weeks shy of age sixteen, he was far from ready for Kaicel. The man threw him against the barn wall, thrashed him, knocked him senseless. When she caught sight of Stanislaus that evening, Julia was aghast and berated her husband for a bully. Without raising his eyes from his plate Kaicel told her to shut up. She saw Stanislaus's hand tighten around his fork and said nothing more, fearing blood at the table. The ensuing hush was broken solely by the clinking of Kaicel's tableware as he finished eating, the scrape of his chair when he departed for the porch.

Julia made Stanislaus promise not to fight with him, not even if the man should hit him again, which he surely would. Kaicel was a brute, she said, not above deliberately and badly harming him.

Still, the boy never again addressed him as "sir," only as "mister," usually in a tone to draw warning against insolence. Kaicel still slapped him on the head in occasional moments of extreme displeasure, but not so often as before nor quite as hard, and always now, it pleased Stanislaus to note, with a wary readiness for counterattack.

In such instances, he would glare at the man and think You *better* be set, you stinky bastard.

SINCE THEIR EARLY childhood, Julia had encouraged her sons to join in her nightly ritual at the piano after Kaicel had removed to the porch. The boys sat to either side of her and she instructed them in the fundamentals of the instrument. Neither of the brothers would ever learn to play the piano well, but they gained a deep appreciation of its classic works. Stanislaus shared his mother's love of Chopin, and his favorite piece was the "Funeral March."

They always capped their evenings with a mix of popular songs both venerable and new, the mother swaying on the bench as she played, the brothers harmonizing on the lyrics of Stephen Foster and the great songs of the Civil War, Stanislaus vastly preferring the earthy die-hard loyalty of "Dixie" to the punishing martial pieties of "Battle Hymn of the Republic." Their repertoire ranged from the quaint "Yellow Rose of Texas" to the much more recent and immensely popular "After the Ball." The younger son's voice was capable, but Stanislaus owned an extraordinary baritone, and it was his mother's dream that his gift might someday gain him a public prominence.

Stanislaus, too, liked to imagine himself famous, though in a far different fashion from his mother. His own ideals were bred of a rapture with dime novelettes. Julia had once discovered a copy in his wardrobe and accused him of degrading his mind. She made him get rid of it but remained unaware of the other volumes he kept hidden under the mattress. The novelettes abounded with hazardous forays and blasting guns and the dust of galloping getaways. The boy venerated the notorious outlaws of an Old West that at this time was in fact far from old. Indeed, in 1886, the year of Stanislaus's birth, Bill Hickok had been dead a mere decade, Billy the Kid but five years, Jesse James only four. Stanislaus was already six when the Dalton Gang was spectacularly slaughtered in Coffeyville, Kansas. For years afterward he heard men speak of the Daltons in timbres of awe. He was profoundly aware that only fifteen years separated him in age from Emmett Dalton, the youngest of the bunch and its sole survivor at Coffeyville, now locked away for life in a Kansas penitentiary. He felt it a low trick of fate that he'd been born a wink too tardy to ride in such legendary company. He daydreamt of being a desperado, a long rider of renown, of being sought for interviews and accounts of his daring exploits. Of posing narrow-eyed and with thumbs in gunbelt for photographs to accompany expositions of him as a highly dangerous but much misunderstood man. Of being the subject of mournful ballads long after he passed from the earth.

YET IF THE day of the Old West was done, the wildness of the West was not. The boy knew there was still much untamed territory on the far side of the Mississippi and by the waning days of the following summer he was determined to light out for it. He had not yet decided on a day for his departure when circumstance took a turn to speed him on his way.

One afternoon in the barn, Kaicel gave him another ringing slap on the ear and it was the one too many. The boy snatched up an empty milk bucket and swung it by the bail, striking Kaicel a glancing blow to the side of the head. Stanislaus tried to hit him again but missed and the man grabbed the bucket and wrenched it away. And now Kaicel advanced on him, swinging the bucket with vicious sidearm sweeps, the boy hopping back from each swipe with his arms flinging outward as if he were doing some rustic dance. A pitchfork came to hand, and Stanislaus brandished it like a soldier at ready bayonet. Kaicel stood fast for a moment, then snarled and flung the bucket at him. Stanislaus dodged it and impaled him.

Kaicel cried out and twisted away, pulling the pitchfork from the boy's grip. It dangled from the man's side, the handle end tapping the floor as he tottered backward, fingers fumbling at the three deep-rooted prongs pinioning his bloody shirt to his rib cage, the upper portion of his breeches reddening rapidly.

He fell to his knees and said, "I am killed." Then folded onto his side, still gripping the prongs, blood darkening the dirt beneath him, legs working slowly as if they might yet somehow bear him away from this terrible strait.

Stanislaus stared down at him for a moment, then snatched up his cap and jacket and ran to his secret niche under the hayloft and extracted his entire fortune, three silver dollars and three more in paper. Then fled.

His mother was in the cackling henhouse and his brother in the privy singing to himself at his ease with a mail-order catalog. Neither had heard Kaicel's yell and neither saw the boy as he raced across the pasture to the fence and hurdled it. He ran into the woods and headed for the rail tracks beyond.

He followed the tracks southward for several miles to where they curved between a long steep hill and a marshy lake and the trains were forced to reduce their speed. He had often fished in this lake and watched the passing trains and thought how simple it would be to board one moving so slowly. He hunkered in the brush and waited, his pulse still thumping in astonishment at what he'd done, with the thrill of being a fugitive desperado, a soon-to-be-wanted man.

Within the hour a freight came chugging round the hill and he laughed to see boxcars with open doors. He waited until the engine went by and then ran out of the brush and up the bed embankment and alongside the train. And was hugely surprised by how much faster the cars were moving now he was so near to them and their great racketing wheels.

An open boxcar came rolling by and he grabbed the iron handle at the bottom of the sliding door with both hands and tried to swing himself up. But he couldn't get his feet into the car and the train was gaining speed and now he was being pulled along like an oversized rag doll, legs flapping and feet glancing off the roadbed, trying for purchase on the air itself. He was afraid to let go of the handle, certain he would be killed or lose part of himself to the wheels. He could not hear his own yells above the rumble of the train. And then he was tugged roughly by the back of his jacket and the seat of his trousers and his shirt collar closed tight around his throat, strangling him. Someone hollered "Turn loose! Turn *loose,* damnit!" But he could not quit his desperate grip. Then a heavy stick jabbed at his fingers and one hand abruptly surrendered its hold and the other slipped loose and for an instant he thought he was falling but was instead hoisted and slung into the car like a sack of spuds.

He heaved for breath and sat up, his neck sore. A pair of men were regarding him in obviously amused wonder. Hoboes, days unshaved and roughly clothed. One with a black patch over an eye and a white worm of scar curving to midcheek from under it, the other holding a walking stick across his shoulders like a yoke.

The one-eyed one showed a greenish grin and said, "Kinda new at this, ain't you, sonny?"

THE WALKING-STICK bo was called Steamer. Bound for New Orleans after a visit to Mackinaw City, though the purpose of the visit he did not tell. The one-eye was Iron George, who jerked his thumb northward when the boy asked where he was from and wagged a finger to the south at the question of where he was going. Stanislaus laughed and said "Yeah, me too."

They shared with him their entire rations of a half-loaf of crusty bread and two tins of sardines and two pop bottles of water. He expected them to ask for money and thought he would lie and say he had none or they might rob him of all of it, but the subject never came up. They all three sat by the open door and watched the country rolling by and he was cautioned to face rearward to avoid being hit in the eye by a blown cinder. The train would arrive next morning in Chicago where both men intended to catch a southbound freight. They told him the best spot just beyond the city railyard for catching one heading westward. But he'd have to improve his boarding technique or he'd not make it anywhere but to a potter's field, and he would be buried there in pieces.

They taught him the various ways to get on different kinds of moving cars and how to jump off a moving train. To lessen the risk of breaking his neck in a crash he was advised to sleep with his feet always in the direction the train was heading. They even coached him in techniques for riding the rods, the framework of metal bars on the undercarriage of a car. It was the most dangerous ride of all and strictly a last resort, but a man never knew when the rods might be all that was available to him and so he ought to know how to do it. Iron George had ridden the rods in Texas some years before for more than two hundred miles and still couldn't believe he lived through it. Steamer had done it once in a Pennsylvania winter for fifty miles he thought would never end.

He listened closely and remembered everything. As the train sped into the rising night they told stories of boes they'd seen killed or maimed under the wheels. Iron George held up for the boy's regard a hand missing the most part of two fingers, lost to a coupler. They told of scraps with brakemen, whom they called "shacks," with yard bulls and smalltown cops. Told of farmers who had run them off their property at gunpoint, sometimes with gunfire, of farmers' wives or daughters who'd fed them, and of a memorable few who'd done more than that. They explicated for him the symbols hoboes inscribed on railside trees, barn walls, fence posts and gates and road signs, warnings to other boes of rough towns and tough cops, bad-tempered farmers and mean dogs, or to inform where a meal could be had and whether it would be free or require payment in labor, or where the nearest hobo camp could be found. They told him he'd need a bindle, a blanket bedroll tied with a loop of rope so he could carry it strapped across his back, that a good bindle always contained an extra shirt and pair of socks, a chunk of soap, a packet of matches. If he didn't have a pocketknife he'd better get one and carry it within easy grab. His makings of a bindle began with Iron George's gift of a small worn blanket he said he no longer needed. Steamer gave him some matches and broke a pencil in two and gave him the piece with the sharpened point. Except from his mother, he'd never met with such generosity.

Deep in the night he woke to the car's easy rocking over the rails. His companions' snores rasped in the shadows. He got up and went to sit by the open door. A high moon lit the trackside pastures and woodlands and sleeping hamlets. The wind rushed cool against him. Cinders streaked brightly orange into the passing darkness like small mute fireworks of celebration. He felt free as a hawk.

Bindle Stiff Days

He was in Chicago for one day and night and that was enough. At the first downtown intersection he tried to cross he went sprawling back onto the sidewalk to avoid being trampled by the horses of a furniture wagon, the driver cursing him for a bumpkin as he lashed the team by.

He had not heard the wagon's approach for the surrounding din. The city was an assault on the senses, the streets a clamorous jam of clattering draft wagons and clanging streetcars trailing crackling electric sparks along the overhead lines, trains screeching and rumbling on the elevated tracks, an assortment of chugging and honking motorcars under the harried guidance of goggled pilots, shrilling whistles of policemen trying vainly to direct the tangle of traffic, cries of newsboys hawking headlines on every corner.

The sidewalks were thronged with a mix of humanity bellowing in a half-dozen tongues. The air ripe with the reek of the multitude, of horse droppings and alleyway garbage, with the stench of the upwind stockyards and slaughterhouses. This mix of stinks fusing with alien odors of tenement cooking and the aromas of bakeries and chop houses and cafés.

He bought a small notebook and wrote a short letter to his mother, saying he was sorry for what he'd done but Kaicel had given him no choice and he did not feel like a murderer. He told her not to worry about him and that he would try to write often. At a post office he bought an envelope and stamp and sent the letter off. He would write to her every so often as he moved about the West, but he feared giving himself away to agents of the law who might examine the letters, and more than six months would pass before he would risk a return address.

On that Chicago evening he went into a saloon and treated himself to a mug of beer and a shot of whiskey, the first of his life not pilfered from Kaicel's unguarded beer bucket or poorly hidden bottles, and then had another of each. He ordered up a steak, having sworn it was the only way he would evermore engage with a cow. Nor would he again touch any teat but a woman's, a happy experience he'd a few times had with a girl, although he'd not yet progressed beyond it. It was a failing he set out to rectify on the completion of his meal. He'd been told that a man could not walk two blocks in Chicago without bumping his nose on a cathouse door. An hour later and for the price of one dollar he knew the rapture of his first coitus. Enjoyed upon a skinny blonde girl who smelled of boiled cabbage and was missing a lower front tooth. She spoke only Polish and giggled at his clumsy way with the language, and he wished he'd paid better attention to his mother's tutoring in it.

He departed the building feeling like a man of the world. So languidly content he took no notice of the ruffians watching from the shadows across the street. Two blocks farther on he was coshed from behind and lugged into the darkness of an alley, vaguely aware of the malodorous slime of the pavement under his face, the hands at his pockets, the low cursing of the assailants and their rapid footfalls as they made away.

The damp dawn found him a quarter-mile west of the railyard, huddled in the brush of a junk-littered swale bordering the tracks. The spot Steamer and Iron George had proposed as the best for catching a westbound train. His head throbbed with every heartbeat and the hair at the swollen bruise on his head was matted with half-dried blood. He was furious he'd been waylaid so easily. See if he let his guard down next time he was in a goddamn city.

The day was breaking red when the train came lumbering out of the yard. Cattle cars, mostly, all of them packed but one. He scanned the train for a watching brakeman and saw none, then ran from the brush and up the crushed-stone embankment, pain pounding his skull. A hatless grayhaired man lurched out of the weeds nearby and started for the train too, but he could not run well and immediately fell behind. Ketchel ran up to the stock car and executed the boarding move exactly as he'd been taught, nimbly swinging himself up to the door and opening it enough to slip into the car. He looked back to see the old bo halted and bent over with hands on knees, a quit man. He slid the door closed. The cattle shuffled uneasily. The car floor was strewn with straw and droppings, but he found a clean corner and gathered more straw into it and settled himself.

"At least you ain't milk cows," he said to the steers.

That afternoon he crossed the Mighty Mississippi into Iowa, his stomach drawing tight as he hung out the door for a better view of the wide expanse of gliding caramel water far below the track bridge. This side of the river the flat dull countryside looked to him like more of Illinois, which had looked mostly like more of Michigan.

But so what? He was over the Mississippi. He was by God in the West.

HE ASSUMED THE hobo name Steelyard Steve and over the next months rode the rails through boundless tracts of western America. He sought respite in hobo camps and was welcomed far more often than not. He held to Steamer's advice and kept his mouth shut unless spoken to. He observed closely. He listened hard.

He rode through Nebraska and Kansas, across the Oklahoma gun barrel into Texas all the way to the Rio Grande. Up to New Mexico and Colorado and Wyoming. Across Idaho and Oregon and down into California. Over to Nevada and Utah. South into Arizona Territory. The untamed beauty of the country was everything he'd imagined. He was agawk at its glorious vastness. Plains of tall grass rolling to the ends of the sky. Mountains like great muscles of the earth. Hills of every color. Rivers deep and swift and fierce. He'd never before known clouds of such tower and breadth, such a blazing nearness of the stars, such intensity of sunrise or sunset. Such heat. Such wind.

He rode past farms with smoke spiraling from kitchen chimneys and men at plowing and at harvest, past meadows with families at picnics, past waving men and boys fishing from trestles, past fields where traveling tent shows had set up, past ferries of pull ropes or poles, past river baptisms in progress, past a Mexican birthday party amid an assembly of shanties where a blindfolded child swatted with a pole at a colorful piñata. Past a hatless girl with blonde hair streaming as she raced her palomino alongside the fence next to the tracks.

He sometimes camped beside rivers jumping with fish the size of his arm and he cursed his bad luck not to have a line and hook. Camped sometimes in deep woods where insects rattled in the trees like tambourines and an owl as big as a cattle dog once swooped within feet of him. Camped sometimes on open prairie where wolf howls woke him deep in the night, his heart jumping with excitement and the hair rising on his nape.

WHEN HE WAS arrested along with three other boes at pistol-point by a yard bull in Alpine, Texas, his first impulse had been to run for it, but an older bo warned against it. "In Texas they'll shoot you for the sport, sonny." They got fifteen days for vagrancy and were put to work with a chain gang grading a stretch of the Fort Davis road. They fed, morning and night, on fatback and beans and bread. A few days into their sentence one of the boes stepped over to a rocky mound to relieve himself and happened on a nest of rattlesnakes. He was so startled he slipped and fell onto it and was struck on the legs, arms, face, everywhere. He stood screaming with a snake thrashing from his chin and one from his thigh and Ketchel snatched them away. By the time he was laid in the truck to be taken to the hospital his clothes were tight on his bloated flesh and his face was a blackening horror, and he died before morning. At the end of their sentence, Ketchel and the other two boes were driven out to the railyard so they could board a west-bound freight. One of the cops said they best never come back to Brewster County if they knew what was good for them. Ketchel would sooner have walked barefoot over burning coals than set foot in Texas again, but he wisely refrained from sharing that sentiment with the cops.

HIS FIRST RIDE on the rods was worse than any he'd been told of. He and a bo named Eight Ball tried to sneak aboard a Santa Fe freight one morning at a whistle stop some forty miles south of Albuquerque, but they found the boxcars locked. So they crawled under one and got up on the rods, one man behind the other. From this precarious perch the crossties seemed close enough to touch.

"I ain't so sure about this," Stanislaus said.

"Don't worry, kid. I done it a dozen times. Just set yourself good and enjoy the ride."

Then the train was moving again and the track bed became a blur and there were no sounds on earth save the rumble and clash of steel and roaring rush of air. But a shack must've seen them get under the car, because a length of chain spilled down between the car they rode and the one directly ahead and started paying back toward them. Attached to the end of the chain was a coupling pin, glancing off the ties and roadbed, whipping around under the car like the head of a crazed iron snake, banging wildly against the undercarriage, clanging off the rods.

Stanislaus had heard of this method some shacks used for clearing the rods of riders. He was forward of Eight Ball and so the coupling pin would reach him first. He did as Iron George had taught him and tucked his head down between his arms to protect his skull as best he could and held on with all his might and hoped he would suffer no broken bone.

He flinched and yelped at the clouts of the pin to his shoulder, to his hip. Then the flailing end of the chain was past him and he looked rearward just as the pin struck Eight Ball in the face and burst an eye and a small ribbon of blood fluttered from it. Stanislaus couldn't hear his own scream as the caroming pin cracked against Eight Ball's elbow and the man fell headlong. But one leg was caught in the undercarriage and for an endless moment he was dragged over the ties and rocky roadbed with large portions of him detaching in quick red rips. And then all of him was gone except the lower leg, torn off at the knee and still jammed in the tie.

Now the coupling pin started lashing back toward Stanislaus and he braced himself once more. Then the chain abruptly straightened and reversed direction and the length of it went shuddering past and vanished. It took him a moment to understand that the brakeman must've lost his hold on it.

It seemed like hours before the train at last halted at the Albuquerque yard but could not have been more than fifteen minutes. He had to force his fingers free of the rods before he could ease himself to the track bed and roll out from under the car. As he hobbled away toward the yard's high iron fence and the sanctuary of the woods beyond, he heard a shouting of pursuers. He made the fence and scaled it, dropped to the other side and ran for the woods as two pistolshots cracked behind him. Then was into the trees and gone.

HE HAD FANCIED becoming a cowboy and riding the range, though he had never sat a saddle or even been astride any mount but Kaicel's aging draft horse. On seeing real cowboys at work on their ponies he knew he would never be one. But he was an expert hand with tools of all kinds, and wherever he went he easily got work. He repaired gates and barn roofs, wagon axles and whiffletrees. He could mend harness and was an able smithy. He took pleasure in the exercise of pitching hay, and his endurance at it was a wonder to every man who witnessed it.

He worked hard and fed well. He relished the comradeship of the bunkhouse, the easy talk and tales of lurid adventure, the Saturday night sessions at poker. He discovered he owned a certain dexterity with the cards and was not above employing it now and then to abet his luck. His adroitness was less than he fancied, however, and on occasion his sportsmanship was called into question. The first time he was accused of bottom dealing he lunged over the table and unhinged the man's jaw with one blow. He'd added pounds of muscle since absconding from his Michigan home and his punch was an awesome thing. Even the foreman was impressed, but nevertheless fired him for a troublemaking cardsharp. That was in Oklahoma.

There were other fights on other ranches, other firings. None of the lost jobs mattered to him at all, as he in any case never stayed on a ranch longer than it took to finish the job he was hired for. He was ever eager to be back on the rails and on the move. To see what might be waiting down the track.

There were fights on the trains, too. And in the railyards and in the hobo camps. Somebody would try to steal his shoes or his bindle. Or would already be in a freight car he boarded and would not want to share it. Or a bull or brakeman would lay hand to him rather than simply order him to hit the grit. He broke noses, teeth, bit off part of one man's ear and almost all of another's nose, drove a knee into various sets of balls. To the cheers of onlooking hoboes, he beat a shack bloody with the same club the brakeman had tried to use on him. But nothing so outraged him in a fight as the introduction of a knife, which happened twice, the first time in a hobo camp outside of Flagstaff, where he dodged the swipes of a

Green River knife until a fry pan came to hand and he laid it hard into the man's ear and then bashed him cockeyed with it. The other time was in a boxcar when a bo tried to steal the bedroll of a thirteen-year-old runaway. Stanislaus interceded and the man pulled a hawkbill. Stanislaus took a gash to a hand before pinning the bo's arm and snapping his elbow joint over his knee, then shoving him from the speeding train.

SHARING A BOXCAR with a graybeard Yank veteran who'd been with Joe Hooker at Antietam, he was enthralled by the man's war tales. Then another old bo clambered aboard at a water stop and as it happened he'd served with Stonewall Jackson. The oldsters locked up in a clumsy fight that had Ketchel laughing until they reeled across the car with their hands on each other's throats and fell out of the highballing train and were gone.

Rolling through New Mexico on a night of windy rain he was witness to a boxcar birth, the woman assisted by her male companion, the infant entering the world with irate squalls. The woman held the babe to her breast and whispered to it as it fed. He asked what they intended to name it, and the man said John L., after his own hero, even though he didn't know what the *L* stood for. Neither did Ketchel. "Lucky," the woman said. "It stands for Lucky."

In Colorado he saw a tramp flogged to the backribs for stealing a chicken. In Wyoming he woke from a nap under a tree in a graveyard just as a funeral procession arrived at a freshly dug grave nearby and when the box was lowered and they sang "Swing Low, Sweet Chariot" he joined in and was acknowledged with tearful smiles.

In Salt Lake City he stood among a downtown crowd and

watched a hotel being consumed by fire, heard the screams of the hapless trapped within, smelled the work of the flames on flesh.

Slowly rumbling through Idaho he saw a man hanging from an isolate tree by a rope around his neck, head queerly angled. Naked from the waist down, crotch a dark ruin, pale legs black-streaked. A raven feeding on his face, another atop his head, while a coyote circled and leaped and snapped its jaws just shy of the bare feet.

In the alley behind a riverfront tavern in Portland he watched two men fight with razors and was amazed at the amount of blood a man could expend before falling dead, the loser doing so a bare minute before the victor.

He was dazzled by his first view of the Pacific and slept wonderfully on a strip of sandy beach until wakened in a panic before dawn by a cold inrushing tide. He was enamored of San Francisco, where he ate his first crab, saw his first real coochie show, sat on a hillside and watched the evening fog drift in.

One San Francisco night he had the pleasure of a whore so lovely he could not believe she was in the profession willingly and offered to liberate her from it by marrying her and never mind that she had been so widely used. She laughed in his face and said, "Jesus, kid, you kill me." She said she'd rather be a whore in San Francisco than the queen of the entire squarehead Midwest. She was still laughing as he departed with his face burning. He went to a waterfront saloon and drank copious mugs of beer that did nothing to assuage his humiliation. A navy sailor came in and sat a few stools away and began telling the bartender what he intended do to the low bastard he suspected of plucking his quail while he was at sea. Stanislaus was feeling sufficiently mean to say loudly that the sailor's quail was probably selling her feathers for fifty cents apiece. The swab went at him and Stanislaus knocked him down four times and the broken-nosed swab said he'd had enough. Stanislaus apologized but the sailor said forget it, he was probably right about the bitch. They took turns buying each other beers and conversed long into the night about the endless mystery of women.

EVERYWHERE HE WENT he heard talk, talk, a motley of recent and not so recent news, accounts witnessed firsthand and reports many times removed from their original source, an endless proffering of hearsay upon a range of topics and doings across the greater republic. . . .

He heard of the two brothers with their flying machine on the beach in North Carolina, an invention that some among the God-fearing likened to the Tower of Babel in its lofty presumption. He heard of the so-called safety razor that made shaving a faster undertaking and gave rise to predictions that American beards would soon be outnumbered by whiskerless cheeks. He heard of the pair of motorists who in the summer just past had made the first cross-country motor car drive, piloting their Winton from San Francisco to New York in fifty-two days. Heard of various bonanzas, of a gold rush in Alaska, of huge oil strikes in East Texas. Heard of massive horrors, of a Chicago theater fire that killed six hundred, of the Galveston hurricane, still spoken of in tones of awe some three years after the fact, that killed six thousand.

He heard of various coal mine explosions in which scores of miners perished. Heard of brutal labor battles in Pennsylvania, Kentucky, Colorado, of street fights between striking workers and police backed by Pinkerton men, of strikers shot down, clubbed bloody, borne away in Black Marias. Heard much repetitious and bitter talk about the killing of President McKinley two years before by a foreign wretch whose name few people could pronounce and nobody could spell, an oily anarchist and prime example of the immigrant trash flooding American shores to spread civic discord and racial pollution, a cowardly bastard who would shoot by surprise a man reaching to shake his hand. And heard much of McKinley's successor, young Roosevelt, hero of the recent Spanish war, a man of the West in spirit and never mind that he'd been born in the East with a silver spoon in his mouth, a man who professed to walk softly and carry a big stick, an attitude Stanislaus greatly admired.

There was constant talk about sports, about baseball's new American League and the first World Series and Boston's defeat of Pittsburgh in the best-of-nine. But no sport was of higher veneration than boxing, and no pugilist more talked about or more revered than James Jeffries, Big Jeff, the Boilermaker, the world heavyweight champion these past four years and more. Stanislaus heard few stories as often as of the pummeling the great Jeff had given to Bob Fitzsimmons for eleven bruising rounds at Coney Island in the spring of '99 to win the title.

And always of course there was talk of women. Of perfidious women and saintly women. Of treacherous women and women treated wrongly and women loved and lost. And in the hobo camps as in the rest of the country, no woman of flesh-and-blood could compare with that celebrated beauty of pen-and-ink, the Gibson Girl. No woman was as popular or as desirable or as utterly unattainable. In her pompadour and shirtwaist and cool self-possession, that national symbol of ideal femininity radiated a wholesomeness so alluring it stoked the lust of every man and boy in America. Many a bo carried a tattered magazine illustration of her to gaze upon in the low light of a late-night campfire.

• • •

ON A FROSTY December eve somewhere in western Wyoming the freight he rode made a whistle stop and four tramps scrambled into his boxcar. They closed the door almost all the way, one of them placing a short strip of rope against the jamb to keep the door from being shut completely, as there was no way to open it from inside. They crouched and watched the bright line of light at the door crack, seemed set to pounce or bolt or surrender, depending on the number and kind of men who might yank the door open and how well armed they might be. But the door stayed as it was and the train at last began rolling.

A match flared and one of them lit a fat stub of candle. They looked at Stanislaus in the murky light where he sat with his back to the front wall of the car. He saw they were of a wolfish breed he had met with before. They usually traveled solo, though from time to time in pairs, but here were four at once, rank beyond the stink of unwashed flesh and clothes. One of them was huge, over six feet tall and Stanislaus judged his weight at above 250 pounds. He had a head like a melon and his baseball cap was slit on the sides to accommodate the massive skull, the hair over his ears shorn to the skin.

Stanislaus nodded. The only one to nod in return seemed the youngest, perhaps only a year or two older than himself. This one asked if he had anything to eat, but his accent was so densely hillbilly he had to repeat the question before Stanislaus understood him and said he didn't, nor tobacco, when the boy asked for that.

They conversed no further with him, settling at the other end of the car and whispering among themselves. After a while they lay down and blew out the candle. The past few days had been rough ones and Stanislaus was weary for lack of sleep, but he stayed awake for a time longer, listening to their sighs and snorts, their shufflings about for a more comfortable lie. When they were finally quiet, he rolled up in his blanket and stretched out with his bindle under his head, though this night he wisely did not take off his jacket or his shoes.

He had no notion of how much time had passed when he woke in the rocking, clattering darkness and sensed their nearness. Before he could get clear of his bedroll they were on him, the melon-head one dropping astraddle of his stomach and knocking the breath from him, pinning his arms with his knees, grabbing him by the hair and banging the back of his head on the floor. Stanislaus lay stunned, hearing their high giggling as the candle was lighted and the car walls leaped up from the dark. He could barely breathe for the weight of the man.

"Set youself on him, Earl," the melon-head said. "Hold them arms."

The Earl one sat on Stanislaus's face and pinned his arms under his knees. The reek of his trousers was gagging. The melon-head's weight shifted down to his legs and Stanislaus felt the man's hands working at his belt buckle. He tried to wrest free and was struck in the chest and told, "Quit fussing." He felt the buttons of his fly rip away and the big man's weight rose off him and now his pants were being tugged down to his thighs. He heard the other two arguing over his bindle and the Earl one said something about his share.

"Raise up so's I can turn him," the melon-head said.

As Earl eased his weight off his face, Stanislaus arched his neck and locked his teeth in his crotch.

The Earl one screamed and lurched into the melon-head and Stanislaus heaved sideways with all his strength and both men tumbled off him, upsetting the candle and plunging the car into blackness.

The Earl one was shrieking and the melon-head shouting "Get him, *get him*!" as Stanislaus crawled fast for the door, pants bunched at his knees. He pulled himself up and yanked the door open just as one of them caught him by the back of the jacket. Stanislaus whirled and punched him in the ear and he fell away. Then another was clawing at him and he snatched this one by the shirtfront and slung him out the door to vanish without a sound.

Stanislaus leapt. He sailed through cold darkness and hit the ground feetfirst and his knees buckled and he went tumbling through scrub brush and soft sand and his head jarred. He was out.

He opened his eyes to a weak sun risen above the mountains, a chill wind stinging his face with grit. He tried to get up but his legs would not function properly and for a terrifying moment he thought he was paralyzed. Then saw that his pants were in a tangle around his shins. It was an effort to sit up and get them unsnarled, and he fell twice before gaining his feet.

Everything hurt. His head was tender to the touch and his fingers came away sticky with gelled blood. But no bones broken, which he thought a wonder. The shoves of the wind were strong and he hugged his jacket to him.

Stark bleak mountains near and far, stretches of rocky scrubland. The rails bare and straight to the opposing horizons.

He remembered the one he'd thrown from the train. He searched and found him about twenty yards back down the tracks, awkwardly supine beside a greasewood shrub. It was the young one who had returned his nod. His eyes were open and his head oddly inclined on the broken neck.

He went through the boy's pockets and found a jackknife with a finely honed four-inch blade, a box of matches, four pennies. He stripped the boy of his floppy denim jacket and put it on over his own and buttoned up both, then found the boy's cap to replace the one he'd left in the boxcar.

He had no idea where he was, whether still in Wyoming or now in Utah. But he knew the direction he'd been coming from, and so followed the rails the other way.

HE ACQUIRED A heavy sheepskin jacket and good woolen mittens and a bandanna to cover the lower half of his face in bank-robber fashion when riding on flatcars or freight roofs, both of which he came to prefer over riding in closed cars, never mind the enveloping black smoke, the live cinders that singed his skin and clothes, the drenching rains or the icy winds whose sudden gusts might loft him from the train. In closed cars his sleep was now always fitful and he was prone to dreams that woke him with a start and his heart at a gallop. He had never yet in his life shed tears, but on such wakings he would have an odd urge to weep. He could never remember what the dreams were about except that they often entailed his mother and sometimes his brother too. He supposed he missed them, but the idea that he might be homesick seemed to him absurd. He had yet to learn that the worst kind of homesickness a man might feel can be for a place he's never been or even heard of, a place he may never know. He was not troubled by such dreams when he slept in the open.

ONE NIGHT NEAR the end of winter, after a brief employment on a Mormon farm, he was in a ramshackle tavern on the outskirts of Boise when he spied the man with the melon head sitting at one of the rough plank tables along the wall. Stanislaus sidled into the shadows and watched him from under his cap brim. When the man got up and went out the back door, he followed, beer mug in hand.

In the alley was the privy, though most men settled for pissing against the fence or the wall. It was dark but he could see the big man standing at the wooden fence with his back to him.

The mug was of thick and heavy glass meant to convey an impression of greater capacity than it actually held. Gripping it by the U-handle, Stanislaus went up behind the man and with an overhand swing clubbed him on the back of the head. The man grunted and fell forward against the fence with his hand still at his dick and slipped down to his knees. He started to turn and Stanislaus swung the mug sidearm and the massive head bobbed with the impact and the man keeled onto his elbows. He groaned and muttered and tried to get up, moving with the awkwardness of a man with a monstrous hangover, and Stanislaus bashed him again and knocked him supine into the pissy mud. He got down on one knee and swung the mug into the man's face a half-dozen times like he was driving home a large nail, the last two crunching impacts stippling his own face with blood. Then stood up and tossed the mug aside.

The man lay silent and unmoving. Somebody in the darkness said "*Jeee*-sus."

He jogged down the alley, vaulted a fence, and loped down the road toward the railyard. Not half an hour later he was rolling north, huddled atop a boxcar against a gelid wind and a stream of acrid smoke. And what he felt other than cold could only be called satisfaction.

The Richest Hill on Earth

By the calendar it was early spring when he hopped off a Utah Northern just before it pulled into the freight yard, but the night was near freezing and felt even colder for the wind. The landscape was illuminated in an eerie ocher light from the gas lamps of the mines and smelteries. Huge plumes of black and gray and orange rising off a stark forest of smokestacks and lacing the air with harsh alien stinks. The "richest hill on earth," Butte was called. It was born of gold and silver strikes but it was copper that made it rich. Meandering under the town was a river of copper fifty feet wide with lodes branching like tributaries, all of it now belonging to the Anaconda Copper Company, which in turn was part of the Amalgamated Copper Mining Company, which itself was a tentacle of Standard Oil. To most residents of Montana, however, Anaconda was simply the Company.

He'd heard talk about Butte everywhere he'd been. Had heard it had the highest smokestack on the planet, the deepest mine shaft, the longest ore train. Every mine had its own name, like the Bluebird, the Lexington, the Spectator, the Diamond, the Neversweat and its famous seven smokestacks. Wherever the Company bored a hole it tapped into a new vein, started another mine, put up another of the colossal elevator rigs called headframes to lower the workers into the ground and haul up the buckets of ore. Gallows frames, the miners called them. Stanislaus had heard enough about the mines to know he would sooner resort to armed robbery than set foot in one, but there was no shortage of men willing to go down the shafts and break the ore out of the rock, men with nothing to bargain with but their physical strength and a willingness to risk their lives. To risk cave-ins, fires, explosions, lung disease from the rock dust, pneumonia from working in the sweltering shafts and emerging sweat-soaked into an icy winter. They came from all over the country, these men, from all over the world, drawn to the ready work. Yankees and rednecks, John Bulls and Dutchmen, Dagos, Chinks, Finns, bohunks of every breed, and above all, Micks. The population of Butte and its environs in this year of 1904 was around fifty thousand, nearly a third of it Irish, most of them named Sullivan.

He'd come to Butte for no reason but to see it for himself. The roughest burg in the West, he'd heard, and the most exciting. He'd heard it said that many a Butte saloon had chosen to brick in their front windows rather than keep replacing the smashed glass, that every day at first light the cop wagon rattled down the streets behind its brace of draft horses and collected the drunks off the sidewalks and from the alleys, the occasional dead. Heard that it was a rare week in Butte that passed without murder. He'd heard the town had the most whores to be found in any four square blocks in the country, the most saloons, the most gambling halls. It had dogfight pits and boxing arenas, vaudeville theaters, burlesque joints. Butte the Beaut, he'd often heard it called, sometimes in mockery and sometimes not.

He hid his bindle in the bushes and headed into town. The crowded streets were in strident carouse, ringing with the cries of doorway shills and a blaring tangle of musical styles issuing from every joint. Ragtime and coochie, waltzes and ballads, banjo plunking of a sort he'd never heard, ringing out a kind of music he would ever after think of as Western hillbilly. It was only a Tuesday, but in a town where the mines operated around the clock and seven days a week, every night was Saturday night.

His hands balled for warmth in his jacket pockets, his face stinging with chill for the rinse he'd given it at a frosty water trough at the edge of town. He relished the raucous high-timing, his eyes brighter than he knew. His first objective was to wash the taste of locomotive smoke from his mouth with a mug of beer. Then he would line the inside of his shirt with newspaper and search for a place to sleep out of the wind. Beyond that, his only plan was to find a job of some sort for a short while, put together a small stake, then get back on the rails.

He was passing a place called the Copper Queen, whose window sign boasted THE PRETTIEST LADIES IN THE WEST—10¢ A DANCE, when the doors sprang open to an eruption of cheers and a fast-moving pair of men, one of them bent forward and being propelled by the other, who had him by the collar and the back of the pants in the customary manner of the bum's rush and flung him into the street, spooking the animals of passing horsemen and wagons. He was a big man, the bouncer, with hair gleamingly pomaded and garters on his sleeves. "And *stay* out!" he said, and went back inside.

The ejected patron rose unsteadily to his feet and set his cap on his head, brushed vainly at his muddy clothes, muttered, "All right, okay, fine and dandy, I get it."

Stanislaus went inside. It was a spacious dance hall and saloon, blue-hazed with gaslight and smoke, boisterous with laughter and shouted conversations and a honkytonk piano. The dance floor was off to one side and dense with couples, the heralded ladies earning their dimes. If they weren't the prettiest in the West, they were the prettiest he'd seen since San Francisco. He was down to his last four bits and couldn't afford even to haggle with a whore, but after the cost of a beer he would still have enough money for a few dances and at least be able to feel a woman under his hands. He had never danced in his life but was certain he could do it better than most of the oafs lurching around on the floor. His mother regarded dancing as an essential social grace and had wanted to teach him and his brother the rudiments. But their first and only lesson had no sooner begun than Kaicel yelled from the porch for them to quit all their foolish stomping around in there or he'd bust up the piano for firewood.

One girl in particular attracted his attention. A strawberry blonde with a sassy way of tossing her hair as she swayed and jigged with a sprightly gusto and seemed to be dancing more with herself than with the oafish partner stomping clumsily at what looked like some altogether different endeavor. As Stanislaus shouldered through the crowd at the bar, he tried for another glimpse of her and in his distraction jostled a man and caused him to spill his drink.

The man glared and said, "Well, shit." Stanislaus started to apologize and the man punched him, propelling him into a clutch of drinkers at the bar who cursed and shoved him right back at the man, who hit him again, dropping him on the seat of his pants amid guffaws and a cluster of dirty pants legs and muddy boots. His jaw ached vaguely but he was not addled and his foremost thought was to get up before the man could kick him. Then various rough hands were helping him to his feet and there was laughter all around and someone said, "Lad can take a lick." So commonplace were fights in Butte saloons that the scuffle drew scant notice from the rest of the room, and the piano man played on.

The bouncer had materialized, armed with a short club. He braced the puncher, whom he called O'Malley, and told him it was time to say good night.

"Fuck sake, Harris," O'Malley said, "the bastard sloshed me whisky out of—"

Stanislaus hit him in the mouth and O'Malley's hat took wing and he crashed against the bar and sat down hard. The startled Harris was too slow in attempting to apply his club to Stanislaus, who butted him in the face and loosed a gush of blood from his nose, then punched him four or five or six times so fast there would be debate among the witnesses about the exact number. Harris's legs quit him and men moved aside to let him fall. His head struck the foot rail and his eyes rolled up white. But now O'Malley was risen and swinging, and Stanislaus hunched his shoulders and fended with his arms. A fist struck his crown and he saw stars but O'Malley yowled with the pain of a broken hand and Stanislaus lashed into him with another blur of punches. O'Malley again went down and Stanislaus began kicking him and he curled up tight with his arms around his head. "Enough! Enough, for fuck's sake!" O'Malley yelled. Stanislaus gave him one more to the ribs and stopped.

The surrounding crowd whooped and applauded the entertainment. The whole room aware now of a good fracas and avid to know what happened, and those who had seen the fight began describing it to those who had not. Somebody clapped Stanislaus on the back and somebody put a foaming mug in his hand and somebody asked his name. He said Steelyard Steve and several of them laughed, knowing a hobo handle when they heard one. He fingered a small lump under one eye and a cut on his upper lip, the only signs he showed of having been in a fight. In two days his face would show no sign of bruise, a remarkable recuperative power that would obtain for all of his brief life.

O'Malley was helped off the floor, his lips raw and distended, an ear like a purple fig, the broken hand already gone big as a bible. He put his good hand to his mouth and tongued out a tooth and regarded it with rue. They slapped at Harris's cheeks and tugged at his ears and someone upended a mug of beer over his face and that brought him around.

Stanislaus spotted the strawberry blonde smiling at him from the edge of the crowd and asked the men nearest him if they knew her name. Gretchel, he was told. Its resonant similarity to "Kaicel," which name he had renounced forever, made "Ketchel" come to mind.

A beefy, silver-bearded man in a cream suit pushed up beside him, introduced himself as Richardson, manager of the place, and asked his name and the name of the mine he worked for. He said he was Steve Ketchel and was no miner and didn't care to be, but he could do with a job.

Richardson's aspect suggested he had witnessed more foolishness in his time than any man should have to. He watched glumly as glassy-eyed Harris was assisted to his feet and someone handed him a bar rag to put to his bloody nose.

"It happens this place is in need of a bouncer, Mr. Ketchel," Richardson said, "and you appear to have the proper aptitude. Pays twenty a week."

"When do I start?"

"Now would be good."

They shook on it. Ketchel asked if he could have a couple of dollars in advance to see him through to his first payday. Richardson gave him two silver dollars and then returned to his backroom office. He made the loan so readily that Ketchel wanted to kick himself for not having asked for more.

AN HOUR LATER the Gretchel girl pushed through the throng to where he stood at the bar with several mugs of beer in front of him, all of them bought by admiring miners. He was half-buzzed and still a little charged with the adrenaline of the fight, and she had to lean close and speak loud for him to hear her through the enveloping din. He'd been giving her the eye all night, she said, and she couldn't help wondering if he was just too shy to ask for a dance.

"All you need's a pair of nickels, honey." Her scent was a heady mix of perfume and woman musk.

"I don't know how," he said. "I never learned."

"Well now, darling, I'll teach you. But like the man said, first things first." She held out her hand and wiggled her fingers. He gave her one of the silver dollars.

It proved less a matter of teaching than uncovering a natural talent. She showed him the basic step-step-close of the waltz and in minutes he was whirling her as smoothly as any swell to the strains of "The Band Played On" and "Daisy Bell." Then came the box step and swaying to "After the Ball" and "Sidewalks of New York." Then the jaunty two-step and some other basic moves and they were bouncing happily to "Won't You Come Home, Bill Bailey?" and "Hello, My Baby." After ten dances he gave her the other dollar and they used up that one too, and she accepted a mug of beer in payment for still another turn.

When he said he was interested in something more than a dance she said she sometimes let a fellow have something more than a dance but it sure cost more than a mug of beer. He asked if she would accept his marker. She said, "Hey, honey, it's not the sort of thing gets sold on the cuff. You welsh on me, I can't exactly take it back, can I?"

He said if he couldn't clear his debt in cash he'd repay her in kind. She laughed and said he might not have any jack but he sure wasn't short on cheek.

When her work shift was done they went to the Buffalo Hotel where she lived, hugging close as they made their way against the biting cold of the wind. The hotel was a block outside of the notorious red-light district he'd heard so much about, including Venus Alley, the heart of the quarter. She told him she'd starve before she'd work in a whorehouse, and shoot herself before sinking as low as an alley crib. She might once in a while be a whore, she said, but she was always her own whore.

Her room was surprisingly ample, impeccably neat, warmed by a radiator. He wrote "I.O.U. $2, Steve Ketchel" on a scrap of paper and handed it to her. She placed it next to a Victor Talking Machine on a table beside the bed, the phonograph equipped with a rigid tone arm and a stationary horn. She said it was her prize possession "of all my worldly goods." He sat in the only chair and watched her select a record, position it on the turntable, crank the machine, and set the needle in the groove.

He recognized the tune as the "hoochie-coochie song," though its correct title was "The Streets of Cairo." He'd never before seen the dance performed outside of a carnival tent or at such close range or by a prettier woman. Or seen the dancer shed *all* of her clothes.

They left the lamp on while they had their sport, and after a short break went at it again in a reprise of gasping and breathless profanities and heaving fits of giggling. She was eight years older than he and hadn't enjoyed herself this much with a man in some time. When she asked if he had a place to live and he said not exactly, she said he could stay with her and they would see how it worked out. He said all right, but only if she permitted him to pay half the cost of the room for however long he was there. She agreed, then went to the dresser and tore up his marker. "No charge for a roommate," she said.

He believed he'd come to the right place.

The next day he recovered his bindle from the bushes. He unrolled it on her bed to reveal his extra shirt and socks, a tin of matches, a piece of soap. "All *my* worldly goods," he said. And laughed when she said there was no reason to sound so proud about it.

IN HIS FIRST week on the job he was tested by a dozen of the town's most eminent toughs, every man of them a miner. They had all heard how he'd put down O'Malley and Harris and they wanted to try him, and each night the place was packed with those who wanted to see the action. The Copper Queen's business boomed.

He dispatched all challengers, knocking them out or beating them into submission, not always without getting bloodied himself. He sent the quitters on their way with a kick in the pants, he dragged the insensate to a side door and chucked them into the alley. The miners marveled at the prowess of someone so young. By the middle of his second week the deliberate trials fell off and he was dealing chiefly with unruly drunks disposed toward threatening the bartender or harassing the piano player or, the most common call for his intervention, taking excessive liberty with the girls.

The Queen's girls doted on him. Like Gretchel, most of them were his elder, some by more than a decade, and as he was only seventeen they tended to mother him in all the best ways. But he was also good-looking and a more capable protector than any of them had ever had, and their impulses ranged beyond the maternal. Gretchel was annoyed by their flirtations and even more by his obvious pleasure in them. But experience had taught her the folly of jealous accusation, and she kept her discontent to herself and hoped for the best.

He lived with her for nearly three weeks before moving in with a girl named Olga Harting who worked at a dance hall a few blocks from the Copper Queen. Gretchel came home from the bakery one afternoon with a warm sack of the cinnamon doughnuts he was fond of and found a note atop the phonograph informing her of his departure and expressing gratitude for her help, saying he would see her later at the Queen.

Callow as he was about women, he had but a vague inkling of the depth of her affection, the intensity of her hopes. When he showed up for duty that evening he was prepared for a mean look, maybe a hard word, but not the drunken wrath he was met by. She berated him for a lowdown bastard and sloshed a mug of beer into his face. He thanked her for the refreshment, then ducked the empty mug she threw and it smashed a mirror behind him. The onlookers whooped, but when she snatched up a slicing knife from the bar-top platter of pumpernickel and salt ham they all drew farther back. She swiped at Ketchel twice before he caught her wrist and disarmed her. She beat at him with the heels of her fists, cursing incoherently, beat at him until she tired, then burst into sobs and ran out.

It was another first-rate diversion for the patrons. Richardson had come out of his office and witnessed the tail end of it, and when Stanislaus asked him not to fire her, he said the thought never crossed his mind, she was too popular with his regulars. He would simply deduct a share of her wages every payday until she'd compensated for the busted mirror.

Gretchel did not speak to him for the next two weeks, not until she deigned to say "Thank you" after he flattened a miner who would not quit pawing her on the dance floor.

HE NEXT TOOK up with a moody, raven-haired girl named Kate Morgan. She had the prettiest legs and shapeliest bottom he'd ever seen. They lived in a room with a small porch in a spacious boardinghouse owned by a former employee of Venus Alley named Miss Juno who kept her nose out of her tenants' affairs so long as they did not disturb the neighbors or do damage to the furniture. They shared the premises with Kate's two cats, a caramel-and-gray called Harry in honor of Harry Longbaugh, better known as the Sundance Kid, a man she had always admired, and a black-and-white named Otto because of a black splotch over its mouth in the shape of a Prussian moustache. She had named them in kittenhood a few weeks before realizing they were both females. By then she felt it wouldn't be right to change their names, thinking it might confuse them.

"Some clever kid I am," she said. "Can't even tell the boys from the girls."

"You must've had your fingers crossed the first time I took my pants off for you."

She threw a pillow at him.

She came from a wealthy ranching family in Wyoming. Her father's success the more remarkable in light of her grandfather having landed in America a penniless cowherd from County Cork. She received a good education and extensive ballet training at a private school in Denver, but she'd been a wild-hearted sort even as a child and, to everyone in the family but her father, something of a black sheep. She was fifteen when her father was killed in a hunting accident, and she despised the man her mother married only a year later. At seventeen she joined with a company of entertainers who traveled in wagons all over the West, putting on shows in rough, remote regions. She was with them for three years, until the day the troupe finished up a stint in Butte, where she stayed behind and went to work on the stage of the Big Casino Saloon. She'd now been in Butte almost as long as she'd been with the troupe.

"Jesus, why Butte?"

"Well now, laddybuck," she said in the brogue she sometimes liked to affect, "with all the harps hereabouts, it's a right bit like the old sod to a lass of Irish root, don't ye know?"

"Cut the malarkey, girl. Why not San Francisco? Why not Denver? Kansas City?"

She said she might well ask him the same question.

He shrugged. "I like the action around here."

She waggled her brow. "I know what you mean, honeybunch, but it's not like Frisco doesn't have plenty of action. Denver too. Bigger action."

"Yeah, and there's a lot more law in those places. A lot more cops. This place feels . . . I don't know . . . freer, somehow. More like . . ." He shrugged.

"The Wild West?" she said, lowering her voice like a conspirator. She pretended to draw a gun from her hip, aimed her index finger at him and flicked her thumb. "Pow!"

He clutched at his heart and fell across the bed, kicking his feet in a death throe. She clapped lightly and said, "Bravo!"

Their room was adjacent to the communal bathroom, and one evening she heard him singing in the tub and was amazed at the loveliness of his voice. He blushed when she told him so, and she kissed him and said he should be proud of such a voice and show it off every chance he had. Every night afterward, he sang to her in bed.

One night she asked if his Christian name was spelled "s-t-e-p-h-e-n" or "s-t-e-v-e-n," and he confessed it was Stanislaus.

"Really?" She sat up in the bed.

"Yep. Polack to the bone."

"Daddy's name was Stanley. When I was little, Ma used to call him Manly Stanley." And then she was crying into her hands over the memory of her fled girlhood and deceased father.

He held her close and said she could call him Stanley if she wanted to. He'd never before thought of using the name, but he liked it. Then sang her to sleep with her favorite song, "I'll Take You Home Again, Kathleen."

[illegible]. She sat up in the bed.

[illegible] Polack to the bone.

The Michigan Assassin

He'd been in Butte less than two months when a local promoter named Tex Halliday asked if he was willing to substitute for an injured boxer on the fight card scheduled for the following night at the Big Casino Saloon. In addition to a bar and a theater, the Big Casino boasted the most popular boxing arena in town, an enormous hall with a regulation ring and enough benches to seat hundreds. Halliday had seen Ketchel in action as a bouncer and thought he might do well in the ring.

"You'd be going against another first-timer," he said. "He's got the weight on you, but I'd say you got the sand on him. You won't even have to hire your own seconds. I got a few fellas who work the corners for fighters who ain't got their own crew."

Although he'd been to the Big Casino once to watch Kate Morgan dance, Ketchel had not gone into the arena. In fact, he had never seen a boxing match, not a real one, with gloves and rules and a referee. His acquaintance with boxing was entirely through hearsay and the pages of the *Police Gazette*, the foremost sporting periodical of the day, which had given him a standard familiarity with such famous heavyweight champions as the legendary John L. Sullivan, Gentleman Jim Corbett, Bob Fitzsimmons, and the present champ James Jeffries, the fearsome Boilermaker himself. But like every boy who liked to scrap, Ketchel had often wondered how well he might fare in a prize ring.

The winner of a Big Casino match always got fifty dollars, Halliday said, the loser no less than twenty-five. Ketchel went to Richardson and told him he was taking the next night off.

PRIZEFIGHTING WAS A rougher endeavor in those days. In some states boxing was altogether outlawed, and in some states where it was not, the police were invariably on hand to put an end to a fight as soon as it seemed a boxer was in imminent danger of being maimed. In most legal venues, however, even a one-sided battering was permitted to continue to its last scheduled round if the boxer getting the worst of it did not get knocked out before then. Or quit. Or, as happened every now and then, fall down dead. Fighters routinely engaged in several matches a month and sometimes fought two or three times within a week. Bouts of twenty rounds or more were commonplace. A fight to the finish—until one of the boxers was knocked out or was otherwise unable to continue—was still legal in some states, and such fights could last for hours. The referee enforced the rules against patently dirty tactics such as low blows and hitting a man while he was down, yet otherwise seldom intervened in the proceedings. Some states granted the referee the authority to name the winner of a fight unresolved by knockout, or to call the bout a draw, but boxers often agreed contractually that if there was no knockout the fight *had* to be a draw, even if it was manifestly one-sided. Other states, particularly in the East, altogether prohibited outcomes by decision, the idea being that a ref without authority to decide an outcome was a ref who could not be bribed. In such states, any fight that ended without a knockout was by default declared "no contest." Reporters could grant a "newspaper verdict," but their opinions were strictly unofficial. Montana was at this time one of the few states that used a scoring system to determine the winner of a match that did not end by knockout.

AS ALWAYS ON fight nights the arena was packed. The clamorous room was moistly hot and smelled thickly of sweat and tobacco fumes and whiskey. The overhead lights were webbed with smoke. Ketchel wore borrowed shoes, baggy red trunks bunched at his waist by the drawstring, a tatty robe imprinted on the back with DR. WATKINS' MIRACLE HEALTH NOSTRUM.

He entered the ring accompanied by the cornermen Halliday assigned to him, a pair of ex-pugs named Hardy and Smith. Smith was missing an ear and his head jerked slightly every few seconds, as if still trying to dodge some of countless blows it had absorbed over the years. When Ketchel asked Hardy how many fights he'd had, he said, "Oh, around fifty, I guess."

"How'd you do?"

"Not too bad. Won them all but about forty."

Halliday had wanted to bill him as "Kid Ketchel," or, better still, "Cyclone Kid" Ketchel, but Ketchel said no, his regular name would do fine. Halliday said all right, then casually asked where he was from. It came as a surprise when Wild Bill Nolan, owner and operator of the Big Casino, introduced him to the crowd as Stanley Ketchel, the Michigan Assassin. As the hometown fighter, he drew loud cheers. There was a scattering of women in the crowd, including Kate, who had begged the night off from the stage manager so she could see Ketchel's first fight. Sitting at ringside she blew him a two-hand kiss and hollered, "You'll kill him, baby!"

That his opponent had the reverse intention was clear enough from his name, Killer Kid Tracy. He was from Helena, and the polite scattering of applause at his introduction was muted by the requisite booing for the outsider. Tracy was only a year older than Ketchel, a farm boy whose success in county-fair boxing matches had convinced him he had what it took to be a top professional. At the afternoon weigh-in he had scaled 163 pounds, a few pounds over the middleweight limit of 160, while Ketchel, at 143 pounds, was just shy of the welterweight limit of 145. Such disparity in size between opponents was not unusual in that day, when catchweight bouts were often agreed to. The light heavyweight class, between 160 and 175 pounds, had only just come into being and would not gain full acceptance for some years yet. He who weighed above 160 was still generally considered a heavyweight.

The fighters' hands had been taped in the dressing room, but the gloves didn't go on until the boxers were in the ring. Each man's gloving was observed by one of his opponent's cornermen to ensure that nothing more than hands went into the gloves. It was not unheard of for a fighter's second to slip a little something, such as an iron pestle, into a glove to add persuasion to his man's punch.

Now everyone left the ring except the fighters and the ref, who gave the standard prefight warnings against illegal tactics and then asked if they had any questions.

Tracy fixed Ketchel with a menacing stare and said, "Yeah, I got a question. Where you want the body sent?"

Ketchel laughed.

"I'm gonna make you famous, Mac, the first of my many victims in the squared circle," the Killer Kid said.

They went to their corners to wait for the bell, and Ketchel asked Hardy, "Say, what's he talking about, squared circle?"

"What you're standing in. They call it a ring but it's got four corners. I still ain't figured it out myself."

In the opposite corner, Tracy opened his jaws so that his second could insert a rudimentary mouthpiece, a tightly sewn roll of cloth to clamp between his teeth to better protect them. He glowered across the ring at Ketchel and punched his gloves together, a figure of ready wrath. Ketchel spurned a mouthpiece and always would.

In those years, the traditional handshake was exchanged after the starting bell. When the gong sounded, Ketchel and Tracy hastened out to mid-ring and touched right gloves, then Tracy snorted and jabbed Ketchel twice to the forehead and that was all the Killer Kid would ever remember of the fight. During the next few seconds he was hit so many times so fast that his head whipped from side to side as if vehemently denying all notion of continuing in this ill-chosen occupation. His mouthpiece sailed out of the ring. Ketchel missed with his last two swings only because Tracy was already falling. The Killer Kid lay spread-eagled and the ref didn't bother with a count. He waved his arms over his head in superfluous indication that the match was over and raised Ketchel's hand. The fight had lasted nine seconds.

Stanley Ketchel grinned at the ovation and winked at Kate, who was beaming up at him and applauding lustily. *Yes*, he thought. *Yes yes yes.*

AMONG THE SPECTATORS at that match was a young boxing coach and manager named Maurice Thompson, who preferred to be called Reece. Later that evening he introduced himself to Ketchel at the Copper Queen, where the Michigan Assassin was celebrating in the company of Tex Halliday and various well-wishers.

Thompson congratulated him on his victory and said he could certainly punch, but he fought like a windmill in an Oklahoma dust storm. His style could use some discipline. What he needed was a manager who could teach him how to box.

Ketchel said, "I bet I know who you got in mind."

"I'm a good coach," Thompson said. "Ask anybody. A lot of fight managers have never had the gloves on, but I've done plenty of amateur boxing, so I know what I'm talking about."

"Yeah, I bet. Thanks, but no thanks. I think I know how to fight."

Thompson turned to Halliday and said, "You tell him."

Halliday said it was hard to criticize a first-round knockout.

"Yeah, against a guy who couldn't box, either," Thompson said. "But you can't knock out a guy you can't hit, and the only way to hit a boxer is to box him." To prove his point, he offered to fight Ketchel on the next week's card even though he himself had never had a professional fight.

"I ain't got the punch to knock down a schoolgirl," he said, "but I'll beat you by boxing. If I do, you let me be your manager. You beat me, I'll let you have my share of the purse."

Ketchel said he had a deal.

The following week, as they came together at the opening bell and shook hands, Thompson said, "Okay kiddo, lesson time."

The match went six rounds and Ketchel never landed a solid punch. Reece Thompson boxed on his toes, weaving and feinting and jabbing, circling one way and then the other, keeping Ketchel off balance, easily darting out of reach of his roundhouse swings. By the end of the first round Ketchel was flustered. By the end of the second he was in a rage. The angrier he became, the wilder were his punches, the clumsier his feet. In round three he fell down from the force of a missed swing, and he fell at least once in every round after for the same reason. The crowd was almost as angry as Ketchel. It wasn't interested in an exhibition of pugilistic finesse, it wanted action, a slugging match, blood. It jeered Thompson and demanded that he stand and fight, but he continued to hit and run, consistently scoring with the jab. In the last round Ketchel grabbed at him in sheer frustration, trying to seize him and hold him still for one good punch. The spectators roared their approval, but Thompson broke free, and the referee warned Ketchel against such alleyway style. Thompson easily won the decision.

When they got back to the dressing room Ketchel accused him of dancing rather than fighting, of deliberately trying to make him look foolish.

"You didn't look foolish," Thompson said, "you looked like a guy who don't know how to box. I wouldn't stand a chance slugging it out with you, but like I said, a slugger can't beat a boxer except with a lucky punch. I'll teach you to box."

Ketchel said it would be a frozen day in hell before he would teach him anything. Thompson reminded him they'd had a deal. Ketchel said the deal depended on a fight and Thompson had refused to fight.

Thompson shrugged and said, "Suit yourself. I'm not the one who might have what it takes be a champ."

The remark stuck with him. For the next few days he thought things over. Then went to Thompson's gym and asked him if he really thought he had what it took to be champion.

"I said you *might* have," Thompson told him. "You got a lot to learn. But as I recall, you have to wait for a certain weather change in hell before I can start teaching it to you."

Ketchel said he guessed Thompson hadn't heard the latest news, about the devil buying himself a pair of ice skates.

AND SO HE began going to the gym every day and training under Mickey Ashburn, who worked for Thompson and helped him to coach his fighters. Ketchel didn't care for the boredom of calisthenics and skipping rope, for the monotony of hitting the heavy and light bags, for any of the exercises Ashburn insisted upon before letting him spar. Sparring was the only aspect of training he enjoyed, even though he was constantly being admonished to jab, jab, keep moving, box, *box*. He heard over and over that a missed punch used more energy than one that landed, that in a twenty-round bout it was stamina that usually decided things and wild punching was a waste of strength. But he had no doubt about his strength, no doubt he could punch all day and night if he had to.

In June he was matched against one Jimmy Quinn. For the first minute of the bout he tried to fight as Thompson and Mickey Ashburn had been coaching him. He stayed on the move, jabbing, searching for an opening before throwing a big punch. Thompson and Mickey hollered their approval from the corner. Then Quinn connected with a hard cross that set Ketchel back a few steps and jolted him into a fury. He attacked Quinn as if the man were on fire and he meant to beat out the flames with his fists. He drove him across the ring and against the ropes, hammering aside Quinn's arms to get at his head, punching so furiously he missed as often as he landed and at one point lost his balance and nearly plunged through the ropes. He kept punching even as Quinn sagged down to his haunches, head jerking under the blows. Not until the seat of Quinn's trunks touched the canvas did the ref finally push between them, permitting Quinn to keel over and be counted out. Ketchel circled the ring with his hands above his head, reveling in the crowd's acclaim.

Thompson ran both hands through his hair and shook his head.

"Yeah," Mickey Ashburn said. "Like leading a horse to water."

It was Jimmy Quinn's first and last professional fight. When he regained consciousness he was permanently blind in one eye.

HE HAD CONTINUED to write his mother regularly, but now for the first time risked a return address, though he was no more specific than "general delivery." He told her of his name change and instructed her to use it on her letters, else they might never reach him, or worse, even somehow help the law to track him down.

By way of her answering letter, addressed to "S. Ketchel," he came to learn there were no warrants for his arrest and never had been, as Thomas Kaicel was still among the living, albeit in chronic pain. He now spent the greater part of each day with a gin bottle, and it was left to Ketchel's mother and his brother, John, to maintain the farm, toiling from dark to dark. Kaicel had lately taken to drinking at the taverns rather than at home, a variation she was glad of, as she much preferred to have him drunk at a distance than drunk in her parlor. She could not help wondering what Stanislaus was doing in such a remote reach as Montana and asked if he would return home now that he knew he was in no trouble with the law. As for changing his name to Ketchel, she only wished that by doing the same she could remove Thomas Kaicel from her life. She would not, however, then or ever after, address Ketchel as

"Steve" or even "Stanley," not even on an envelope. To her he would always be Stanislaus.

He wrote back that he was employed in a gymnasium, but he would return to the farm if Kaicel were abusing her. He hoped the offer would comfort her, and hoped even more she would not take him up on it and force him to disappoint her. He was vastly relieved when her next letter admitted that although she was tempted to allege mistreatment in order to draw him home, she could not bring herself to deceive him. The fact of the matter, she said, was that Kaicel seemed to have lost all inclinations except for the demon rum, even his keenness for bullying. Still she hoped Stanislaus would at least come for a visit sometime soon, and she would continue to pray for his safety. She closed with the news that John had begun to court a lovely young neighbor girl named Rebeka Nelson.

HE BOUGHT HIS first suits and some candy-striped shirts, a stylish derby. Kate Morgan presented him with a pocket watch. She taught him the sartorial trick of wearing gray-green neckties to compliment his eyes. They took afternoon walks through town, hearing the screech and growls of the gallows frames, the whistles and clangor of the trains bearing ore to the smelters. Kate liked everything about summer in Butte except for the higher stink it raised from the scores of privies along the shantytown alleys at the bottom of the hill.

He had never seen so many cripples in one town. All of them former miners. Men with missing fingers, missing a hand, an arm. Faces disfigured with burn scars. Here and there an eye patch. It seemed half the people who worked in town had limps. One day he and Kate turned a corner and had to hop aside to avoid being bowled over by a pair of legless men scooting side by side along the walkway on little roller platforms, arguing loudly whether Jeffries the Boilermaker was the equal of the Great John L. in his prime.

Everywhere in town they heard coughing. The "song of the mines," Kate called it, although she herself had a chronic need to clear her throat and was sometimes taken by seizures of hacking that left her red-eyed and breathless and had permanently rasped her voice. The first time she had such a coughing fit in Ketchel's presence, she said she guessed she better quit her job at the Neversweat mine before it killed her.

Almost all the downtown buildings were of brick or paintless stone and stained by smelter fumes. The surrounding mountains were black and gray, the hills streaked sickly yellow with tailings of ore. On good days the sky was the color of old tin, more often looked like a lid of dirt. The air was a tan haze and smelled of dirty pennies. A bird was a rare sight. Yet every Sunday that Ketchel and Kate rode the trolley to the Columbia Gardens at the edge of town to rent a rowboat on the lake and listen to the band concert and dance at the pavilion, the park was packed with happy crowds.

Sometimes he and Kate took dinner in the Finlen Hotel, which she informed him was the swankest to be found in all of the West between Denver and San Francisco. Sometimes they ventured into the sizable Chinatown to regard the Celestials and wonder at their catlike speech, the mysterious orthography of their signs and posters, the peculiar odors permeating the neighborhoods. They dined on fried rice and egg rolls and savory exotic dishes whose ingredient meats Kate advised him it was best not to inquire into, considering the rumors of what so often became of cats and dogs in Chinatown.

They attended the theater and delighted in the vaudeville acts, in the comic skits and acrobatic dogs and jugglers and magicians. At the Broadway he saw his first moving picture, a short film featuring a locomotive that sped head-on toward the camera and sent spectators scrambling from their seats to get out of its way. When *The Great Train Robbery* came to town the theater was packed every night, and Ketchel was hardly the only one who attended its every showing. No dime novel he'd ever read roused such vivid images in his head as were projected onto the white sheet screen for twelve thrilling minutes. At the end, when one of the outlaws pointed his six-shooter at the audience, some among them gasped and Ketchel felt the room's collective cringe, and when the gun discharged with a puff of smoke he flinched too. Even on subsequent viewings, each time he stared into the bore of the bandit's revolver he felt the same exhilarating dread.

A few days after the movie left town, he looked into the muzzle of an actual pistol, cocked and aimed at him across a span of some ten feet as the crowd in the Copper Queen parted from the line of fire. It was the first time a real gun had ever been pointed at him, and yet the situation felt somehow familiar. The man with the gun was a miner with a grievance regarding a dance girl but perhaps was neither so cold-blooded nor so drunk as to be oblivious to the consequence of murder. Maybe that was why he hesitated to pull the trigger. Or maybe it was simply a paralyzing disbelief as Ketchel walked up to him without a word or blink and snatched the gun aside so abruptly the man inadvertently squeezed off a round through the front window and into the side of a passing dry goods wagon. Ketchel wrenched the gun from his grasp and backhanded him with it, opening his cheek to the bone and knocking him to his knees. Then dragged him by the collar to the door and slung him into the street.

The ejected miner never returned nor made claim for his six-shooter, so Ketchel kept it. A single-action .45-caliber Frontier model Colt. And Kate Morgan, who'd grown up the only girl among five brothers on the family ranch and learned much about guns from an early age, taught him how to shoot it.

They went to the garbage dump outside of town and fired upon numberless cans and bottles. He was elated to discover he had a knack, and he laughed like a happy child when she called him a natural-born deadeye. He stood poised with the gun tucked in his waistband and stared narrowly at an empty bottle of James E. Pepper whiskey atop an empty oil drum and said with low menace: "I told you this town wasn't big enough for both of us, Bad Jim." Then yanked out the Colt and fired, reducing the hapless Bad Jim Pepper to shattered glass.

"I'm Jesse James!" he shouted. "I'm Bob Dalton!"

"Yes, yes, you are!" Kate happily yelled.

A rat emerged from a pile of scrap and rose on its hind legs as if to have a better look at the cause of all this clamor. Kate spotted it. "Bushwhacker on your right, Jesse!"

Ketchel whirled and fired at it and missed, the bullet ringing off a rusted axle. The rat remained upright and staring. It had been shot at more times than Ketchel could know and it had grown confident in its long experience with poor marksmanship. It twitched its whiskers.

"Bedamn if the rascal's not funning you," Kate said.

The rat turned and started to walk away in no hurry at all. Ketchel shot it and it went tumbling and then lay spasming until he stepped closer and with his next bullet removed half its head.

"I guess he'll think twice before giving you the razz again," Kate said. Then saw Ketchel's face. "What?"

"Ah, hell. That was lowdown."

"What was?"

"Shooting him in the back."

She put a hand over her smile.

He said, "I'm serious."

She laughed so hard she lapsed into a spell of coughing.

The first time he went out on the streets with the gun tucked in his waistband under his coat flap, he wore a new pair of tooled cowboy boots and a boss-of-the-plains hat pulled low over his eyes. Kate held close to his arm and whispered, "Now I know how Wild Bill's woman felt."

And he smiled a crooked smile in the manner of the storied pistoleers he idolized.

HE FINISHED OFF Kid McGuire in the final minute of the first round, the knockout punch snapping McGuire's head sideways with such force he would have to wear a neck brace for the next two weeks. A week later he fought Kid Leroy and the only time this Kid touched him was when they shook hands at the opening bell. Ketchel then belabored him for a half-minute before landing one to the stomach that doubled Leroy over and clubbing him behind the ear to end it.

Thompson rebuked him after both matches for continuing to fight like a hooligan.

"Christ's sake, Reece," Ketchel said, "I bet most managers are *glad* when their guy wins."

Only two days after the Leroy bout he substituted for an injured fighter against an opponent named Young Gilsey. He forced himself to box, to jab and sidle, to circle his opponent, to exercise finesse rather than simply whale away. He reaped praise from Reece and Mickey as they tended him between rounds. "You see? You can do it," Thompson said. "Never said I couldn't," Ketchel said. But then in the fourth Gilsey connected with a hook to the eye that made Ketchel wince and he retaliated like a man amok. Twenty seconds later Gilsey went down for the count. Ketchel ignored Thompson's reproving glare and raised a fist high in appreciation of the crowd's acclaim.

He fought twice in September, knocking out tough Bob Merrywell in four rounds and then dropping Jimmy Murray in three. The day before the Murray fight, Kate baked him a chocolate cake in Miss Juno's oven and put eighteen flaming candles on it and sang "Happy Birthday." As a present, she gave him a shoulder holster for the Colt.

In October he fought a rematch with Merrywell, a free-swinging affair that had the crammed arena howling with excitement from the opening bell and ended with Merrywell crashing to the canvas unconscious in the middle of round three. Yet Thompson was so displeased with Ketchel's persistence in his alley style of fighting that he matched himself against him again, a ten-rounder this time, telling Ketchel he needed another firsthand boxing lesson. Ketchel shrugged and said, "Sure thing, Reece," secretly certain that this time he would knock Thompson silly. But once again he was frustrated by Thompson's style of fighting in constant retreat and only sporadically closing in to score with quick jabs before again scooting out of Ketchel's range. As before, Thompson was steadily booed for refusing to slug it out, but as before, he won the decision. And believed he had made his point. "I keep proving it to you, kid, a slugger can't beat a boxer. When you gonna start doing like I say?"

During the next two months he had four fights and won them

all by knockout. One of the bouts was in Miles City and one in Lewiston, his first fights outside of Butte. His reputation was spreading throughout Montana.

But he continued to fight without discipline, and Thompson continued to disparage him for a clumsy brawler. "You still don't get it, do you? I guess you just ain't *smart* enough to get it."

That Thompson truly believed such mockery would serve good purpose merely underscored his misunderstanding of Stanley Ketchel's nature. Ketchel veiled his anger with an expression of sincerity and said he knew he'd been a disappointment, but he thought he was starting to catch on. "Don't quit on me, Reece. Let's go another ten rounds, you and me. I'll show you I can box."

Thompson said okay, one last time, but only on two conditions. If both of them were still on their feet at the end of the fight it would be declared a draw, because he did not want to add another loss to Ketchel's record. Plus, Ketchel had to promise that if he didn't win this time he would henceforth fight *exactly* as Thompson instructed him to.

Ketchel said they had a deal.

As Thompson expected, the fight went the distance and was ruled a draw. He had not, however, expected to confront such a disciplined display of boxing skill. Had not expected the jarring Ketchel jab that countered every jab of his own. Nor the nimble Ketchel footwork that repeatedly worked him into the corners or against the ropes where Ketchel each time rocked him with punches before he could manage to escape. The more seasoned observers in the crowd could tell that Ketchel was letting him off the hook each time, that he was not so much interested in scoring a knockout as in giving the man a thrashing. Thompson went down at least once in every round. He was unrecognizable at the final bell but was cheered for his fortitude. An unmarked Ketchel congratulated him on avoiding a knockout and then fired him as his manager.

Stanley Ketchel would have sixty-four fights of record and lose only four, and it is one of the quirks of boxing history that two of those losses were to Maurice Thompson, the only two bouts Thompson ever won in a total of eight professional matches.

HIS MOTHER WROTE to announce John's Christmas Day marriage to Rebeka. The newlyweds would live with her on the farm. She was happy to report that Rebeka was as strong and industrious as she was pretty and kind. Kaicel's opinion of the marriage was unknown for the simple reason that he had been missing for more than a month. He'd sometimes been absent for a few days at a time, but when he still hadn't shown up or sent word in almost two weeks, she had dispatched John to Grand Rapids to make inquiry at the police station and at the hospital. He even asked about him in all of the taverns on the road between town and the farm. But no one knew where he had gone. Her keenest fear was that, despite her hopes and prayers, the man might yet return.

Ketchel was delighted to learn of John's marriage, and Kate contracted his high spirits. They celebrated the wedding that night along with the arrival of the New Year.

A Season of Wrathful Sorrow

He now trained at Freddie Bogan's gym, and his new manager by handshake agreement was Joe O'Connor, a short blocky man of soft-spoken disposition, a photographer by profession, with a small portrait studio on Main Street. O'Connor was a lifelong boxing devotee who had for years been managing local fighters as a sideline, but he'd never managed one with the talent and championship potential of Ketchel.

"I can handle the business end of things," he told Ketchel, "but you need a hell of a better trainer than me. I think I know just the man."

He sent a wire to Billings, and a few days later Pete Stone arrived in response to it. Lean and whitehaired and goateed, of indeterminate age, Stone had been an old-time bareknuckle boxer of repute and was now widely regarded as the best cornerman in the northern Rockies. O'Connor had offered him the job of Ketchel's chief second, and, having already seen Ketchel in action twice, Stone had accepted. He first saw Ketchel fight in Miles City, where he knocked out Jimbo Kelly in the opening round. Then, a week later, in Lewiston, where tough Kid Lee floored him in the eighth with a perfect shot to the chin and every man in the place was sure the fight was over. But Ketchel got up at nine, and half a minute later he trapped Kid Lee against the ropes and pounded him into helplessness, ending it with an overhand right that fractured Lee's jaw and dislodged two sideteeth and mackled his vision for days.

Ketchel needed to work on his boxing skills, Stone told O'Connor, he needed better discipline in the ring. Those things could be taught. But you couldn't teach a punch like his and you couldn't teach his endurance and you for goddamn sure couldn't teach his killer instinct. You were born with such gifts or you were not.

When O'Connor introduced them, Ketchel asked Stone how old he was. The old man was cutting a plug of tobacco and took his time about fitting it in his cheek before saying, "About as old as I look."

Ketchel laughed. "Man, you look like Noah's big brother."

Stone's brown grin webbed his eyes with wrinkles. "Well, in that case, I'm older than I look."

Ketchel liked him. He said Stone's little white beard and the way he worked his chaw reminded him of a goat. Stone said "Baaa." And the Goat was his nickname from then on.

Unlike Thompson, Pete the Goat conveyed his sparring-session instruction in terms of admiration. "Let the guy know he's fighting a goddamn jungle cat, Stevie, let him *know* it. You're too quick for him, he can't hit you, you're too smart. Play with him, move in quick and cut him up some and jump away. That's the ticket. Jungle cat! Now work to the body, work to the body. Beat the heart out of him. Make him bring his hands down, then work to the head. Beat the heart out of the bastard, Stevie, beat the heart out of him while you get his measure and *then* tear into him with everything and finish him. You're a goddamn jungle cat!"

"Yeah, yeah, *yeah*!" Ketchel said as he thumped his sparring partner with two hooks to the ribs and drove him into the corner with an uppercut.

And three days later knocked out Kid Thomas in the first forty seconds of their fight with a combination of hooks to the head that repositioned the Kid's nose and afflicted him with a sinus condition for the rest of his days. Afterward Ketchel explained to the Goat that he'd gotten the man's measure pretty fast. "So I gathered," the Goat said.

Two weeks after that, he boxed impressively for four rounds against Jack Bennett before cooling him in the fifth. The Goat clinched him around the neck with a hammerlock. "What are you, kid! What *are* you?"

"Jungle cat!" Ketchel yelled. "Goddamn *jungle cat!*"

JOHN L. SULLIVAN'S final prizefight was on the first of March in 1905. Except for an exhibition match in 1896 the Boston Strong Boy had not fought in the twelve and a half years since losing the title to Gentleman Jim. He was now forty-six years old and weighed a leviathan 273 pounds. His hair had gone gray, his face was jowled and dewlapped. He did not really need the money, but he yearned for the old adulation. His opponent was James McCormick, half his age and 200 solid pounds. In the opening round McCormick landed several good punches, but mostly was in retreat as Sullivan lumbered after him, throwing one roundhouse atop another, most of them hitting nothing but air, some few striking McCormick's defending arms and making the man wince. The warhorse was blowing hard when he returned to his corner at the end of round one. His crew was alarmed he might be courting a heart attack. But a minute into round two, one of those great fists found the point of McCormick's chin and that was all she wrote. The crowd gave the grizzled hero a lusty and prolonged ovation.

The fight took place in Ketchel's home town of Grand Rapids, Michigan. His brother, John, was in attendance and wrote Ketchel an excitedly scrawled three-page letter packed with detail. He said Sully had a rummy's red nose and wore every hour of his life on his face and was grossly fat, but still had a punch like a mule kick.

"Next time we see each other," he wrote, "you can shake the hand that shook the hand of the Great John L."

ONE FEBRUARY EVENING, after a vigorous session in the gym, he took Kate to Kelly's Chop House for supper. He was still heated from the workout and the shower afterward, and steam issued from under his jacket collar as they made their way arm-in-arm through the frozen night. She said he looked like he was on fire under his clothes.

They were drinking hot rum and cold beer, waiting for their steaks, when she broke out in a coughing fit that coated the fingers at her mouth with blood.

Over the next weeks, she underwent examination by every doctor in Butte, and then Ketchel escorted her to Helena for another opinion, then to Billings, then to Boise. All diagnoses agreed on a rapacious throat malignancy too far advanced to be treated. The most optimistic of the doctors gave her little more than a year, the most realistic said she could not hope for three months.

"They're full of shit," Ketchel told her on the train ride back from Idaho. "All of them. If they were any good they'd be set up in a big city and making plenty of jack, not sawing bones in some rathole mining town."

He'd been told of a prominent cancer specialist in Denver, and he wanted to take her there. But Kate said she needed to rest up a little and think things over.

"What's there to think about?" he said. "I *know* it's not serious, but whatever it is, the sooner some smart doc checks you, the sooner you'll get the right medicine and be fine." He could not have admitted his terror of the possibility she'd been correctly diagnosed.

"Please, Stanley. I just need a few days to catch my breath before—" She was interrupted by a coughing jag and turned her back to him. When the fit passed, she was gasping and had to blow her nose, dry her eyes, wipe her mouth. She tried to hide it from him but he glimpsed the bloodstains on the hankie.

She chuckled and said in her inflated brogue, "By Jaysus, laddie, 'catch my breath' did I say! I believe I made a wee joke."

She didn't tell him so, but she knew the doctors were right. She could feel it. At her insistence, and while Ketchel was not in the examining room, the Boise doctor had graphically described the dreadful end in store.

THREE NIGHTS AFTER their return from Idaho, he was fetched at the Copper Queen by a resident of the boardinghouse who could tell him only that there had been a gunshot.

He found her on the bed in her best robe, freshly bathed and redolent of perfume and talc, her hair beribboned, a powder-burned red hole in her breast and his Colt fallen at her side. A note on the pillow provided her family's address in Cheyenne and said she loved him and wished him happiness, and that although she knew he'd miss her a little "(At *least* a little, I hope!)," she also knew they were two of a kind and neither of them really needed anybody. It ended with: "Sorry I won't be there to see you KO Jeff." Its appearance in the note was the only time the word "love" had ever passed between them.

Someone had fetched the sheriff. Ketchel let him come in and see her. Let him read the note. The man offered his condolences and accepted Ketchel's assurance that he would take care of things, then left.

He sat by the bed and held her hand until it was cold in a way no living hand could ever be. In the company of her corpse he felt more alone than he'd known it was possible to feel. Felt as if she'd killed something in his own heart as surely as she had stopped hers. When the undertaker announced himself at the door, Ketchel said to go away or he'd break his neck. The cats watched him all night from the top of the wardrobe but at first light they were gone and he would see them no more. That morning he sent a telegram to Cheyenne and then shipped the body in ice on the afternoon train.

He then returned to the room and stayed there, drinking from the bottle, softly singing the songs she'd liked best. He slept with her clothes at his face, breathing her scent. He woke in the night to new kinds of darkness.

Pete the Goat and Joe O'Connor stopped by to offer condolences, then let him alone. Then after another two days O'Connor went to see him again. He accepted Ketchel's offer of a drink and did his best to promote a bluff masculine stoicism, telling him he smelled worse than some dead men he'd had a whiff of and maybe it was time to get himself cleaned up before the landlady mistook *him* for dead and called the undertaker to cart him away.

"What we need is something to wash down this whiskey. What say we go to a chop house, pal, and get us a big thick—"

"Joe?" Ketchel said.

"Yeah, kid?"

"Thanks. Now go away."

O'Connor sighed and nodded, patted Ketchel's shoulder and left.

HE KEPT TO the room for a week before finally rousing himself and moving to another boardinghouse. The day after that he showed up at Bogan's gym. He had trained only sporadically during Kate's illness, and now it was late March and he had not fought in nearly two months. O'Connor and the Goat were glad to see him, but neither thought he was ready to resume training immediately.

"You been boozing for days and you look like hell," the Goat said. "I bet you ain't slept ten minutes at a time or ate more than a bite. You need some proper rest and a few regular meals, kid, then we'll get back to training."

O'Connor agreed. Ketchel didn't. He wanted to spar. He wanted to hit somebody. They were arguing about it when Tex Halliday came in and said Ketchel was just the man he was looking for. He offered him a spot on the program the following night. A twenty-five-rounder against Sid LaFontise, a miner who'd been preparing for his first pro match for the past seven weeks.

Pete the Goat said hell no, Steve was in no condition to fight, especially not a twenty-five-rounder, and especially not against LaFontise. Pete had been in Thompson's gym recently and seen

LaFontise sparring. The man was a hardcase hitter with plenty of natural talent.

"Give us two, three weeks to get ready," O'Connor said, "and you got a match."

Halliday said he needed somebody for LaFontise by tomorrow.

"I'll take it," Ketchel said. Since Kate's death, he'd been feeling an unfamiliar and inexplicable tension, and he thought a good fight might set him straight.

O'Connor protested. "Goddamnit, who's the manager here?"

"Who's the fighter?" Ketchel said.

He was knocked down three times in the first round, twice in the second, he went down once in each of the next three rounds. By which time his eyes were battered to beets, his nose was streaming blood, his lips cut and bloated. Just before the bell for the ninth he threw up into the sponge bucket. Then his timing began to come around, his punches to find their mark. He knocked LaFontise down for the first time in the twentieth round, then again in each of the next three rounds. And floored him for the count in the twenty-fourth. The walls of the Big Casino quivered with the exultations of the crowd. And as Ketchel stood in the ring with his fist raised high, he knew that what he most loved about fighting was its clarity. He could not have expressed it, but he understood as surely as he'd ever understood anything that when you knock a man out you resolve matters with an absoluteness impossible to rhetorical arguments or philosophical disputes. A knockout was pure truth.

Still, it was the worst beating he'd yet absorbed, and Pete told him not to blow his nose for a few days or he'd make his eyes blacker. Ketchel secretly welcomed the pain. It was physical, could be dealt with and endured. But as always the bruises healed with amazing swiftness.

The following month he went to Miles City for a twenty-rounder against a hulk named Rudy Hinz who had a twenty-five-pound advantage and bragged he couldn't be knocked out with a brick. Ketchel agreed to a draw if the fight went the distance. Then tried to break Hinz's skull with his fists, knocking him down thirteen times, but Hinz each time beat the count. "I *told* ya!" Hinz crowed when it was over. But his mauled mouth made him almost unintelligible and his eyes were so swollen he had to be led from the ring like a blind man.

In May he fought a rematch with LaFontise and knocked him out so soundly the man could not recall his own name for a half-hour after being revived.

THERE WAS A distant cast about him during this period of his life, except when he was fighting, and then he seemed near to insane in his ferocity. So ruthless was he even with sparring partners that the Goat ordered him to take it easy before they all quit. As a favor to Richardson he still worked as bouncer at the Queen three nights a week, but he now took a fiendish gusto in quelling disturbance, and the only way a troublemaker could leave under his own power was by outrunning him to the door. The natural fury of his violence had become a red wrath, and O'Connor and the Goat both knew its engine was incessant grief. But they knew too there was nothing for it. He would overcome the sorrow of losing Kate or he would not.

The first time O'Connor saw him slip the Colt along with his clothes into a locker before a workout he said, "Why you carrying *that* around?" Ketchel said, "Protection." O'Connor wanted to ask from what, but didn't.

Then came a fight against Curley Rue in a two-dog town called

Gregson Springs. No one knew much about Rue except that he talked tough and claimed he'd had plenty of fights here and there, none of them on the official record. That he could take a punch is beyond dispute. Ketchel floored him at least once in eight of the first ten rounds, but Rue got up each time, and Ketchel grew enraged at his failure to knock him out. At the start of the eleventh he pinned Rue against the ropes and pounded him steadily for an everlasting fifteen seconds, continuing to make a jellied smear of his face even after it was obvious to everyone looking on that Curley Rue was out on his feet. When he finally stepped back to let him fall, Rue fell over like a plank.

"Get up now, honyocker," Ketchel said.

Curley Rue was carried unconscious from the ring. A week or so after the fight, a rumor reached Bogan's gym that he had died of the beating.

O'Connor didn't believe it. After several tries, he was finally able to get a phone call through to the promoter of the fight, who was also the local constable at Gregson Springs, and asked if it was true. The constable said he didn't know. He said Rue had regained consciousness in the dressing room but wasn't what anybody would call alert and he had trouble forming coherent phrases. At his own insistence he was helped to get dressed and transported to the depot and he got aboard the train for Lewiston. The next day, word started going around that he'd changed trains at Lewiston and shortly afterward died in the coach car. But nobody knew which train he'd been on or where he'd been headed or where he called home. None of the railroad agents knew of anybody having died on a train recently. Nobody even knew where the story got started.

"Ten to one the guy ain't any deader than you or me," the constable said. "I figure it's one of them stories somebody makes up for the sheer hell of it and next thing you know a whole bunch of people are swearing it's true." He promised to let O'Connor know if he should learn anything about the matter for certain.

Ketchel didn't see why O'Connor was so rattled. "It's either true or it's not. But if it's true it ain't like I murdered him. It was a legal fight."

"Of course it was, Stevie. That's not the point."

"What is?" Ketchel said. "Nobody held a gun to the guy's head and made him get in the ring."

"He might be dead, for Christ's sake."

"And if he is, what's anybody supposed to do about it?"

O'Connor gestured in vague exasperation. "I don't know!"

"Then what are we talking about?"

O'Connor turned to Pete the Goat, who was paring his nails with a pocketknife. "What do *you* think?"

The Goat pondered the question. He shifted the chaw in his cheek. "Well, I'll tell you, one of the first fights I ever saw, bareknuckle I'm talking about, back when I was a kid, my uncle was working a corner and let me sit next to him. My uncle's fighter was a fella called Moe, and in the fifth round he some way or other knocks an eye out the other guy's head. Swear to God. There wasn't much blood, a smear of it under the empty socket is all, and the eye's hanging halfway down the guy's cheek on some little stringy veins, I guess they were. You never saw nothing like it. Anyway, the ref stops the fight for a minute to try and figure out what to do. He asks the pug can he keep on fighting and the pug says yeah, but not with his eye hanging down like that because he can still see with it and it's showing him his feet while the other eye's showing him what's in front of him and the whole thing's terrible confusing and starting to make him dizzy, which I found easy to believe. His cornermen all have a close study of it and they don't see any way to put the eye back in his head, so the pug tells them to just go ahead and pull it off and hold on to it so he can give it a proper burial later on. So they do, and the pug says that's better, at least he's not seeing in two different directions at once anymore. The ref asks is he sure he wants to go on with the match and the pug says yeah. Now, you'd figure a fighter with two eyes has got a pretty big advantage over a guy with just one, but turns out my uncle's fighter, this guy Moe, had a delicate stomach. When the ref tells them to resume fighting, they swap a few jabs and Moe lands one on that empty socket, then steps back with this kinda sick look, then bends over and starts puking. And while he's doing that, the one-eyed guy steps up and hits him with an uppercut from down around his ankles and Moe goes about a foot in the air and comes down like a sack of bricks. You coulda gone out and had yourself some supper and a cigar and still got back in plenty of time before he woke up."

He paused and spat a streak of tobacco. "Boxing's a rough game. Kinda funny sometimes, kinda strange sometimes, kinda sad sometimes. But all the time rough. Like the man said, it ain't for everybody. Anyhow, that's what *I* think." And went back to paring his nails.

Ketchel grinned like a mule chewing briars.

O'Connor glared from one to the other. "Jesus Harrison Christ, I ask a goddamn simple question. . . ."

IN TRUTH, KETCHEL was not sure how he felt about the rumor that Curley Rue had died in consequence of the beating he'd given him, and because he was not one to be unsure about himself the uncertainty made him angry and troubled his sleep for the next two nights. Then late the following afternoon came the news that James Jeffries had retired, the only heavyweight champ up to that time to retire undefeated. And Ketchel recalled a recurrent dream he used to have about Jeffries, a dream he'd never told to anyone except Kate.

The particulars were always the same. It was a fight to the finish for the heavyweight title and they slugged it out all day and all night, beating each other bloody into the 212th round while spectators came and went and the faces at ringside changed continually. But at the bell to begin round 213, Jeffries could no longer muster the strength to raise his arms, and Ketchel set himself and threw a tremendous overhand at big Jeff's unprotected jaw. But on every occasion of the dream, in the instant before the punch struck he woke up.

Kate had not been uninformed about boxing and knew the might of Jim Jeffries and that at his fighting weight he outscaled Ketchel by sixty pounds, and she was aware of Ketchel's veneration of him. She was delighted by the dream. She said she believed the only reason he always woke up before the punch landed was that he respected Jeffries so much he wanted to spare him the humiliation of a knockout, even in a dream.

"You think so?" Ketchel said. "Boy, wouldn't that be something? To knock out the Boilermaker! I mean, that man is a goddamn killing machine."

"Well, so are you, Mr. Michigan Assassin."

"Yeah, but . . . Jeffries! He's the biggest of them all."

Kate smiled and kissed him. "Oh baby, he's no bigger than you, he's just taller and weighs more."

Since Kate's death, he had not had the Jeffries dream nor occasion to recall her response to it. But when he got the word of Jeffries' retirement, he remembered. He lay in bed that night and remembered the dream and remembered telling Kate about it and remembered her wonderful kiss and bold green eyes and confident insistence that he was no less powerful nor even smaller than Jeffries, the physical difference between them be damned.

The recollection was akin to recovering from a brief but unsettling episode of amnesia, a return to full awareness of who he was, and he suddenly felt like both laughing and crying. And did both. Then slept soundly.

HE HAD SIX more fights in the rest of that spring and summer and won them all by knockout, fighting as fiercely as ever. And in two of those fights he had his opponent on the ropes and beaten to helplessness, at which point he both times ceased his attack and let the man fall for the count.

Miss Molly Yates

He met Molly Yates one morning when he took breakfast in the Silver Hill Café for the first time. Along with the family house, she had inherited the business after her parents were killed in a train derailment returning from a trip to Denver. She was tall and auburn-haired and twenty-five years old. She knew who he was before he introduced himself, having seen his picture in the local newspaper and heard her customers talk about him.

He went to the Silver Hill for breakfast every morning thereafter, and they would converse for an hour or two every time. He learned she'd had a high school sweetheart she planned to marry, but two months after graduation and going to work in the mines he was killed in an explosion, and for almost a year she thought her heartbreak might kill her too.

He'd known her for three weeks when she invited him to supper at her home on the following evening. He arrived freshly barbered and in a new suit. After they dined they repaired to the parlor and she played the Victrola and they danced. He thought she might slap him for his sudden kiss and was instead surprised by the fervor and finesse of her own kiss in return. She unpinned her hair and let it spill onto her shoulders in a dark abundance. And then they were naked in her candlelit bed.

She afterward told him she had known several men, as she phrased it, since the death of her betrothed, though never again a miner. She had discovered the particular enjoyment of physical intimacy without emotional investment. She said she hoped he did not think her wanton.

He said he thought she was just what the doctor ordered.

"Well, in that case," she said, rolling atop him, "I believe it's time for your medicine."

IN NOVEMBER HE became an uncle when a daughter named Julia Josephina Kaicel, who'd been nicknamed Julie Bug, was born to John and Rebeka. Although the farm continued to provide a living for his mother and his brother's family, Ketchel had in recent months been sending cash in his letters to her, and he now enclosed even more than usual, directing her to use the money to pay the legal costs of a divorce from Kaicel, who at this point had been missing without word for almost a year. He had spoken with an attorney in town and been advised that his mother very likely had grounds on the basis of desertion.

HE COULD FEEL himself sharpening under the Goat's rigorous regimen. His footwork quickened, his defenses improved. He was using his jab to better effect than ever. Still, his most potent asset, ever and always and excepting perhaps a nearly maniacal determination, was the flurry, a two-fisted salvo of punches one behind the other and linked tightly as a chain. A flurry at once punished an opponent and kept him on the defensive, unable to counterpunch in the midst of the attack. Few fighters owned both the hand speed and the reservoir of energy necessary for throwing more than a few effective flurries in the course of a long fight, but Ketchel's hands were fast as vipers and he was a phenomenon of unflagging stamina. The locals liked to joke that while some fighters were pretty good at the old one-two, Ketchel was the master of the old one-two-three-four-five-six.

He and Molly kept company whenever he wasn't at the gym or working at the Copper Queen and she wasn't taking care of business at the café. He repeatedly asked her to come see him fight but she steadfastly refused, saying she did not care to witness violence and had no desire to see him get hurt.

"It's usually the other fella gets hurt," he said, trying for a laugh but not unaware that he was bragging, wanting to impress her.

He fought six times in December, including three fights in a single week, and won them all by knockouts. Then asked Joe O'Connor when he thought he would be ready for Tommy Ryan, who had been the middleweight champion for the past seven years but who was now thirty-five years old and had not defended his title in a year.

"I can take that old man," Ketchel said.

O'Connor said a lot of other middleweights felt the same way and all of them wanted a shot at Ryan. Ryan, however, didn't seem inclined to accept anybody's challenge, and the odds were that he would retire without ever fighting again.

"Don't worry, Stevie," O'Connor said, "the breaks'll be coming our way real soon. For now, we just stay sharp and ready."

Right, Ketchel said. But he'd earned a rest and meant to have it. He persuaded Molly to take a short vacation to San Francisco with him right after Christmas.

IN CONTRAST TO Montana's glacial winter, San Francisco's December seemed almost mild, never mind the chill Pacific breeze. They took breakfast every morning in the glassed-in gallery of the hotel café. On their second day in town the newspaper front pages were full of the Idaho bombing murder of Frank Steunenberg, who had been hard on miners' unions during his governorship of that state a few years earlier. The Industrial Workers of the World, commonly called the Wobblies or the "I-Won't-Works" and widely regarded as a union of red agitators bent on the destruction of the American Way, was suspected in Steunenburg's killing. Ketchel said he bet every miner in Butte was talking about this news. He began to read the report to her but she asked him to please don't. The whole thing sounded too awful and she did not want to know about it.

They had a wonderful few days. He showed her around this city he loved so dearly, taking her to the wharves, to the park, out to the beach where he'd spent his first night on the coast and been soaked by the tide. They ambled through a Chinatown so much larger than Butte's she joked that she felt as though she'd been shanghaied.

New Year's Eve was their last night in town. Molly wore a stunning blue dress he'd bought for her in the city's best dress shop. They dined at an elegant restaurant with blazing chandeliers and waiters in tuxedos. The champagne came to the table on a wheeled tray, in glass buckets of shaved ice. The dessert came in a dish of flames. They afterward went dancing in a posh club and joined in the raucous midnight cheering. They were both slightly tipsy as they started back to the hotel.

They were on a deserted street of closed shops and only two blocks from the hotel, skyrockets still bursting in sprays of bright color, firecrackers banging loud as gunshots, when a pair of men stepped from the darkness of an alley and blocked the way. In the weak light of a distant corner lamppost Ketchel saw the small pistol one of them held and the long-bladed knife in the hand of the other.

"Your money or your blood," said the one with the gun.

"Oh my God," Molly said softly.

"Anything you say, gents," Ketchel said. "Easy does it. Here's my wallet."

He reached into his coat and pulled out the Colt, cocking it in the same motion, and shot the gunman in the throat, the muzzle-blast bright yellow. The man's hat fell away and his gun clattered on the pavement as he staggered back and collapsed in the alley.

Ketchel pointed the Colt at the other man and he dropped the knife and raised his hands. "Oh Christ, mister, not me."

"Get," Ketchel said.

The man turned and ran down the sidewalk and around the corner and was gone. The crack and pop of fireworks continued in the surrounding streets.

He was exultant, marveling at his own coolness, at his steadiness of hand. At having pulled the gun without hesitation or doubt of purpose. He knelt beside the robber in the alley darkness and heard the man's small gargling gasps. He could not make out his features.

"You hear me?" Ketchel said. The man said nothing. Was likely unconscious, likely dying.

"Can't say you didn't have it coming, Mac," Ketchel said. He stood up and tucked away the revolver. He looked at the little pistol lying at the foot of the alley and chose to leave it there. Let the cops know the bastard had not been unarmed.

Only now did he remember Molly. He turned and saw she was gone.

Back at the hotel he found the room door locked from inside, and she did not respond to his rapping and request to open up. He crooned through the door that everything was all right, he understood why she'd run away, she didn't have to be ashamed of being afraid of them.

To which she answered in a small voice that she was scared of *him*. He was a frightening man and it scared her even more that she hadn't seen the truth about him until this evening.

"Scared of *me*? What . . . what're you talking about?"

"That gun . . . I had no *idea* . . . And you just . . . oh, God."

"Hey now, darling, it was a damn good thing I had it. Come on, sweetheart, open up."

She said nothing more nor undid the lock. He asked her to let him in so they could discuss it in private. "I can explain," he said, although he did not see what there was to explain.

He was smacking the door with his palm, beginning to lose his patience and entertaining thoughts of shouldering his way in, when a boisterous quartet of drunks came up the stairway. They grinned at the sight of him leaning on the door, and as they passed by him one said, "Good luck, chum. I been in that doghouse a time or two meself."

Ketchel was the only one who didn't laugh. He watched them go reeling down the hall and had an impulse to run after them and knock them all on their asses. Then pictured himself as they saw him and felt like a dope.

The hell with this, he thought, and repaired to the hotel bar downstairs.

He woke to a gentle shaking of his shoulder by the early-shift bartender. He was seated with his painful head on his arms at a table next to a window glaring with morning light. He went up to the room and found she had packed her clothes and gone. She left a note saying she was taking an earlier train back to Butte and asked that he please not seek her out.

HE DID SEEK her out, of course. First at the café, where she disappeared into the back room when she saw him come in, and later at her house, where she stood behind her locked front door and said that if he did not leave her alone she would ask the police to intervene. The mention of police did the trick. It obliged him to consider the chilly prospect of discussing with them the cause of her estrangement and the incident of New Year's Eve. There was nothing for it but to let her be.

He never returned to her house, did not again set foot in the Silver Hill Café. As far as he would ever know, she told no one in Butte, maybe told nobody anywhere, what happened to bring their brief association to an end.

A little over three months later, all the news was of the apocalyptic quake and fire that razed San Francisco. When he saw in a newspaper photograph the smoldering remains of the very hotel where he and Molly had stayed during their visit, he could not help but feel that he was looking at the wreckage of more than a building.

HIS MOTHER WROTE that the petition for divorce had been submitted. All she could do now was wait for it to make its slow way through the legal system and meanwhile hope to heaven that Kaicel did not show up before it was granted.

Ketchel didn't say so, but he was sure they had all seen the last of Thomas Kaicel. In a recent dream he'd seen himself fighting with him in a boxcar of a rumbling freight, throttling him, pitching his lifeless body into the passing night. Wherever Kaicel might be, Ketchel knew in his bones the man was dead. And had a strong sense that he had died badly.

HE APPLIED HIMSELF with renewed zeal to achieving greater proficiency at his trade, and by autumn had won another seven matches, all of them against opponents larger than himself. He had now won thirty-five fights and every one by knockout. His only losses remained the two decisions to Reece Thompson. He was twenty years old and a solid 150 pounds, and there was no worthy opponent in the region left for him to fight, not even among the heavyweights.

But in those days before radio he remained unknown to the world beyond Montana. O'Connor and the Goat agreed that he was ready to climb the ladder. It was time to move to California, the center of big-time boxing. They agreed to make the move at the end of the year.

Among the enduring topics of national interest at this time was the shooting murder of the famous architect Stanford White in New York City a few months before. The crime had occurred at the roof theater of the Madison Square Garden. The killer was Harry Kendall Thaw, a rich young man of dubious sanity whose motive was reported to be outrage over White's "ruination" of a woman now Thaw's wife, never mind that the alleged ruination had occurred five years earlier and that she had become Thaw's wife only a year ago.

The woman in the scandalous triangle was Evelyn Nesbit. She was twenty-one years old on the occasion of the killing. She had been a showgirl, a model for photographers, for painters and illustrators. Even before the infamous crime, her face if not her name had been renowned as the subject of Charles Dana Gibson's immensely popular illustration, *The Eternal Question,* in which her exquisite profile was framed within a question mark shaped by the lush fall of her hair.

Ketchel thought Evelyn Nesbit was as beautiful in the newspaper photographs as in Gibson's drawing. He saw in her face an abused innocence that inflamed his imagination. As she was for countless other American males from blushing boys to palsied old men, she was the object of his most passionate sexual fantasies, and he readily understood why a man would kill for her. Sitting at supper in Montana, beholding a picture of her taken in New York and printed in a Denver newspaper, he was thickly heartsick with desire.

SHORTLY BEFORE KETCHEL made his move to California with O'Connor and the Goat, middleweight champion Tommy Ryan announced his retirement. There was immediate and wide debate about who should be recognized as the division's new champ. In point of fact, the matter had been in dispute since the year before, when Hugo Kelly of Chicago claimed the championship on the basis that Ryan refused to fight him. It was not much of an argument, in that Ryan had refused to fight anybody since 1904. Still, a number of sportswriters supported Kelly's claim to the title. Others, however, insisted on Jack (Twin) Sullivan as the middleweight champ, and some argued for Joe Thomas, a hard hitter in San Francisco who had only recently turned pro and in his third fight kayoed the welterweight champ.

"The division's a hell of a mess," Joe O'Connor said, tossing aside *The Sporting News*.

"Don't fret about it, boss," the Goat said, "Stevie's gonna sort it out all nice and clear for everybody, ain't you, kid?"

"Bet your ass," Ketchel said. "I'll whip them all. The sooner the better. Then we'll go for Burns."

It was his first mention to them of an ambition he'd confided to no one but the late Kate Morgan. To be the heavyweight champion. Until recently that meant having to beat Jim Jeffries, which Ketchel hadn't believed he could do till Kate persuaded him otherwise. But now Jeff had hung up his gloves, and the new champ was Tommy Burns. Tommy Burns, for Christ's sake. A man no taller than Ketchel himself and but fifteen pounds heavier. Ketchel knew he could dismantle Tommy Burns, could make a red smear of him, he had not the slightest doubt of it. But he also knew he'd never get a match against him without first winning the middleweight title. A fight between champions would be too profitable for Burns to turn down.

At the mention of Burns, Pete the Goat beamed and winked at Ketchel, but O'Connor was quick to invoke caution. "Whoa now, laddie," he said, "let's keep our shirts on. You're a natural middle and the best of them, no question, and you'll soon enough prove it. But the heavies . . . well . . . the heavies are another matter. Let's don't try to shoot down the moon, hey?"

Ketchel was about to say "Why not?" but didn't. It wasn't something he was going to argue about. Not now nor when the time came.

Under the Bear Flag

They departed Butte on a frozen gray morning, and late the following afternoon arrived in sun-bright San Francisco. They set up their training camp in Colma, a mile or so south of the Frisco city limit, and they wasted no time issuing a challenge to Joe Thomas.

Thomas was amenable to a match, but he was already contracted for two bouts. The earliest he could fight Ketchel was the Fourth of July. Ketchel chafed at the delay. He was afraid Thomas might lose one or both of the fights before their own. Only if he was the first to beat him would Ketchel be in prime contention for the title.

Thomas wouldn't lose either bout. The first would be a draw and the second would be scrubbed after his opponent broke a hand in a saloon fray three days before the fight.

In the meantime, Ketchel kept busy. He trained diligently. He rose early six mornings a week to do roadwork. Then calisthenics and chopping wood. Then hitting the heavy bag, the speed bag. Sparring. He ate well and went to bed early and slept free of disturbing dreams. In the span of two months in spring he had his first three California fights and won them all by knockout.

He and the Goat occasionally went into San Francisco for a vaudeville show and to view nickelodeons, to treat themselves to seafood. On his first visit to Frisco since he'd been there with Molly Yates, he was astounded by its degree of recovery from the smoky rubble in the newspaper pictures some nine months before. The resurrected city still showed dark scars and it had a much altered aspect, but its charm was indestructible. He grew to love all of central California, its splendid weather, its picturesque countryside. He thought the state flag beautiful and bought one and tacked it on the wall above his bed.

HE HAD WRITTEN to his mother and told her of his move to California, and she had written back to say she was glad he'd left the wilderness, as she referred to Montana, but chided him for moving in the wrong direction and placing himself even farther from her. She saved the happy news for the end of the letter, where she told him the divorce decree had been granted. She wrote, "I feel so freeeeee!!!!" And added in a post script that she had very proudly changed her name to Ketchel. John had petitioned the court to do the same.

MIDWAY INTO 1907 the question of who should rightly be recognized as middleweight champion was still unsettled. Within two months of retiring, Tommy Ryan changed his mind. But after boxing Hugo Kelly to a draw and then losing a decision to a featherweight opponent—a *featherweight!*—he clearly read the handwriting on the wall and again called it quits, this time for good. As for Kelly, following his draw with Ryan he fought a draw with Jack (Twin) Sullivan, and both he and Sullivan continued to lay claim to the title.

To further complicate the matter, a young middleweight named Billy Papke was making a name for himself in Illinois. Since turning pro the year before, he had won all fourteen of his fights, ten of them by knockout. He fought in Peoria but often trained in Chicago, and hence had attracted much national attention. A number of sportswriters around the country thought he was destined to be the middleweight champion. He had been quoted as saying he could lick any middleweight in the world and would prove it just as quick as he was given the chance.

THE FIGHT WITH Joe Thomas was in Marysville, some forty miles north of Sacramento and just below Yuba City. The day before the match, Ketchel, O'Connor, and the Goat took the train to Yuba and checked into a hotel. At dinner that evening they were waited on by a striking brunette, Sandra by name, who smiled at Ketchel's jests and boldly returned his flirtations. By the end of the meal she had agreed to meet him for coffee at a café down the block when she got off duty.

O'Connor and the Goat argued against the impromptu date, urging Ketchel to rest up for the next day's fight. Ketchel told them not to fret, he was only going to have coffee with the girl and try to arrange a date with her for another time. He laughed and patted Joe on the shoulder. "Go on to bed, mother. I'll be back before you've counted a hundred sheep."

O'Connor could have counted thousands of sheep before he next saw him, which wasn't until after eight o'clock the next morning. Joe was sitting with his head in his hands, the Goat slumped in a chair and staring glumly at the wall, when Ketchel came through the door, saying, "God almighty, boys, what a night! She wrung me like a dishrag, I'm telling you!"

He had lipstick smears on his face and was missing the collar of his shirt. He smelled of booze and sex and perfume.

"Sweet Jesus, you're boiled as an owl!" O'Connor said.

"Nah," Ketchel said. "I *was* boiled, but now I'm only about parboiled." He cackled like a schoolboy sharing a joke.

O'Connor berated him for a goddamned fool as they hustled out to the street and hired a cab. Pete the Goat slipped the driver an extra dollar and said they were in a hurry and the man snapped the reins on the team to move them into a lope.

On the ride to Marysville the Goat wiped the lipstick off Ketchel's face and neck with a spit-wet handkerchief like a mother tending an unkempt child. O'Connor spoke of trying to postpone the fight but Ketchel wouldn't hear of it.

"I'm fine, Joe," he insisted. "I'll take him apart."

They made it to Marysville in time for the weigh-in, four hours before the fight. Ketchel's debauched night had robbed him of a few pounds and he tipped the scales at 146. Joe Thomas weighed in at an even 150. Thomas wore his hair thick and curly on his crown and razored to the skin several inches above his ears, a style he believed evocative of menace. His face looked made of pocked concrete. Like everyone else in the room except O'Connor and the Goat, he was amused by Ketchel's disheveled appearance, his bloodshot eyes, the reek emanating from him, even more pronounced when he stripped for the scales.

"Good Christ, man," Thomas said, "you smell like you just come from Sadie's whorehouse."

"I did," Ketchel said. "Sadie said to give you her best and tell you she still ain't found anybody to clean the chamber pots as good as you did."

The crack got a laugh from the sportswriters on hand, but Thomas wasn't amused. "You'll be laughing out the other side of your face when I'm done with you, farmboy."

Like Ketchel, Thomas had been a saloon bouncer before putting on the gloves, and right from the start their match was rough as a bar fight. They butted heads, used elbows at close quarters, beat at each other's kidneys in the clinches, scraped at each other's cuts with the laces of their gloves. The ref warned them twice and then said, "All right, you boys have it your way." At the end of eighteen rounds Ketchel was tired and it showed as he slumped onto the stool to be swabbed and watered by the Goat. O'Connor continued to berate him for his dissipation of the night before. "It's guys like you give Polacks the reputation for stupidity," he said. Ketchel spat into the bucket and said, "Say now, I didn't come here to be insulted." The Goat completed the old vaudeville dialogue with, "Oh, where you usually go?" and they both laughed. O'Connor shook his head and muttered, "Clowns, I'm working with goddamn clowns." Ketchel and Thomas knocked each other down five times in the course of the twenty rounds but were both on their feet at the final gong. The ref raised a hand of each man and declared a draw. The arena resounded with the chant of "Rematch! rematch!"

Both boxers favored another fight as much as the fans, and the sooner the better. Within a week the contracts were signed for a Labor Day rematch at Sunny Jim Coffroth's Mission Street Arena in Colma. They both preferred a fight to the finish but California law would not permit it. It did, however, allow for a match of forty-five rounds, virtually the same thing, since it was a rare occasion in which one boxer did not do in the other or quit from exhaustion before the forty-fifth round.

Ketchel trained more assiduously than ever. During his free hours he comported himself like a monk. Thomas trained with equal discipline. The accounts of their previous match drew sportswriters from all over the country for this one, many of them eager for their first look at these two contenders for the middleweight title.

The fight lasted more than two hours under a warm midafternoon sun, and for most of it they were slugging toe-to-toe. In the seventh round Thomas scored the first knockdowns, twice flooring Ketchel for a count of six. In the eleventh, he gashed Ketchel's eyebrow with a headbutt. Ketchel returned the foul in the twelfth, and now both men's faces were streaked with blood. The referee might as well have been warning a pair of pit dogs for all the heed they gave him. Ketchel went down again early in the fifteenth, but thirty seconds later unloosed a terrific flurry that sent Thomas's mouthpiece lofting over the ropes and dropped him for a count of eight. After twenty-five rounds both of them were still hitting hard enough to spray sweat and blood off each other's heads. In round thirty Ketchel would not remember getting knocked down nor even the first six seconds of the ref's count, would recall nothing of the time between missing Thomas with a punch and then being on one knee and hearing the ref shout "Seven!" The brief loss of consciousness was like an absent portion of a spliced film in which everything in the picture is abruptly repositioned by the sudden forward jump in time. At "Nine!" he was up and swinging, and half-a-minute later drove Thomas through the ropes and into the laps of sportswriters who heaved him back up to the apron so he could re-enter the ring, his broken nose streaming blood. And now Thomas at last began to flag. At the gong for round thirty-two Ketchel almost ran across the ring to tear into him with an astounding ferocity for this late stage of the bout. Thomas went down three times and could not beat the count after the third.

No reporter present had ever seen a rougher fight, and yet, despite the cuts over his eyes and a pair of fat lips, Ketchel seemed improbably fresh when the hacks were admitted to his dressing room. Thomas by contrast looked as if he'd been thrown off a cliff. He nevertheless wanted to fight Ketchel again. He was sure he could beat him in a twenty-rounder. He hoped Ketchel would be sport enough to give him a rematch. Sure thing, Ketchel said.

The handful of sportswriters who had argued for Thomas as the middleweight champ now began calling for Ketchel's recognition as king of the division. Asked if he considered himself the champ, Ketchel said, "That's not for me to decide. All I'll say is, I sure don't think of anybody else as champ."

He celebrated for three days and nights with Sandra at her place in Yuba City. When he finally got back to the Colma camp he was nearly limping in cheerful exhaustion. He slept most of the next day, getting up only to eat or make use of the outhouse. The day after that he went into San Francisco and opened his first bank account. That second fight with Thomas was his biggest payday yet, and forever more he would always carry large sums of cash in his pockets. He bought some spiffy new suits and ties and several pairs of shoes. A week after the fight, he boarded a train for Michigan.

HE HADN'T TOLD the family he was coming. His mother shrieked on opening the front door to see him standing there with his arms open wide. They had not seen each other in more than three years, and she flung herself on him and wept. He returned John's bear hug and back slaps and then was introduced to Rebeka, who proved even prettier than his mother had said. Julie Bug, now almost two years old, stole his heart at first sight. They talked and joked through supper, and afterward John showed him the scrapbook in which he'd pasted newspaper reports of his two matches with Joe Thomas. As word of his visit spread through town over the next few days, neighbors and other local well-wishers stopped by to introduce themselves and say how proud they were of him.

His mother could not stop beaming. He remarked that she seemed somehow younger than when he'd last seen her. She said it was the joy of seeing him again, and of Kaicel's blessed disappearance from their lives. Perhaps so, but it was something more, too, as he perceived when they were joined for Sunday dinner by a well-tailored man whom his mother introduced as her dear friend Mr. Barzoomian. She herself addressed him as Rudy. He was reserved but polite, well spoken with a slight accent, impeccably barbered, his nails manicured. His single incompatible feature was a thin crinkled scar that curved from the hair above his ear to the tip of his moustache. He told Ketchel his people had come from Armenia. In addition to a store that sold the finest furniture in Grand Rapids, he owned a number of rental properties, including the offices of the legal firm that had handled his mother's divorce, and which was where they had met. He was a childless widower and lived in an apartment above his store. Ketchel liked him, and soon felt comfortable enough to ask where he'd got that honey of a scar. A Turk, Barzoomian said, as though it explained everything.

Ketchel stayed for two weeks and grew nostalgic for the country of his boyhood. Even before he boarded the train back to California, he had already determined to buy himself a homestead not far from his mother's.

HIS THIRD FIGHT against Joe Thomas was in mid-December. This one under electric lights in Recreation Park in San Francisco. It was another thriller. To add to the drama, most of the bout was in a thunderstorm that shorted out a measure of the electrical power and cast the ring in a sort of eerie twilight. Ketchel almost ended it in the first round when he dropped Thomas with a head-snapping left, but by the end of the round Thomas was trading him blow for blow. Despite being drenched the crowd stayed put. Squinting against the blowing rain, the fighters ripped at each other from round to round without another knockdown until the thirteenth, when Ketchel dropped Thomas again. And then again in the fifteenth. But then in the eighteenth Thomas connected with a left that sent Ketchel sprawling. He scrambled up and charged into Thomas and they clinched and stumbled and fell down in a cursing, splashing tangle. The referee added some cursing of his own as he warned the fighters against such barroom style. In the nineteenth round Ketchel dropped Thomas twice. And when the gong sounded at the end of the twentieth, he was pounding Thomas on the ropes and kept at it until the ref yelled in his ear that the fight was over. By then the rain was coming down so hard and the lighting was so poor that the announcer had to crawl into the ring to see which man's hand the ref was holding up before he could announce Ketchel's name to the spectators.

THE WAY JOE O'Connor saw it, because Hugo Kelly and Jack (Twin) Sullivan were both persisting in their claim to the middleweight championship after having fought each other to a draw, whoever beat either of them could rightly claim the title for himself. The sportswriters concurred. Since Kelly was already contracted to a match with Papke at the end of December, Ketchel challenged Sullivan.

Jack Sullivan, however, was not eager to get in the ring with Ketchel, not after what he had done to Joe Thomas. But Jack's twin brother, Mike, who was the welterweight champ of California, was avid to fight Ketchel. He was absolutely sure he could beat him, because a fighter of finesse, which Mike Sullivan considered himself to be, could always outscore a slugger. Maybe Jack thought so, too, or maybe he was only stalling for time, but, whatever the case, he said he would fight Ketchel only if Ketchel could first beat brother Mike.

O'Connor sighed at the condition but agreed. Ketchel said, "What the hell, whatever it takes. Just line them up and let me at them."

HE CELEBRATED THE arrival of 1908 with a pair of slim-hipped sisters named Ruby and Rose he met at a party in San Francisco. They claimed to be full-blood Arapaho Indians and they looked it, with sharp cheekbones and quick black eyes and raven hair that hung to their high round bottoms. Whatever their surname, he didn't catch it and didn't care. To him they were simply the Arapaho Sisters. He danced with both of them at the same time. The other people on the floor applauded their bohemian abandon and three-way grace.

As the midnight hour was greeted with fireworks and howls and bellowed song in the streets beyond the sisters' apartment window, Ketchel and the girls, all three of them drunk and their faces streaked with war paint of lipstick and shoe polish, were nakedly abed and deciding on the next sexual configuration they might compose.

MIKE SULLIVAN ANNOUNCED to the assembly at the morning weigh-in that he was going to give young Ketchel a major boxing lesson. Like his twin brother Jack, Mike was bald on the crown but had thick dark hair on the back and sides of his head. Ketchel stared at the bald spot and snickered. Sullivan asked him what was funny, but Ketchel only shook his head.

"Loss for words, eh, boy?" Mike Sullivan said. He winked at the reporters. "I suppose the lad's gone simple. A few too many to the head, eh? Damned shame in one so young."

Four hours later the bell rang to begin the bout and Mike Sullivan strolled out of his corner as casually as if he were about to ask Ketchel for a light. They touched gloves and Sullivan jabbed Ketchel twice and threw a right that missed and Ketchel countered with a hook to the belly they heard in the back rows of the arena. Mike Sullivan doubled over like he'd been gored, his hands at his midsection and his mouthpiece falling from his mouth in a string of saliva. Ketchel punched him in the jaw like he was throwing a sidearm fastball. A tooth shot from Sullivan's mouth in a streak of red spit and he spun with his legs in a twist and fell on his ear and lay unmoving but for a shuddering right heel as he was counted out.

Jack Sullivan was in his brother's corner as chief second and brought him around with smelling salts. Mike's eyes looked like fogged pink glass. "Jesus, Jackie," he said, his breath whistling through the new gap in his teeth, "if I ever had a worse idea than to fight this fella I can't remember what it was."

Jack Sullivan patted him on the shoulder. "Oh hell, Mikey, you were out of your class fighting a middleweight, that's all." But his doleful aspect was owing chiefly to the thought that he had to fight Ketchel next.

As it turned out, Jack fared better than Mike, at least in the sense that he made a longer fight of it, lasting almost twenty rounds. It could also be argued, of course, that he fared worse, in the sense that the longer he lasted the more severely he was abused. After nineteen rounds Ketchel had knocked him down four times and Jack's resemblance to his twin had turned vague. His nose was offset and bloody, his brows were puffed, his ears like raw beef. And yet he had for the most part succeeded in keeping his distance from Ketchel's strongest punching range. As the last round got underway he thought he would at least be able to say he was on his feet at the final bell. He tried to stave Ketchel with the jab, tried to keep out of knockout range, but then the ring abruptly tipped backward and his next awareness was of Mike helping him up and back to his stool. In the opposite corner Ketchel was posing with ready fists for the photographers, then raising his hands high at the cheering that only now began to penetrate the persistent ringing in Jack Sullivan's ears.

"He got you with a right," Mike said. "Christ almighty, Jackie, it was about the fastest, hardest punch I ever seen."

Hardly in the mood to share his brother's admiration of Ketchel's might, Jack Sullivan responded with the uncharitable observation: "I guess so, since you never saw the one he hit *you* with."

In his dressing room Ketchel told reporters that as far as he was concerned he was now the middleweight champion, seeing how Hugo Kelly and Billy Papke had fought to a draw in December and Papke then defeated Kelly in a rematch in March.

But what *about* Papke, the newshounds wanted to know. Didn't the Illinois Thunderbolt, as he called himself, have a claim to the title after beating Hugo Kelly?

Oh hell, no, Ketchel said. Papke hadn't fought anybody but bums and has-beens. "But I know you fellas won't be satisfied till I take care of that squarehead, so we got some news for you." He turned to O'Connor. "Tell them, Joe."

O'Connor announced that he and Papke's manager had come to terms for a match between their fighters. In less than a month, the sixth of June, to be exact, they would meet in a ten-rounder at the Hippodrome Arena in Milwaukee.

"We wanted twenty rounds but they would only go for ten," O'Connor said. He gave a shrug of theatrical dimension. "Guess they're afraid their man ain't got the juice to keep up with Steve."

A reporter asked Ketchel for his assessment of Papke, and Ketchel said he had never seen him fight. "I know he's got a big mouth, always yakking about he's the best there is and so on. Mouth that big will make a good target. Say, I hear he fights with no pants on, is that true?"

Several reporters affirmed it was, that Papke wore only a jock-strap in the ring.

"Ignorant squarehead probably can't figure out how to put on a pair of trunks," Ketchel said.

When his remark was conveyed to Papke at his training camp in Chicago, he wanted to know where the Polack got the nerve to call anybody else ignorant. "I hear he wears cowboy boots. I bet it's because he's too goddamn stupid to tie a shoelace."

By the time they met at the weigh-in for the first of four fights they would have against each other in the span of only thirteen months, there was a sizable enmity between them, these two young men whose mercurial natures were remarkably similar. Who had been born within the same week. Who had both grown up in the Midwest and known harsh circumstance. Who would both come to tragic ends.

The Illinois Thunderbolt

They each tipped the scale at 154, then took questions from reporters. One of them asked Papke why he didn't wear shorts in the ring.

"Because I move around better without them," Papke said. "Sure hope it don't make any of you boys blush."

Ketchel said the problem with Papke not wearing shorts was that his ass and his face looked so much alike you'd have to see if his toes were pointing up or down in order to know if he was on his back or his belly while he was getting counted out.

Only Papke and his crew did not laugh. Papke said he had thought about wearing shorts for this fight but wanted to make it easier for Ketchel to kiss his ass.

Ketchel put a hand to his ear and said, "How's that, mein Herr? To *kick* your ass? Much obliged."

At match time the Hippodrome was standing room only. The odds favored Ketchel, eight to ten, but most of the Milwaukee crowd was pulling for Papke. He had beaten Hugo Kelly in this arena three months earlier, and as an Illinoisan he was practically a local boy. As the ref gave them his instructions, Papke glowered and Ketchel grinned.

At the bell's first clang they hustled out to the center of the ring and Papke reached out his right hand to touch gloves, and all in one smooth move Ketchel tapped Papke's glove with his left hand and hit him with a right cross to the forehead that sat him down hard in an explosive uproar from the crowd. Papke was up at the count of three in a cursing rage and they pounded at each other without pause for the full duration of the round. It was that kind of fight all the way. By the start of the fifth, Ketchel had knocked him down for a second time and both of Papke's eyes were cut. But the Thunderbolt was as tough as his reputation held and in the fifth he connected with a roundhouse that dropped Ketchel to one knee for a seven count. In the sixth Ketchel had Papke's hair jumping with head punches and almost drove him through the ropes at the end of the round. In the seventh he trapped him in a corner and knocked him down again. But Papke rebounded in the eighth, scoring with several jarring combinations. In the last fifteen seconds of the ninth Ketchel loosed a demonic flurry that drove Papke across the ring and nearly dropped him, but Papke hunkered against the ropes with his arms helmeting his head and lasted the round. They fought in a frenzy through the tenth and were still trading blows like berserkers when the final gong sounded. They ignored the bell and kept on swinging and the ref pushed between them and caught a punch in the face and went down. Then the seconds were pulling the fighters apart amid vehement cursing and brandished fists and the cops clambered into the ring just in time to prevent a donnybrook. The referee was helped up and took a moment to regain his senses and feel of his bruised cheek, then raised Ketchel's hand.

None of the sportswriters in attendance disagreed with the decision or that Stanley Ketchel was now the undisputed middleweight champion of the world.

Papke's manager, Tom Jones, went to Ketchel's dressing room and shoved past the reporters to congratulate him and then ask for a rematch. A twenty-rounder next time.

"This is the same mug who wanted no more than ten rounds this time," Ketchel said to the hacks, and the reporters laughed and scribbled in their notebooks.

Jones said maybe Ketchel was scared of going a long one against Billy.

Ketchel said he'd love to go twenty rounds with him. He'd love it if they got back in the ring right that minute and fought to the finish so there'd be no chance at all of Papke being saved from a knockout. "A dummkopf like him, his head's solid rock. It takes a little time to make gravel out of it."

The reporters scribbled faster.

"Illinois Thunderbolt," Ketchel said. "Illinois Beer Fart's more like it."

The reporters guffawed.

It had been a lucrative fight, however, and both parties knew a rematch would rake in even higher profits. Within a month they would come to terms for a twenty-five-rounder in Los Angeles in September.

MILWAUKEE BEING SO close to home, he had promised his mother he would pay her a visit before returning west. The morning after the fight, he took a ferry across the lake. John met him at the dock with a wagon, and though he'd already learned the outcome of the match, he couldn't get enough of hearing about it. He made Ketchel recount it in every detail.

Barzoomian was visiting at the farm too, and that evening after supper he told Ketchel he had asked Julia to be his wife and she had accepted. They had not yet announced their engagement, however, because they wished first to receive his blessing. "I wanted to ask you man to man," Barzoomian said.

Ketchel was impressed with the man's gallantry and pleased by his formal recognition of him as head of the family. He gave the Armenian an affectionate tap on the arm and said of course they had his blessing. Then whirled his happily crying mother all around the room. They promised to let him know as soon as they had set a date.

WHEN HE RETURNED to California he bought a motorcar, a costly Locomobile of ninety horsepower, touted by its manufacturer as "the best built car in America." It was also one of the fastest. He loved its name and repeatedly joked that it meant "crazy car" in Spanish and was so called because it was made by lunatic engineers in a Mexican madhouse.

He was still in a mood to celebrate and thought it would be great fun to do it in the company of the Arapaho Sisters. His cap pulled low and tight, his duster buttoned to the neck and his eyes bright behind his goggles, he drove up to San Francisco with both the top and the windscreen down, rocking over the dirt road and raising rooster tails of dust behind him.

He stored the car in a livery just off Market Street and started off on foot for the girls' apartment a few blocks away. As he was waiting to cross a busy intersection, a streetcar went clanging past and he glanced up at it just as a young blonde woman in a window seat turned and looked out at him. She was hatless, her hair in a loose braid over her shoulder, and of only standard prettiness, but her smile seized his breath. The moment was made electric by the guileless cast of that smile and the frank attraction in her stare. Then the trolley was around the corner and out of sight. Not until the traffic policeman finally gave Ketchel's side of the street the signal to cross did it occur to him to try to catch up to the car, board it, and introduce himself. Too late for that. When he dashed around to the next block, jostling other pedestrians and begging pardons, he saw that the street was acrawl with trolleys and who could say which one she was aboard or even if she were still on it? He caught sight of his reflection in a store window and thought, Well now, ain't you a silly son of a bitch? But his skewed smile was no match for his rue. For the rest of his life he would have sporadic dreams of this girl he'd glimpsed but for a moment.

THE ARAPAHO GIRLS were excited to see him and happily broke the news of their engagement to a pair of rich brothers, owners of a merchant shipping line. The double wedding would take place the following month.

He tried not to show his disappointment, thinking it wasn't his day. He congratulated them on their good fortune and said their fiancés were a couple of lucky stiffs.

"Yeah they are," the Ruby one said. She exchanged a look with her sister, and then said: "But you know what? The lucky stiffs are in Boston on business."

"Waaaay off in Boston," the Rose one said.

"Till late next week," the Ruby one said.

"So why the long face, baby?" the Rose one said.

Their brightly mischievous grins incited his own.

Their spree lasted five days. They played various games of their own invention, including Rape the Redskin and Turn the Snake Purple and Make the Paleface Prisoner Do It, the last of which entailed one of the girls holding Ketchel's unloaded revolver to his head and threatening to shoot him if he didn't strictly obey her sister's demands regarding a variety of sexual pleasures, all of them contrary to conventional morality and several in violation of the California penal code.

On the final night of their frolic, they drunkenly ventured into the foggy evening to replenish their whiskey supply and happened upon a tattoo parlor. The girls exhorted him to get one on his buttock. A red heart with an arrow through it, SQUAW inscribed directly above the arrow and LOVER just below it. The idea seemed perfectly swell to him at the time.

He'd been back at the Colma camp for more than a week before Pete the Goat finally noticed the artwork one day when Ketchel came out of the shower. The Goat's laughter drew O'Connor's attention, and Joe caught a glimpse of the tattoo just before Ketchel yanked up his shorts.

"Oh Christ, what was *that*?" O'Connor said.

"I ain't sure I want to hear about it," the Goat said.

"Good," Ketchel said, "because neither of you mugs is going to."

They never did.

HE HAD TWO fights before the rematch with Papke. The first in San Francisco against Hugo Kelly, who had been born in Italy and whose true name was Micheli. He now made his home in Chicago and thought the name Kelly more befitting to a Yankee pugilist.

This was a time of vast European immigration, and Hugo was not the only boxer in the U. S. who'd been born with a surname ending in "-elli" or "-ski," "-ĉek" or "-witz," or any of a thousand other "foreign" names before switching to a moniker that sounded American, and by this point in the republic's history an Irish name met the requirement. An excellent boxer, Kelly predicted he would take the title from Ketchel by means of superior style and finesse. His confidence was misplaced. In round three Ketchel knocked him so utterly insensible that one reporter wrote that you could almost see the stars twinkling over the supine Kelly's head.

The other fight was with Joe Thomas, their fourth and final match. In order to get it, Thomas had to let Ketchel have 75 percent of the purse, a dear price to pay for a public trouncing and humiliation. Through the first round Ketchel buffeted him from one end of the ring to the other, knocking him down four times. Thomas went to his corner as much forlorn as battered. His cornermen remonstrated with him to quit. He couldn't. Not after only one round. Less than half a minute after the bell for round two the smelling salts were at his nose.

For all the ease of his victory on this occasion, Ketchel's first three fights with Thomas would remain among the most grueling of his career. To say they were tough on Thomas is to understate the matter. Ketchel had pummeled him into palookahood. Joe Thomas would fight fourteen times more and win only once.

THE SECOND KETCHEL-PAPKE fight took place on Labor Day at Jim Jeffries' Athletic Club in Los Angeles, and the great Jeffries himself served as the referee. He was in shirtsleeves and vest and wore a straw boater with a black band. In his four years of retirement he had been farming alfalfa and managing his boxing club.

He had gained more than fifty pounds, most of it in a sizable paunch. Yet he remained an impressive specimen, the bulge and play of heavy muscles evident under his clothes, and he was as widely revered as ever. It was one of the thrills of Ketchel's life to shake Jeffries' hand when they were introduced at his club a few days prior to the fight. They'd had their picture taken together, Jeffries in a smartly tailored suit and his usual boater, Ketchel in a motorcar duster and a railroad engineer's cap he had lately come to favor.

On this Labor Day of perfect Southern California weather they were the subjects of cameras again, this time in the ring and in the company of Billy Papke. With Jeffries standing between them, Ketchel and Papke struck a pose of squaring off, Ketchel in baggy gray trunks, Papke in but a black jockstrap. As the cameras clattered around them Ketchel said he hoped Papke wouldn't chafe his ass when he hit the canvas. Jeffries chuckled. Papke glowered and spat at Ketchel's feet. Ketchel laughed.

Then the picture-taking was done and Jeffries gave the fighters the usual admonishments against illegal punches, asked if there were any questions, and sent them to their opposite corners. Each man ground the soles of his shoes in the resin box in his corner to gain better purchase. They bounced on their toes and rolled their heads to loosen their neck muscles and regarded each other across the ring. The bookmakers favored Ketchel at three to one.

At the gong, Ketchel trotted to mid-ring and put out his right hand for the shake. Without giving the extended hand a glance Papke walloped him on the jaw, catching him flatfooted. Ketchel felt himself falling, felt the back of his head strike the canvas under the sudden blue sky. Addled and only vaguely aware of the riotous outcry, driven by instinctive imperative to get up fast and by alarm that he might be too slow about it, he scrambled up before Jeffries had even begun the count. And stood directly into a Papke overhand that dropped him back down. And once more got up too quickly and was knocked down again. Now feeling as if he were deep under water, his limbs encumbered with heavy clothes. But up at the count of eight and driven against the ropes, feeling his head jarring but stunned beyond pain. And then sitting on the canvas and slumped on the bottom rope, faintly hearing Jeffries' count through the mad din, seeing his chest streaked red and not comprehending it as blood from his broken nose. His mouth tasted of rust. Up at nine and his head instantly jolting. Then down again. The arena rolling halfway over and then slowly righting itself like a ship in a bad sea. He pushed up onto a hand and knee like a sickly runner at his mark, saw the Goat and O'Connor in momentary focus at the corner apron, eyes huge and mouths moving, but could not hear them. Jeffries bellowed "Eight!" into his ear and he rose at nine into another onslaught and went tumbling still again. Of all the shocks of that opening round, none surpassed the fact that he got through it. O'Connor and the Goat helped him to his stool and the Goat set grimly to stemming the blood. "Oh Jesus," O'Connor said. "That lowdown son of a bitch. Oh Christ." Some of the ringside reporters already composing their diatribes against Papke's treacherous gambit and never mind that there was no official rule about shaking hands. A flagrant violation of sportsmanship if not of the regulations. Other of the hacks would remind readers of Ketchel's batting aside Papke's hand at the beginning of their first match. The minute of rest between rounds was woefully insufficient to unstun Ketchel's reflexes. His eyes so mauled by the end of the fifth round Jeffries had to steer him to the corner. The Goat lanced the bloated lids to restore a degree of red-hazed vision. Ketchel reeling through the rounds, missing punches by a foot. Clinching as much to keep from falling as to keep from being knocked down. At the end of the tenth Jeffries said at his ear it'd be no disgrace to toss the towel. "Go to hell," Ketchel said. It remains one of boxing's great stories of endurance that he lasted as long as he did. By the twelfth round there was argument among the ringsiders about the exact number of times he'd gone down, and early in the round he was floored again. Papke glared down at him like he wanted to kick him, wanted to grab up a stool and club him with it. Ketchel up at nine, swaying, nearly blind. Papke snarled and hit him as if trying to drive his fist through a wall. Ketchel was on all fours, bloody snot and spit webbing from his face, struggling to rise, when Jeffries counted ten.

In the dressing room forty-five minutes later Ketchel's disfigured eyes were concealed behind dark glasses, but the raw distended cheeks and gross purple lips and lumpy swollen ears were in full evidence to the assembled reporters. When one of them asked about Papke's "sneak punch" at the start of the fight, he said he wouldn't call it that. "I should've been ready." His nose so clotted with blood his voice seemed to come from a well.

Did he want another go at the Thunderbolt? Of course he did. Sooner the better. Joe O'Connor would be in contact with Tom Jones, Papke's manager, every day from now until the rematch was a deal.

"He needed twelve rounds to finish a blind man," Ketchel said, his voice so low the reporters at the back of the pack had to ask those in front what he'd said.

Papke of course crowed. He told the reporters he'd always known he was the better man and he guessed everybody else now knew it, too. He bristled at the mention of a sneak punch. "There wasn't nothing sneak about it. If that bohunk's saying so, he's a damn crybaby. When the bell rings, the fight's on and you better guard your ass. You seen how he did last time when I went to shake his hand. Ain't my fault he wasn't set. Wouldn'ta mattered if he was. He was lucky in the first fight and I proved it."

Would he give Ketchel a rematch? Before Papke could answer, Tom Jones said sure they would, but Ketchel would have to wait his turn, just like he made Billy wait after the first fight. "I told Hugo Kelly we'd give him first crack after Billy won the title."

But shortly thereafter the deal to fight Kelly foundered, and Papke agreed to a third match with Ketchel, on Thanksgiving Day in Colma.

"YOU'LL KILL THE kraut next time," his brother, John, told him in a letter. "They'll need a mop and pail to collect him for the morgue."

His mother expressed equal certainty, albeit in less graphic terms, that he would regain the championship. She did not tell him she prayed daily that he would give up boxing and take up a less anguishing trade. Nor that, although John had hidden from her all photographs of this fight, she sensed he had been badly hurt, sensed it as a mother can, and had cried for him in the privacy of her bedroom.

The crux of her letter was to inform him that she and Rudy had decided they preferred a quiet civil ceremony rather than a church wedding with friends and family in attendance, and so had eloped. They had been married four days at the time she wrote the letter. She hoped he would not be cross with her for not telling him until after the fact, but neither had they told anyone else. John and Rebeka had been vexed when they found out, but had since forgiven her and joined in her happiness. She wanted him to know, too, that she had asked to retain the Ketchel name and Rudy had no objections. They planned to buy a house in Grand Rapids. John and his family would remain on the farm. She enclosed a small photograph of herself and Barzoomian on their wedding day, and one of Julie Bug playing with a handsome gray kitten she had named Stanley in honor of her uncle.

Ketchel wired his best wishes.

And prepared for Papke.

THE ELEVEN WEEKS and three days between their second fight and their third was the longest wait of his life. He did not leave the camp property during those three months. His cuts and bruises healed with their usual uncanny quickness, and he trained like a Spartan every day except Sunday, when the Goat limited him to calisthenics and shadowboxing. After supper he would play a few hands of nickel-ante poker with his crew and read the newspapers before going to bed at eight o'clock sharp. He read of Henry Ford's new motorcar called the Model T and its ingenious assembly-line method of production, read of Orville Wright's airplane accident in Virginia that injured Wright and killed his passenger, the first recorded air crash fatality. He read about William Howard Taft's election over William Jennings Bryan to become the twenty-seventh president of the United States and was sorry his revered Teddy had chosen not to run. He was astounded to learn that Taft weighed over three hundred pounds, and thought it funny when he heard somebody call him the Great White Whale of the White House.

He was at his roadwork before sunrise. After breakfast he made a rattling blur of the light bag for thirty minutes, then beat the heavy bag for an hour. He threw boulders. He climbed trees. He napped in the afternoons with a brine-soaked towel on his face to toughen the skin, and, because Pete the Goat said John L. himself had done it to harden his knuckles, with his hands hanging down either side of the narrow cot into buckets of horse piss. "Just don't get them mixed up," he told Pete.

During those long eleven weeks he did not permit himself even a glass of beer, a single puff of a cigar. He shuttered his mind against so much as a passing fancy about women. In the last two weeks before the bout, he berated his sparring partners for not applying pressure on him, then flattened them when they did, sometimes knocking them out despite the oversized training gloves he wore. Neither O'Connor nor the Goat made an effort to restrain him. He was honing a fine fury and they would do nothing to distract him from it. Onlookers were in awe of his single-mindedness.

When a reporter told him of the devastation Ketchel was wreaking on sparring partners, Billy Papke sneered. "Christ, anybody can kayo the guy he spars with. He's just putting on a cheap show for you guys."

THEY FOUGHT FOR the third time in less than six months on a cool and bright Thanksgiving Day. Papke was the bookies' pick at four to five, but Colma was Ketchel's home ground and he stood in heavy favor with the crowd. Ketchel in his customary black trunks posed for the prefight pictures in his usual stance, bent slightly forward with his left arm extended and his right hand drawn back and ready. Papke wore a white jock and faced Ketchel with his fists up, his aspect bordering on smirk. A towering flagpole loomed over the ring and a California bear flag fluttered overhead. Referee Jack Welch, Sunny Jim Coffroth's top referee, then gave them the usual instructions. They ignored his direction to shake hands before going to their corners for the opening gong.

The first round was so fierce it brought the spectators to their feet and not a man of them sat down again till the clang of the bell. Papke fought gallantly and well, but Ketchel was a fiend unchained. He floored Papke near the end of the first and for an instant looked as if he would spit at him. He knocked him down again in the third, and again in the fifth. By the ninth round the Ketchel crowd was howling like a massive wolf pack at the smell of blood. In a clinch near the end of the tenth, Ketchel told Papke the next round would be it. Papke told him to eat shit. Ketchel broke the clinch and clubbed him with a left that spun him halfway around and into the ropes just as the gong sounded. In the eleventh a Ketchel uppercut found Papke's chin, and dropped him onto his bare bottom. Papke was up at eight but stumbling like a rummy, the crowd roaring with a sense that the end was near. Ketchel whaled at his ribs with lefts and rights to bring his hands down, then hooked him to the jaw and sent him sprawling with his feet slinging high. The tumult was deafening. Referee Welch's right arm rose and fell as he shouted a count that could barely be heard by the ringsiders. Papke started to rise, fell over, made it to all fours at the count of six. To one knee at seven. He later insisted that he misheard Welch's count. He told the reporters he was waiting for "nine" before he got up, but he never heard Welch say it. He heard "Eight!" and then "Ten!" and it was over. The news guys nodded sympathetically as they made their notes. And among themselves agreed that even if Papke had beaten that count he wouldn't have beaten the next one. It had been Ketchel's fight from start to finish.

Ketchel told the reporters he believed Papke's story about the count. "It's hard to hear real good with all those birdies singing in your head."

Papke wanted another match, of course. But after having defeated him so decisively, Ketchel felt no need for a fourth fight any time soon. As the first champion ever to lose the title and win it back, he was now the best known middleweight of all time, and he had large ambitions. More than seven months would pass before his final meeting with the Thunderbolt.

NEW YORK WAS the place for them now, he told O'Connor.

"Maybe the place for you," O'Connor said, "and you can have it. I was in New York once for four days and it felt like goddamn forty."

Ketchel called him a rube and said he shouldn't think so small. New York was where the big money was. New York was where he could really make a name for himself.

O'Connor said that Ketchel had already made a name for himself and it often enough appeared in the papers all over the country, which last he'd heard included New York. And the last time he'd looked, a dollar in California was the same size as a dollar in New York.

Maybe so, Ketchel said, but there were a lot more dollars to be had in New York and a lot more things to spend them on.

Round and round they went. After a couple of weeks, what began as a difference of opinion had grown into an argument. He decided to go see his family for Christmas and visit with them for a time, and he told O'Connor to think things over while he was away.

O'Connor said there was nothing to think over. "You do what you want, kid, but I ain't going to New York and that's final."

As Pete the Goat drove him to the depot in the Locomobile, Ketchel told him he should think things over too.

"I ain't got to think nothing over, either," the Goat said. "I like New York. I'm with you."

"You been to New York?"

"More than once."

"I didn't know that."

"There's lots you don't know," the Goat said. "Tell me, where am I from?"

Ketchel stared at him.

"I ever been married? I been to war? I ever done time?"

Ketchel shrugged. Then said: "You were a bareknuckler, I know that. A good one, too, so they say."

"Yeah, kid. So they say."

The Colonel

His mother's new home was large and bright and comfortably furnished. Draped across the parlor wall was a white banner with red letters proclaiming WELCOME HOME, CHAMP!

He had never seen his mother so happy. When he hugged Barzoomian in greeting and said, "Good to see you, too, Dad," the man blushed through his smile.

On Christmas Eve the whole family, including John and Rebeka and Julie Bug, attended a dinner party at the home of Rollin P. Dickerson, whom Barzoomian described as a man of various and highly successful enterprises. His house was at Pine Lake, a few miles north of Grand Rapids. He had bought the place the year before and furnished it through Barzoomian. Mr. Dickerson was also an avid sportsman and very eager to meet the middleweight champion.

Barzoomian drove them there in his spanking new Model T touring car. They drove across the river and followed the Belmont road to Dickerson's estate, passing through a wide front gate onto a property dense with pines and bare maples. A wind-rippled lake, dark green and cold-looking, was visible through the trees. The lane ended at a circular drive in front of a long, two-story house of red brick and black ironwork. John gave a low whistle and said, "Posh."

Ketchel thought it was a beautiful place.

He was surprised when his mother rather than Barzoomian made the introductions. It turned out that Dickerson, whom she called Pete, had been raised in Grand Rapids and they had known each other since they were children. He was a short, portly man of around forty, with recessed thinning hair and the look of a former athlete gone to fat. His stickpin and ring were fitted with small diamonds. He told Ketchel he'd been following his career with interest and had been to two of his fights, the one with Thomas under the lights and in a rainstorm in San Francisco, where he happened to be visiting on business, "the only fight I ever been to where there was a chance of drowning," and the one with Papke in Milwaukee. He said Ketchel was the greatest fighter he'd ever seen and would no doubt be champion for a long time. "You've made your mother awfully proud," he said.

He ushered Ketchel about the room and introduced him to the other guests. The men all expressed admiration and some tried to convey their own manliness through the force of their handshake. One fellow put so much into it Ketchel felt obliged to respond in kind, and the man's face twitched and paled before Ketchel unhanded him.

The women all greeted him warmly, and some let their hand linger in his.

Everyone addressed Dickerson as "Colonel," and Ketchel asked him if he had been in the army.

"Only for as long as it took to settle the Spaniards' hash," Dickerson said. He'd shipped to Cuba with the Rough Riders. "Teddy was the colonel, I was a lowly private. But when I got back home my pals took to calling me colonel as a joke and the damn thing simply stuck."

As an avid admirer of Theodore Roosevelt, Ketchel was impressed. "You kill any Spaniards?"

"I did. Three, to be exact."

"With a rifle?"

"Trusty .30-40 Krag, a real humdinger. Show it to you after supper."

"The army let you keep it?"

"I wouldn't exactly say *let* me, but . . . I have my methods."

After dinner the colonel conducted him to the den for a private brandy and cigar. The superb cigars were regularly shipped from a master roller in Tampa, where Dickerson had first savored them while training for Cuba. There were various rifles on wall mounts and the colonel took down the Krag-Jörgensen and handed it to Ketchel so he could work its action and dry-fire it.

"A well-made firearm's a work of art," the colonel said. "Back home, I've got a hundred guns, pistols and long arms both, all kinds. Muzzleloaders, cap-and-balls, the latest Winchester. Got a Mauser machine pistol, by damn."

"Back home?" Ketchel said.

The Pine Lake house was actually a vacation place, the colonel told him. His real home was in a region of Missouri called the Ozarks, where he had lived now for more than twenty years. He had a house in Springfield, where his timber business was headquartered and where he owned a mortgage bank and a jewelry store, but his main residence was on a ranch of more than eight hundred acres some forty miles from town. Just for fun he raised corn and a little wheat, and there were several tenant houses on the property for the farmers who worked his fields. He said Ketchel must come and visit him there sometime. Ketchel said it would be his pleasure.

Dickerson was curious to know how much he liked living in California. Ketchel said he liked it fine, but what he'd really like was to have a home not far from his mother.

"Would you be content with a house like this one?" Dickerson asked.

Ketchel said such a place would be perfect. Did the colonel know of one like it for sale?

"No need of one like it," Dickerson said, "you can buy this one." He said he had recently decided to sell the place and would gladly let Ketchel have it for less than its market value.

Ketchel thought he was joking, but Dickerson assured him he was not. He had grown up in this region and had always loved the proximity of the forest and Lake Michigan, and for many years now he had been making one or two annual trips back here to hunt and fish. He had a cabin up in the woods and kept a boat stored in a lakeside yard in Grand Haven. During these visits he always spent a few days in town, as well, hobnobbing with old chums. After all those years of staying in Grand Rapids hotels he'd finally bought this house. But even though he'd made use of the place twice in the past year, he had decided such brief visits did not warrant the year-round expense, and he had anyway come to realize he actually preferred putting up in hotels whenever he went to town.

"The place is yours if you want it, Mr. Ketchel. We can get the deedwork started tomorrow."

"Call me Steve," Ketchel said.

Two days later the house was his, and Dickerson was now the guest in it. The colonel observed that the property's only lack for Ketchel was a training facility. The following week there came a delivery of two wagonloads of boxing apparatus and equipment, including a regulation ring, together with a hired crew to set it up in the rear of the house.

Ketchel was flabbergasted by the gift. Dickerson said it was his pleasure to be of some small assistance to such a great world champion.

He trained in his backyard camp every day, damn the mild hangover he might be carrying from a late night with the colonel. He did roadwork in the morning before the sun came up, his breath billowing on the damply cold air. Then did calisthenics and worked with the heavy and the light bags. One afternoon he deigned to spar with several thrilled members of the Michigan State University boxing team who had stopped by to pay their respects. Despite his best effort to pull his punches, he hit some of them harder than he meant to and made them see stars. No matter. A bruised eye from the fist of Stanley Ketchel was to them a black-and-blue badge of honor.

THEN CAME THE report from Australia of Tommy Burns's humiliating loss of the world heavyweight championship to Jack Johnson, the first Negro to win the title.

The news made the colonel both angry and forlorn. "A nigger champ! Jesus! Who'da believed things could come to such a pretty pass?"

The vast majority of America shared his sentiment. Jim Jeffries was being implored from all sides to put on the gloves again and cool the Texas coon.

Ketchel's main reaction to the news was to rue his missed chance to take the title from Burns, whom he knew he could have beaten handily. Unlike Burns, Johnson was a genuine heavyweight. But although they called him the Galveston Giant he wasn't as big as Jeffries.

"Tell you one thing," he said to the colonel. "It wouldn'ta taken *me* fourteen rounds to put Burns away. Hell, the boogie didn't even knock him out."

IN THE FIRST days of the new year they went to Dickerson's hunting cabin on Big Blue Lake in the Manistee Forest and each bagged a buck, the colonel's an eight-point, Ketchel's a ten. Dickerson sent the heads to be mounted by a Grand Rapids taxidermist and both would go on the wall over Ketchel's fireplace.

The colonel gave him two of his rifles as gifts, a .44-40 Winchester that had once belonged to an army cavalry scout who reputedly killed a score of Apaches with it, and a.22 Remington bolt-action with a shoulder sling. The colonel called the .22 "ideal for popping varmints." Ketchel showed him his frontier Colt and demonstrated his proficiency with it by shooting the head off a squirrel at a range of about twenty feet.

Some days after that, they drove to Grand Haven in Dickerson's motorcar and then went fishing in his boat. They buffered themselves against the freezing lake wind with mufflers and fur caps and parkas, plus a couple of bottles of rye. They returned to the docks in the redness of late afternoon, half frozen but happily crocked, with more than a dozen muskies and pike.

When the colonel asked about his plans, Ketchel said he wanted to have some fights in the East because of the better publicity, but it meant he would have to cut ties with Joe O'Connor. Dickerson said he was pals with a few fight managers who would be overjoyed to handle the middleweight champ. The cleverest of them was probably Willus Britt, whose main fighter was his own brother, Jimmy, who just a few years earlier had been lightweight champ for a while. Willus was a Californian, and most of his brother's fights had taken place on the West Coast, but he was also familiar with New York and its sporting crowd and he had been wanting to set up a camp in New York for some time. In fact, Dickerson said, the Britt brothers were in New York at that moment, preparing to go to England for a match.

"Suppose I wire Willus in the morning and see if he's interested in handling the one and only Michigan Assassin?"

Ketchel said that would be just fine. Then added: "Tell me something. Is there anything you can't take care of?"

The colonel laughed and said he was sure there was, he just hadn't run into it yet.

The following day, after trading several telegrams with Willus Britt in New York, they had things all worked out and closed the deal on the telephone. Britt said Ketchel was doing the smart thing, coming to him, that they would do well together. He was eager to get acquainted but was about to leave for London, where his brother Jimmy would be fighting. He would return to New York in the first week of March. He gave the name of a hotel where they should meet and promised he would have a big-name match set up for him by then. "See you in New York, champ," he said, and rang off.

"The man works fast," Ketchel said.

The colonel said that was a fact. "They call him Whirlwind Willie."

Ketchel then sent a wire to Pete the Goat: SELL CAR PACK MY

STUFF STOP BE NYC 3 MARCH BARTHOLDI HOTEL 23 AND BROADWAY STOP STEVE.

Then dispatched one to Joe O'Connor: OFF TO NYC NEW MANAGER STOP GOOD LUCK STOP SK.

O'Connor wired back: NO SURPRISE.

IN JANUARY HE agreed to a three-round exhibition match in the Grand Rapids armory for the benefit of his hometown fans and simply to stay sharp. "You rest, you rust," Pete the Goat always said.

His opponent was an itinerant boxer named Tony Caponi, who happened to be in town. The first time he heard the name, Ketchel said, "Tony Caponi? Sounds like some kinda wop candy."

For most of the exhibition, and by agreement between themselves, they made it look good by popping jabs into each other's shielding gloves and throwing smacking hooks into each other's arms that sounded harder than they actually were. But with less than twenty seconds to go in the bout, Caponi suddenly sprang at Ketchel and landed a stunning cross to the jaw, igniting a blast of cheers at this best punch of the match. Caponi's smile made clear the punch had been no accident, and Ketchel was outraged at his violation of their deal. His retaliatory effort to knock out Caponi had everyone on his feet and yowling for the final fifteen seconds. Caponi reeled under the assault, wincing at body blows and head-bobbling hooks, and was barely saved by the bell. The armory rang with ovation.

The announcer thanked both boxers for an exciting match and said he was sure everyone agreed it was a draw. Ketchel forced a smile. Caponi had recovered sufficiently to grin through bloated lips and shake his fists over his head as though he'd won a title fight.

Over drinks with Dickerson that night, Ketchel made light of the whole thing, but the colonel said he shouldn't shrug it off, that it should be a lesson never to underestimate an opponent, even when the contest is of little import and we know the other fellow's our inferior. That we should be at our wariest against our inferiors.

"More than once I've seen the better fellow get the worst of it for not taking the proper caution against somebody he didn't think was worth it," the colonel said. "The minute he turned his back, the other one got him from behind with a bottle or stuck him in the short ribs with a knife. You were a saloon bouncer, you know what I'm talking about. It happens that way if a man isn't careful. I know you know it already, Stevie, but the trick is not to forget it for even a minute."

AT THE END of February he said goodbye to his family and Dickerson drove him to the depot to catch the morning run to Chicago, where he would change trains for New York. Barzoomian's nephew, Aram, who worked for him at the furniture store and had been living in the apartment upstairs, had agreed to live in the rear quarters of Ketchel's house and take care of the place in his absence.

The colonel carried his bags into the coach. They shook hands and each made a clumsy move to hug the other and they bumped heads and laughed, then embraced warmly and patted each other on the back.

"If you need anything," the colonel said. He gestured ambiguously. "You know . . ."

Ketchel nodded and patted his shoulder. The colonel got off the coach and they waved at each other through the window. The conductor took up the stepstool and hollered "Boooarrrd!" and the train hissed and steamed and jerked forward with a shuddering clash and began to chug away.

"Remember what I said!" the colonel called after him. "Whatever you need, son!"

Ketchel shook a fist in the window and nodded.

DICKERSON'S ADDRESS OF Ketchel as "son" derived from a paternal regard that went beyond the figurative. Ketchel himself had reached that realization during their hunting trip. They were in the lake cabin, sitting in ladderback chairs close to the coal oil stove, drinking whiskey from tin cups, and Dickerson was telling a joke about a whore with a wooden leg. Ketchel was sniggering at the joke's setup when the word *father* suddenly sounded in his mind.

He told himself it was only a stupid, drunken notion. And then knew, simply *knew,* it was true. The colonel was his daddy. He was no less stunned by the insight than by his failure to have arrived at it earlier.

Dickerson saw the expression on Ketchel's face and knew the cat was out of the bag. He let the joke fall away and said, "What's on your mind, son?"

They talked for the rest of the night, though it was of course incumbent upon the colonel to do most of the talking. He told Ketchel everything. Told of his earliest memories of skinny Julia Oblinski and of the beauty she turned into at fourteen. Told with a careful delicacy of their meetings in the barn. Told with no small degree of heat of the fight with Kaicel on the last night he saw her for twenty-two years. He had already told him of the move to Missouri at age seventeen and his success as a young entrepreneur staked by his father, proving himself Captain Jerry's equal at making money with every venture he put a hand to.

He'd never married. However foolish it might sound, he said, it wasn't till he'd known dozens of women that he came to understand how much he loved Julia Oblinski. As so often happens, it was an understanding come to roost too late. Through a hired investigator he learned she'd married Kaicel and borne him children. He couldn't help but believe she'd made the best of a bad bargain and what was done was done.

Yet he never stopped thinking of her. She especially came to mind whenever he paid a visit to his boyhood country to hunt and fish and spend a few days at a poker table with old friends. Each time he came to Grand Rapids he thought of looking her up, seeing how she was. But to do so, he felt, would be folly. She was married and a mother. To intrude on her life would have served only to complicate matters, perhaps open old wounds. He could not even ask his friends about her, as none of them had known of their involvement, and he would not risk staining her reputation even at this late date through a misplaced confidence in a poker pal.

And then a little over a year ago he was visiting Grand Rapids and playing cards with some cronies when the subject turned to boxing and somebody told him if he'd been in town a month earlier he could've met Stanley Ketchel, who'd been there visiting his mother. By way of an interview in a local newspaper, the people of Grand Rapids learned that Ketchel had been born among them, that his real name was Kaicel, that his mother lived on a little dairy outside of town. He was the greatest excitement to hit town since the Great John L. staged his last fight there more than three years earlier, and a number of the locals immediately claimed, some even truthfully, that they remembered him as a boy. Some of them, including two of Dickerson's friends, had gone out to his mother's farm to introduce themselves and shake his hand and say how proud he'd made them. He was a polite kid, the colonel's pals said, and awful damn handsome for a boxer with a slug-it-out reputation.

"Everybody was saying how wonderful it was you're from Grand Rapids and how proud you'd make the town if you got to be champ," Dickerson said. "But the minute I heard you were Julia's first kid, something started eating at me. After the game broke up I went back to the hotel, but I couldn't get to sleep. I told myself there was no reason to be thinking what I was thinking and to quit being a fool, but by morning it was all I had on my mind."

Ketchel was absorbed by the tale. The colonel paused to light a cigar and peered at him over the flame as if trying to gauge his reaction. "Then what?" Ketchel said.

"I went to the Grand Rapids public records office and looked up your birth date," the colonel said.

And found it was eight months after Julia's marriage and almost exactly nine months after the last time he had seen her. Dickerson thought and thought about it on the trip back to Missouri, then went to the Springfield library with the only photograph he had of himself and dug through issues of various sporting papers and found a clear, close-up photo of Ketchel's face. It was taken just prior to the second fight with Joe Thomas, not quite a month after his twenty-second birthday. Next to it the colonel placed his own picture, taken when he was thirty-five years old. He studied them for some time, looking from one to the other, but could reach no conclusion. When he'd owned a full head of hair the resemblance might have been easier to judge. Was there a true similarity in the shape of the mouth, in the set of the eyes? He couldn't tell.

The following month he went to San Francisco to attend Ketchel's third fight with Thomas. He bought a ringside seat near

Ketchel's corner and had a pretty good gander at him when he arrived at the ring. The rain was already falling and the electric lighting was poor, but in his close view of Stanley Ketchel's face he saw nothing to refute outright the possibility that they were of the same blood.

Finally, there had been nothing for it but to go to Julia Oblinski Kaicel. He motored out to the farm on a frozen Saturday morning. It happened that John and his family had gone to the city for the day and she was alone at the house. She did not recognize him when she came to the door, only squinted curiously and said, "Yes?"

He removed his hat. "Hello, Julia."

They stood at the open door and stared at each other. He felt an enveloping rush of warm air from the house. She was now thirty-eight years old and appeared to him even lovelier than she had at fifteen. "I wish only to know the truth," he said to her.

She said, "Please, come in."

They sat in the kitchen and had a long conversation punctuated but once by a mutually surprising moment of shared tears that ended in shared laughter. He confessed his realization of love for her and that it had come too late. She in turn confided that for the first few years after he'd gone, she had sometimes imagined his return and what might happen if he somehow came to know the truth about Stanislaus. Those reveries had slowly waned, and then many years ago ceased altogether. And Kaicel had vanished. And she met Rudy Barzoomian, who had since asked her to marry him and she had said yes. She said she loved Rudy, and Dickerson saw the truth of it in her eyes.

"That's how it goes, son," Dickerson told Ketchel. "I love your mother dearly and I'm truly glad she's happy. My hard luck it's with somebody else. I had it coming."

With regard to Stanislaus, he and Julia decided that they would not volunteer to him the truth of his paternity, but neither would they withhold it if he should ever ask. If the opportunity should ever come for father and son to meet, they would let the thing go as it would. That was the real reason Dickerson decided to buy a home in Michigan. To be ready for the opportunity.

"That's about it," the colonel said. He told Ketchel he was not a devout man but had prayed they would be friends. "I can't tell you how happy I am, son. It just kills me that we've come to know each other and get on like we do. I hope nothing I've said changes that."

"Hell, Colonel, I've never had a better friend."

They both brushed at their eyes and went red in the face. "Christ almighty," the colonel said, "between me and you and your mother we make a pretty bunch of crybabies, now don't we?"

They were of course bound to keep the matter a secret. "It would do injury to your mother's reputation, son," the colonel said. "It's not fair that it would, but it's how it is, it's how people are."

As for Barzoomian, Julia had admitted to Dickerson that she had not yet confessed the truth about Stanislaus to him. She did not want to marry him with a lie of omission on her conscience, but she had been afraid to tell him. She could not say how he would respond.

Dickerson assured her that whether she told Barzoomian or did not, he respected the bravery required of her to make the decision, and she could count on his own abiding allegiance to whatever choice she made.

She told Barzoomian. Told him that very night. The man had sat and listened attentively, and when she concluded by saying in all sincerity that she would not blame him in the slightest if he should choose to withdraw his proposal, Rudy Barzoomian, that good man, took her in his arms and said, "Julia Ketchel, I do not withdraw," and initiated the deepest kiss they had yet shared.

Thus did they come to an accord, Dickerson and Julia and Barzoomian. Ketchel's reaction to the whole business was also amply clear. For most of the trip to New York, he stared out the coach window at the passing world and could not stop smiling.

Sidewalks of New York

He arrived in Manhattan on an early morning and checked into the Bartholdi Hotel, where Pete the Goat had already been for two days. Willus Britt showed up later that afternoon. A natty little slick-talker given to bowler hats, French cuffs, and red ties, Britt was overjoyed to be managing Ketchel. During supper at a chop house next door to the hotel, he told Ketchel and the Goat that in the morning they would all be moving to a training camp just north of the Manhattan limits, a quiet, nicely wooded training place near Woodlawn Inn. As he'd promised, he had already arranged for Ketchel's first match in New York, a big-money nontitle bout in only three weeks at the old horse market arena on East Twenty-fourth Street.

"Three weeks ain't long to get in top shape for a big-time fight, kid," Britt said.

"Who is it?" Ketchel said.

"Philadelphia Jack O'Brien."

They all grinned.

"Damn well done," the Goat told Britt. "Philly Jack's as big-time as they come."

"Yeah he is," Britt said. "But remember, New York doesn't allow decisions. You knock him out or it's officially no contest."

"Got it," Ketchel said.

IT WAS HARD TO believe a spot so near to the teeming commotion of Manhattan could be so tranquil, greenly wooded, sparsely neighbored.

"Quiet as a graveyard," the Goat said, making the obvious joke, since the camp property was bordered by the Woodlawn Cemetery.

Every day at dawn Ketchel and Jimmy Britt did their roadwork along the dusty lane flanking the graveyard and traded greetings with curious gawkers on passing wagons. When they got back to camp they chased chickens inside a large wire pen for an hour, feeling like fools despite the Goat's insistence that the exercise sharpened their quickness and agility. In the afternoons they punched the bags and sparred a few rounds against each other. Jimmy Britt, a lightweight with a reputation for quickness of hand, was astonished at Ketchel's superior punching speed.

When he wasn't engaged with his training regimen, Ketchel was in Britt's tow in the city. The first order of business had been at a clothing store specializing in Western wear. Under Britt's guidance Ketchel acquired a variety of outfits befitting a Man of the West as perceived by Willus Britt, the model of Stanley Ketchel he would present to the Eastern press. They went to a photography studio where Ketchel first posed in his boxing trunks and gloves, striking various classic stances, and then according to Britt's instructions changed into an ensemble of cowboy boots and jeans, a logger's jacket of checkered flannel, a denim work shirt open at the throat, a bandanna knotted around his neck, a miner's cap on his head.

He beheld himself in the mirror. "Sweet Jesus, I look like some jackleg who don't know whether to chop a tree, shovel shit, or kick a cow. Nobody I ever knew wore a getup like this. Not a miner, not a cowboy, nobody."

"And not ten people in New York know that besides you," Britt said. "Leave the packaging to me, kid. I know what sells."

He posed Ketchel before a plain pale backdrop, hands behind him, the cap set far enough back on his head to avoid shadow on his handsome face, angled slightly toward the sidelight as toward a radiant future.

During the next two weeks they made the rounds, paying visits to every big-name sportswriter in New York as well as many of the lesser lights of the local sporting world. Ketchel comported himself well in the interviews, smoothly delivering pat responses learned from constant rehearsal with Britt. Britt passed out photos by the handfuls, photos of Ketchel the Boxer, Ketchel the Westerner. His name began appearing in the New York papers, in Boston, in Philly, almost always accompanied by his picture. By the time of Stanley Ketchel's fight with Philadelphia Jack O'Brien, every boxing fan in the East could have recognized him a block away and could have told you his life's story, told you how he'd lost his father to smallpox at age thirteen and been forced by his family's poverty to ride the rails in search of work so he could send money home to his mother and little brothers and sisters, how he'd been unjustly jailed for vagrancy at fifteen and spent six months on a work farm staffed with cruel guards and to this day was still shy about exposing his bare bottom even in a boxing dressing room because of the whip scars it bore, how he'd gone to work in the Montana mines at sixteen and in the same year became a smalltown hero by saving a little girl from a burning house, how he'd escaped from the mines by dint of his fists and the job they got him as a dance hall bouncer protecting the girls from drunken brutes, how in that same year he'd entered the ring for the first time and found his true calling.

He strode the sidewalks in a euphoric awe of towering, pounding, fast-moving, big-voiced New York City. He'd never seen so many gorgeous girls, so many embodiments of the Gibson Girl. Some of them returned his smile in passing and some ignored it, some frowned in affront and some blushed fetchingly and some seemed to dare him to do more than smile, and those were the ones who made his breath go deepest. Girls winked from doorways to dance clubs that he knew were more than places to dance. He suggested to Britt they go into one and relax with a dance or two, wet their whistles while they were at it.

"Wet your wick, you mean," Britt said. "Listen, kid, I know lots better places than these dives, but I don't want you to even dream of booze or babydolls till we've done our business with Philly Jack."

PHILADELPHIA JACK O'BRIEN was so well known at this time that he figured in a standard vaudeville skit wherein one fellow attempted to physically intimidate another by turning to his own pal and saying, "Tell this mug what I did to Philadelphia Jack O'Brien." The pal would say, "Tell him what you did to *Philadelphia Jack O'Brien*?" The first guy would say, "Yeah, tell him what I did to Philadelphia Jack O'Brien." And then lean closer to his buddy and add in a stage whisper: "Just *don't* tell him what Philadelphia Jack O'Brien did to *me.*" Rim shot, chortles.

A droll fight journalist of a later day would call O'Brien the *Arbiter Elegantiarum Philadelphiae.* He was a superb defensive boxer, awesomely fast of foot and hand, with the reflexes of a fly. He would entertain saloon crowds by standing with both feet on a handkerchief and his hands in his pockets and betting one hundred dollars that, without stepping off the hankie, he couldn't be hit in the face by any man in the house who wanted to try for ten seconds. There were many takers, none ever successful, and O'Brien always spent his winnings on drinks for the house. A natural middleweight, in 1905 he won the championship of the newly established light heavyweight division, but the weight class was not popular and he never had occasion to defend the title.

At the time of his first fight with Stanley Ketchel he was thirty-one years old and had won ninety-six fights and lost only five. As evidence of his hardiness it is worth noting that on five different occasions he fought two matches in a single day. And once, feeling especially energetic, he fought and outscored a different opponent in each round of a six-round bout.

Philly Jack was even more of a rarity in that he was given to elevated diction and, outside the ring, the manners of a gentleman. He exercised both qualities at the weigh-in, offering Ketchel his hand and saying, "I'm honored to make your acquaintance, sir. Considering your admirable record and the reported intensity of so many of your engagements, you present a remarkably unblemished countenance, I must say."

Ketchel said, "Yeah, well . . . thanks, I must say."

Jack laughed along with everyone else and said, "I'm very much anticipating our competition. I'm certain it will be highly spirited."

"You betcha," Ketchel said.

THE FIGHT WAS set for ten rounds and they both scaled 160 even. The majority of the hacks covering the bout thought O'Brien would outbox Ketchel, but few believed he had the power to knock him out. Ketchel, on the other hand, had a dynamite punch but no one thought it likely to connect with Philly Jack's jaw. The betting favored the fight lasting the full ten rounds and perforce being ruled no contest.

O'Brien's longtime popularity in the East had most of the crowd pulling for him, including most of the reporters. He won the first eight rounds on almost every scorecard, and some of the hacks had already written their leads giving him the newspaper decision. Through most of those eight rounds, he'd retreated from Ketchel in a circling glide, warding with an expert jab, intermittently scoring with sharp, flashy punches to the head that each time roused roars from his partisans. Though Ketchel's jab was working well, too, O'Brien nimbly dodged his strongest head punches, and so he belabored O'Brien's midsection, making him wince at least once every round. To judge by appearances at the end of the eighth, Ketchel was the worse for wear, both brows cut and swollen, cheeks welted and nose bleeding, while O'Brien showed only a bloated upper lip and a small cut under an eye. In truth, O'Brien's ribs were in anguish from Ketchel's pummeling, and the inside of his mouth felt to his tongue like it had been razored. For the past two rounds he had been swallowing blood. Even O'Brien's cornermen were unaware of the severity of the mouth cuts until late in the ninth when Ketchel landed a hook to the stomach that blew out a spray of blood together with O'Brien's mouthpiece. O'Brien clinched and held on till the end of the round. His alarmed cornermen told him to keep his distance from Ketchel for the last three minutes of the match, and try O'Brien did, valiantly staving off Ketchel with the jab and even scoring sporadically as he retreated, but now every punch he threw was a torment to his ribs. Ketchel bulled after him, loosing wild flurries short of the mark, unable to breach the defending jabs. But as the last seconds of the round were ticking away, O'Brien's agonized jab faltered, and Ketchel swooped in and struck him ferocious hooks to heart and chin and O'Brien crashed to the canvas in front of his own corner as if he'd been dropped from the rafters. He lay unmoving with his head in the resin box. The arena resounded like a madhouse in flames as the ref started counting. He arrived at "Five!" before the gong began clanging like a fire alarm and saved Philly Jack from a knockout.

The fight was ruled no contest.

WHEN HE CAME out of the shower, a wire had arrived from the colonel. Dickerson had his own telegraph line at the Springfield office and had received round-by-round reports as the fight progressed. His message read: NO CONTEST MY ASS STOP KAYO IN MY BOOK STOP CONGRATS CHAMP STOP RPD.

Not until the following day, when several reporters showed up to ask his opinion of the newspaper verdicts, did Ketchel learn that a number of the hacks had given the decision to Philadelphia Jack on the basis of his having won the most rounds.

"Jesus Christ!" said Willus Britt, and went into a blue fit of profanity.

The Goat just shrugged. "Newspaper verdicts don't count for nothing."

Ketchel, too, made light of it. "Listen, fellas, just be sure and remind everybody that O'Brien ended up flat on his back in dreamland."

The reporters laughed and made their notes and went away. But in truth Ketchel was nettled, and the more he thought about it the angrier he became.

"What kind of stupid bastards could give a verdict to a guy who's out cold at the end of the fight?"

"Newspaper stupid bastards," the Goat said. "Hell, Stevie, forget about it. Their opinions don't matter none."

But Ketchel would not be placated, and he soon worked himself into a state. By God, he'd settle this once and for all. He wanted another fight with O'Brien.

Britt was all for it and said he would see about setting it up.

THE FOLLOWING DAY he went to a high-class haberdashery. The manager was alarmed at the sight of him coming through the door and about to telephone for the police before learning from his chief salesman that the man with the freshly bruised face was none other than the world middleweight boxing champion. When he departed, Ketchel was wearing a custom-tailored suit of superior weave, impervious to Britt's argument that he should maintain his Man of the West public image rather than turning into Dapper Dan the Broadway Man. He had ordered three more suits to be delivered to the Hotel Bartholdi.

He plunged into New York's pleasures, Britt having told the truth about knowing where some of the finest recreations could be had. They patronized exclusive sporting houses staffed with stunning girls, and Ketchel enjoyed a different one every night, sometimes two in one night, sometimes two at the same time. They went to fancy nightclubs where he wowed onlookers with his dance floor acrobatics and drew cheers when he danced with two partners at once as he'd taught himself to do with the Arapaho Sisters.

At a club one night, someone who'd heard he was a good singer passed the word to the bandleader, who requested that Ketchel come up to the bandstand and honor them with a song. And he did, belting out a rendition of "Hello, My Baby" that had the patrons bouncing in their seats and nodding at each other, and they rewarded him with prolonged applause.

When he returned to the table they were sharing with five drunkenly happy girls, Britt said, "Christ, kid, you ain't just a boxing champ, you're a goddamn *star*."

One of the girls said, "Willie, mind your language! Ladies present!"

Britt regarded her with bleary half-closed eyes. Then looked at the other girls. Then looked around behind him. He raised the tablecloth and peered under the table. Then looked at Ketchel and shrugged.

And they all burst out laughing, pounding the table, stamping the floor, heads back and teeth bared, laughing till their bellies cramped.

AROUND THIS TIME he met a hatcheck girl named Jewel. He told her she had a lovely name and started to introduce himself but she said she knew who he was. "The minute you walked in here, everybody was saying your name and that you're some kind of boxing champion."

Ketchel apprised her that he was the middleweight champion of the world.

"Well, I don't know very much about boxing," she said, "but you must be pretty good at it to be a champion."

"I'm pretty good, yeah."

She was slender and her shirtwaist clung to a fetching bosom. Her eyes were gray blue, her waist-length hair light brown and braided and adorned with a blue ribbon. She had a hint of Southern accent he thought delightful.

When he asked her last name she seemed reluctant to say. "What's the big secret?" he said. "Is it Vanderbilt? You the black sheep?"

Worse than that, she said, it was Bovine. She had the good humor to chuckle along with him. He said the name sure didn't fit her.

She thanked him for the compliment and said she supposed she should be grateful it wasn't something worse. "Like the poor daughter of that governor in Texas named Hogg. He went and named her Ima, can you imagine?"

Ketchel said she was making that up, but she swore she was not.

"Well, if you don't like your name, why don't you change it?"

She gaped at him. "*Change* it? But . . . it's my name. You can't just go and change your *name*."

He said you sure could, lots of people did it. Maybe so, she said, but it didn't change the truth of what their real name was and it didn't change who they really were. So why do it? Changing your name was just a kind of lie.

He raised his hands and said, "You win, girl." Then asked if he could take her out on the town sometime.

"I'm not . . . *that* kind of girl, Mr. Ketchel." He followed her gaze toward the ballroom door where Britt and the two chippies they'd brought were waiting for him.

"Of course not," Ketchel said. "That's why I'd like to squire you sometime."

"*Squire?* My, how elegant." She said she'd consider it.

The next day he went back to the club to see her. She said she was still considering. The next day he was back again and she said all right, she'd have coffee with him but that was all.

So they had coffee and talked. He learned she was from Cumberland, Maryland, and had been raised by an aunt and uncle after being orphaned at age ten. She'd come to New York with her best friend because they both wanted a more exciting life than they could ever hope to have in Cumberland. They had also considered going to Washington, D.C., and Baltimore and Philadelphia, but they figured if they wanted excitement they might as well go to the most exciting city of all. They shared a room in a boardinghouse near Central Park. He walked her home and bid her goodbye on the sidewalk.

The day after that he called on her and they went for a stroll in the park. The day after that he took her to supper. The day after that he took her to supper again and then persuaded her to come see the hotel where he lived and have coffee with him in the café next door. When they'd had their coffee he persuaded her to come up and see the view of the city from his room. When they were in his room and looking out his window he put his arm around her and drew her to him and kissed her.

"Please, Stanley," she said. But returned his next kiss as well. "Please," she said, almost panting now, "I'm not that kind of girl."

"Of course not." He gently steered her toward the bed.

He'd known she would prove no virgin and she didn't. She was in fact ardently adroit.

Some time later, as they lay holding each other in the dark, she whispered, "I have to tell you, Mr. Ketchel, you really know how to *squire* a girl."

"Well, now, I must say you squire pretty good yourself, Miss Bovine."

"Oh, *you*!" She swatted his arm, and they giggled like naughty kids.

When he woke in the morning she was not in the room but her clothes were on the chair and his robe was missing from its hook behind the door, so he knew she had gone down the hall to the bathroom. The sun was bright against the yellow window shade and the room already warm. He kicked off the bedcovers and was drowsing on his side when he heard the door open and close behind him. He felt her sit on the edge of the bed, but she did not lie down nor say anything.

"Having morning regret?" he said.

"No, I'm reading."

"Reading? Reading what?"

"Your behind."

He jerked the sheet up and rolled over to face her. "Ah hell . . . that thing . . . it, ah . . ." He made a vaguely dismissive gesture.

"I bet there's a good story *behind* that work of art."

"Not one you'll hear from me."

"I believe you're blushing, champ."

"Hell I am. I'm just getting hot for you again, toots."

She screeched with laughter as he yanked open the robe and pulled her to him.

ONE EVENING, TALKING with a barman who had not recognized him and whom he'd told his name was Tex Halliday, he learned about a poker game in a joint a few blocks north and over by the Hudson. He said he was interested, so the barman made a telephone call, then told him there'd be a chair for him at that night's game and gave him directions to get there. He wore the most lavish handlebar mustache Ketchel had ever seen. Ketchel tried to thank him with two dollars but the man wouldn't accept it.

Back at the hotel he asked Britt if he wanted to go along, but Willus said no, it was no neighborhood in which to venture. "I don't want you going there, either."

"Listen, Willie, I lived in Butte for three years. There ain't a street in New York rough as that town."

But Britt was adamant. The last thing they needed was the kind of trouble to be found in waterfront joints.

"Yeah, okay, you know the town better than I do," Ketchel said. "Guess I'll just get me a beer and turn in early." Then went downstairs and out the door and hopped aboard a streetcar.

The game was in a pool hall in an industrial neighborhood of darkened warehouses locked down for the night. The air smelled ripely of the river. The hall was doing meager business that evening, only two of its dozen tables in use. The players all stared at him when he entered. One asked his name and he said Halliday, and the man pointed toward a door in the rear. It opened to a smoky room lighted only by the funnel-shade lamp hanging above a lone table where six men sat at cards. There was one empty chair. The dealer, shaggy-haired and wearing a green visor that shadowed his eyes, nodded him toward it. The door he'd entered was the only one. There were no windows.

When the hand in progress was finished, the dealer told Ketchel, "Five card stud, nothing wild, two-buck ante, no bet limit. Strictly cash. I'm the only dealer, I don't play."

Ketchel nodded and was dealt into the next hand.

Conversation was minimal, the dominant sounds the faint clacking of pool balls in the other room, the dealer's riffling shuffles, bets and raises and calls for cards, an occasional profanity as a man tossed in his hand.

An hour later, Ketchel was down more than a hundred dollars and was certain the dealer and one of the other players, a man in a checked suit, were working as a team. And figured as well that the barman who'd steered him here was probably in cahoots with them. He was both outraged and excited. Play him for a patsy, would they?

He presumed the dealer and the checked-suit man were armed, and so had to pick his moment carefully. He waited until the end of the next hand, and as the checked suit leaned over the table to rake in his winnings and the dealer began to gather the cards, Ketchel eased his right hand off the table and under his jacket for the Colt at his left hip. His intention was to get the drop on them and exact a fine for being cheated—all the money he'd lost plus all of theirs seemed fair enough. But the dealer was quicker of eye than Ketchel had guessed and made a grab into his vest the moment Ketchel's hand left the table. A derringer was just clearing his vest as Ketchel shifted in the chair and fired twice from under the table. In the close confines of the room the gunshots were ear-stopping and cards jumped from the sudden holes in the tabletop and one bullet shattered the dealer's elbow and the other removed a portion of his cheekbone and the derringer thunked on the floor as Ketchel whirled toward the checked suit who was raising a five-shot bulldog. Both pistols fired and Ketchel felt a soft brush at his ear and the checked suit pitched over backward and took the chair down with him. The bulldog round punctured the chin of John L. Sullivan, squared off on a wall poster behind Ketchel, who would later see in his hotel mirror the minute nick in the top rim of his ear.

His heart was heaving. The dealer was slumped over the table, holding his bloody face with his good arm and swearing hugely. Ketchel stood up in the acrid haze with the Colt cocked. The man in the checked suit lay awkwardly on his side in a widening mat of blood. His mouth was moving without sound and his eyes were very bright and seemed to be searching the ceiling and then they went still and the light drained out of them.

The other five players sat unmoving, their eyes on Ketchel and their hands spread wide on the table. Not a man of them seemed unfamiliar with precarious moments.

He kicked the bulldog across the floor and then the derringer, then told one of the men to take off his coat and put all the money on it and tie it up tight. The man hastened to do it.

Ketchel tucked the bundled coat under his arm and said, "They were cheating you boys, too, but I'm the one did something about it, so I'm the one gets the prize." He nodded at the maimed dealer. "You might settle up with him."

He opened the door slightly and peeked into the front room and saw no one. On the edge of one of the pool tables were two undrained mugs of beer and a smoking cigarette.

He went out and closed the door behind him, then hurried across the poolroom, holding the revolver close against his leg. He paused at the front door and took a deep breath and stepped outside, set for anything.

The street lay deserted. He jogged four blocks before coming to a corner where a trolley was making a stop, and he hopped aboard.

He got off a block from the saloon where the barman had tipped him to the game, then went around to the saloon's alley door. The door was kept locked from inside except when the saloon waitress periodically opened it to check for neighborhood children who nightly presented themselves to have beer buckets filled for the men of the house. The alley was dank and reeked of slops and garbage and the cobbles were slick under his shoes. Two small boys were sitting on the stoop under the back door's dim overhead light with their empty growlers and chucking brickbats at a cluster of garbage cans to try to flush out the rats rustling within. Ketchel joined the game, heaving a whole brick and knocking over a can, its rancid contents spilling together with a pair of rats the size of weasels. The boys whooped and hurled rocks at them as they scooted into the darkness.

The doorlock rattled and the door swung open and the blowsy waitress said, "Growlers?"

Ketchel hopped up on the stoop ahead of the boys and pushed her back into a storeroom. "*Say now*, what's this?" she said. "I'll fetch the barman with his shillelagh on ye."

"The big lug with the handlebars?" Ketchel said.

"Big enough for the likes of you."

"Do it," Ketchel said.

She went to the door between the storeroom and the barroom. "Terrence!" she called loudly to be heard over the player piano within. "It's a bully one here."

He faintly heard the barman curse and tell her to come tend the counter.

"You'll be sorry now, bucko, you don't scoot away quick," she said, and vanished into the barroom.

He set his bundle on a crate and stood to one side of the door with his back to the wall. The boys were watching from the alley doorway.

The barman entered with a blackthorn in hand. "All right, now, who's the hardcase asking for it?"

Ketchel sprang, seizing the shillelagh with one hand and driving fast, hard punches to the barman's kidney with the other. The man grunted and sagged to his knees and Ketchel wrested the club away. He gripped it like a bat and swatted him in the ornate moustache with a glassy *pop* and teeth rang off a stack of beer mugs shelved across the room. The barman crashed onto his side and groaned wetly.

One of the boys said, "*Wow-wee!*"

Ketchel grinned at them and said he hoped the son of a bitch had a taste for soup because he was going to be living on it for a while. He handed the club to one of the boys, snatched up his bundle, and made away.

The money in the coat amounted to less than nine hundred dollars, a pittance compared to his recent purses, but it seemed to him as sweet as any money he had ever come by.

The next morning at breakfast Britt asked if he'd slept well. "Like a top, Willie boy, like a top," Ketchel said.

FOR ALL HIS good-timing in the nightclubs and with Jewel Bovine, he had been training daily, preparing for another go against O'Brien, working hard to perfect certain tactics meant to offset Philly Jack's superior footwork and keep him within punching range.

But it was now May and O'Brien had still not agreed to a rematch. Britt had been trying to pressure him through various sportswriters in New York, telling them O'Brien was afraid to fight Ketchel again after what Steve had done to him the last time, and some of the hacks had begun asking in print if Britt might be right.

O'Brien scoffed at the notion. In an interview with a Philadelphia reporter he said that although Mr. Ketchel had landed a spectacularly lucky but inconsequential punch in the last few seconds of their bout, it hardly outweighed the fact that he had out-boxed Mr. Ketchel throughout the match.

"Inconsequential?" Ketchel said, when Britt read the passage to him and the Goat. "That inconsequential punch knocked him colder'n a damn mackerel!"

"Oily-tongue son of a bitch," Britt said.

"I notice he didn't say anything about fighting you again," the Goat said.

All the while Ketchel was trying to get another fight with O'Brien, Billy Papke was badgering Ketchel for a rematch of their own. Frustrated by O'Brien's persistent stalling, Ketchel finally said okay to another go with the Thunderbolt. A twenty-rounder on the fifth of July in Colma, California, where they'd had their second and third fights and would draw the biggest gate.

A FEW DAYS after the news went out that Ketchel had signed to fight Papke, O'Brien's manager, Butch Pollack, sent a wire offering Ketchel a rematch on three conditions. The fight had to be in June, in Philly, and for only six rounds. That was the deal. Non-negotiable. Take it or leave it. Britt and Ketchel had one day to give him an answer or the offer would be withdrawn.

"Those clever bastards figure you won't fight O'Brien just a few weeks before having to take on Papke," Britt said. "And if you don't, O'Brien's off the hook for a rematch. He can say he made you an offer and you said no and as far as he's concerned that's that."

"But in case you say okay," the Goat said, "he wants a short fight. He knows you can wear him down in ten rounds, but figures he can keep away from you for six."

"Goddamnit, who they think they are, telling *us* take it or leave it," Britt said. "To hell with them! *You're* the champ. You don't have a thing to prove against a washed-up—"

"Tell them we'll take it," Ketchel said.

Resolutions

At the weigh-in, O'Brien was his usual silver-tongued self. "Well, my good fellow, we meet again. I've no doubt this engagement will prove as lively as our previous one, but I assure you I have no intention of getting resin in my hair this time."

The reporters smiled and jotted their notes.

"Good to see you, too, Philly," Ketchel said.

In the first minute of the fight, Philly Jack understood he was being bested at his own quick-footed game by this younger man with the harder punch. Ketchel had learned the trick of cutting off the ring and blocking O'Brien's escape moves, each time jolting him with lefts and rights to the head, with stinging hooks to the ribs. At the end of the first round, Philly Jack's face was a mess. Goodly sums had been wagered that he would still be on his feet after a mere six rounds, but when he went down for the third time in round two, it was apparent to every witness that an early end was at hand. Ten seconds into the third round Ketchel floored him with a right lead to the head, then stood looming as the ref counted and Jack struggled to his feet. The moment O'Brien came upright, Ketchel hooked him with a combination to the belly and jaw, and he crumpled again. Barely conscious and functioning instinctively, O'Brien tried mightily to rise as Ketchel stood by, set to hit him. Sensing an imminent killing if Philly Jack should make it up, referee Jack McGuigan stopped counting and waved an end to the fight, ruling it a knockout. Nobody protested the uncommon action. Every man present had seen Ketchel poised over the struggling O'Brien like a slaughterhouse worker with a ready hammer.

Meeting with reporters after he was showered and dressed, Ketchel was asked if he thought Philly Jack was still as smart a fighter as he used to be.

"Oh sure," Ketchel said. "Philly's a real smart fighter. He was thinking all time. And all the time he was thinking I was socking the shit out of him."

The hacks laughed and wrote it down, though of course "shit" would yield to such printable euphemisms as "dickens" or "heck" or "tar." It was such a swell quote that in years to come it would be attributed to at least a dozen other boxers.

If the referee had let Philly Jack continue, another reporter inquired, would Ketchel have eased up his attack so as not to cripple O'Brien, or maybe even worse?

"Oh you bet," Ketchel said. "I would've given Jack every chance in the world to recover so that maybe he could get in a lucky punch and knock my teeth out or break my nose, maybe knock me down and keep doing it till my brains oozed out my ears. Oh sure, you bet I would've taken it easier."

There were a few uncertain titters and crooked smiles, but the only one to laugh out loud was Pete the Goat.

LESS THAN FOUR weeks later, on the fifth of July, he fought Papke under a blistering sun in Coffroth's arena. They did not speak a word to each other at the weigh-in, but reporters on hand remarked that their glares spoke volumes.

"Theirs is no mere pugilistic rivalry," wrote one, "but a blood feud rooted in an abiding mutual hatred."

It was a fight with none of the finesse Ketchel displayed so capably against O'Brien. Referee Billy Roche would himself assert that he had never seen two men in the ring with such evident desire to kill each other. More than one reporter described the match as a dogfight. For more than an hour, for twenty rounds and from bell to bell, the fighters punched without pause. There were moments when they seemed on the verge of tearing into each other with their teeth. There were no knockdowns, though at one point a Ketchel roundhouse wobbled Papke's knees and only the Thunderbolt's desperate clutch of the ropes kept him from hitting the canvas. The final round the most brutal of the bout, both men streaked with blood and swapping punches as vehemently over the span of the last three minutes as they had in the opening round. And as in their first fight, they did not let up even at the repeated clanging of the bell and again had to be separated by their seconds, who again very nearly became embrawled.

Referee Roche declared the bout for Ketchel and none of the hacks at ringside took exception in their reports.

Papke of course believed he'd been wronged, that at the very least the match should have been judged a draw. One more fight, he told anyone who would listen, one more fight with Ketchel was all he asked.

He would not get it.

KETCHEL AND BRITT and the Goat celebrated his win over Papke deep into the night in a trio of adjoining suites in a deluxe San Francisco hotel. In their company were four young and lovely and lively girls leased for the evening from a Nob Hill madam of Britt's acquaintance. The two girls tending to Ketchel were solicitous of his cuts and bruises and kissed them tenderly, cooed over him like sweetly salacious nurses, marveled at his show of lusty energy just hours after having fought a vicious twenty rounds.

The first editions to carry reports of the fight were strewn throughout the parlor, as were bottles of champagne, whiskey, beer. The girls had snipped out newspaper photos of the fight and Ketchel had autographed them, writing on half of them, "To Cynthia, the only true love of my life," and on the other half, "To Annabelle, the only other true love of my life."

When Cynthia presented one to him that showed Papke landing a jab on his cheek, he said, "Not this one," balled it up and lobbed it through the window. The girls intended to frame the clippings and put them on their walls in the Nob Hill house.

Sometime after midnight, he left the girls dozing in the big bed and went into Britt's suite and found him reclining with a girl named Francie in a steaming bathtub foaming with bubbles and laced with scented oils. Britt was puffing a cigar and sipping a flute of champagne, his derby slanted over one eye.

"Hiya, champ. Like the man said, this is the life."

"Listen, Willie, I been thinking."

"Hell you have. I know what you been doing."

"There ain't a middleweight left to fight."

Britt sat up, sensing what Ketchel had in mind. The Francie girl made a low whine of protest at being discomfited and then re-accommodated herself to him. "I guess not, kid. You beat them all. Hell, you beat the light-heavy champ."

"Yeah, I did. And I think—"

"*I* know what you're thinking, Stevie!" the Goat called from the adjoining suite.

Ketchel looked toward the door. "Oh yeah?"

"Nosebone time!"

Britt arched his brow at Ketchel. Ketchel grinned. Britt laughed. "I gotta admit, kid, I've been doing some thinking along that line myself. I just didn't have the balls to be the one to bring it up."

The Francie girl snickered without opening her eyes and murmured, "You got plenty enough, baby, and you bring it up just fine." She did something with her hand under the bubbles and Britt winced and slapped at her arm. "Hey, tootsie! Careful with the jewels."

"Think the dinge'll go for it?" Ketchel said.

"Hell yes, he'll go for it. He's dying for a big-money match, and you're the biggest draw in the country. Know what else I think? I think you can take him. Hell, kid, I *know* you can take him."

Pete the Goat came in with a lanky and very naked brunette riding him piggyback. "I know that too," he said.

"Oh Jesus, I just got a great idea," Britt said.

"Hear them wheels grinding, champ?" the Goat said, and winked at Ketchel.

"If we play this right," Britt said, "if we by God play this right . . . we can make a real killing."

He told them what he had in mind. The Goat said it sounded good to him.

"Yeah," Ketchel said, "fine."

"Well all right," Britt said. "I'll track the boogie down and then see about—"

"Do it," Ketchel said.

AND SO. A few weeks after his fourth fight with Papke, Ketchel and Britt met in a San Francisco hilltop restaurant with Jack Johnson and his manager George Little and a shameless Australian redhead named Sheila. They sat at a secluded table next to a window overlooking a blue fog rolling in from the bay. Willus Britt laid it out plain and simple, and they came to an accord. They would sham a draw and clean up with side bets. And then have a rematch and make a real killing on the gate. They'd need a goddamn freight train to haul away the dough. . . .

IN THE THREE and a half years since Kate Morgan's death, he'd not had his old dream of James Jeffries. But for six months now he'd been having one almost exactly like it. It differed in only two details. In this one he was again in a fight that went on and on for two days and the faces of the ringsiders kept changing, but now he was always fighting Jack Johnson. And unlike the Jeffries dream, from which he always came awake just before landing a roundhouse to Big Jim's jaw, he didn't wake from this one until the punch struck. Struck and felt . . . *perfect* . . . and Johnson fell.

He always woke from this dream in transcendent elation. If I could do that, he would think, if I could do *that* . . .

Just land that *one big punch* . . .

Well. He would simply and irrefutably be the best.

The best as best could get.

The heavyweight boxing champion of the world.

That's who he would be.

Him.

The Galveston Giant

October 16, 1909. The James W. Coffroth Arena, Colma, California.

The day is dazzling blue under a warm autumn sun. The outdoor arena is packed to capacity with ten thousand paid spectators, more than two thousand others turned away, the ring a small tan island in a sea of white skimmers.

The announcer is the venerable Billy Jordan, his walrus moustache thick and white. Colossal cheering greets his introduction of Stanley Ketchel, the "Michigan Assassin," middleweight champion of the world, who enters the ring at 170 pounds and with a record of forty-nine wins, three losses, four draws. He spins in his corner, his robe swirling, raises his fists over his head in recognition of the ovation, bounces on his toes, rolls his head on his neck.

When Jordan directs the spectators' attention to the opposite corner of the ring, the boos rumble like thunder. Jack Johnson, the "Galveston Giant" and heavyweight champ, weighs 209 pounds. Winner of fifty-eight bouts, loser of six, fighter of twelve draws. His head smooth as a burnished cannonball. His gold teeth bared at the squall of insults and catcalls. He shakes his hands together over his head in mock thespian fashion as though acknowledging applause, and grins at the louder heckling.

The boxers shed their robes to their seconds. Both are splendid specimens of leanly sculpted muscle and both appreciably free of obvious scars, a striking detail in light of the many fights each has had at this point in his career, and especially remarkable in Ketchel, given the carnage of so many of his previous contests. His trunks are black, Johnson's butternut, with his usual red-and-white-striped bandanna tied to a belt loop at his hip.

Now that they are in the ring, the difference in their size is profoundly apparent, and makes clear why the Negro is the bookies' heavy favorite. For many bettors it is a day of keen dilemma: should they hope to win their bet at the cost of a continuing Negro champion, or hope to rejoice at the boogie's defeat and to hell with the loss of their wager?

The fighters position themselves for pictures. Johnson jokes with the photographers, says every side is his best side, "Even this one here," turning his back to them and wagging his buttocks, cackling at his own highjinks. Amid the chattering of shutters and clattering of photo plates, he faces Ketchel with fists upraised and smiling broadly. Ketchel poses in his customary semi-crouch, sideways to Johnson and holding his left arm outstretched toward him, his entire body seeming as cocked and ready as his right fist. Also on hand to record the fight is a motion picture crew.

Now everyone departs the ring but for the principals and the referee, the esteemed Jack Welch, hatless and portly, in shirtsleeves and tie and buttoned vest. He delivers the standard warnings and instructions and then directs them to shake hands and come out fighting at the bell. The fighters tap gloves and Johnson says, "Showtime, Mr. Stanley."

"Okay, Stevie," Britt tells him back in the corner, "it's a nice twenty-round workout for you boys, that's all. Just make it look good."

Ketchel nods, his eyes on Johnson in the opposite corner.

The gong sounds.

The crowd roars as the fighters come together in the middle of the ring and Johnson opens his mouth to make a jibe and Ketchel tries to knock out those gold teeth with the first punch of the fight.

BECAUSE THE DAY will not dawn on which Jack Johnson does not expect a double cross from one direction or another, Ketchel's breach of their agreement does not take him entirely by surprise, though he does not expect it in the opening seconds. For all his feline quickness in turning his chin from the blow, it catches him hard on the neck and wobbles him rearward to a detonation of cheers as Ketchel rushes after him, hammering with lefts and rights. Johnson retreats from the assault, warding it with his arms. Over in his corner George Little says, "What the *fuck*!"

Willus Britt and Pete the Goat are agape.

But in his haste to press the advantage, Ketchel is punching too wildly, and Johnson, with his back against the ropes, counters with three snapping jabs to forehead and mouth and nose that stop him short, and a right cross to the cheek that jolts him into a greater caution.

They circle each other, sidling and feinting, Ketchel feeling the blood running hot from his nose, dripping off his chin. Johnson smiles and says, "Any way you wants it, little man, okay by me."

Ketchel bores in with fists churning but Johnson defends artfully and scores with another combination to the head, driving him back.

"What the *hell're* they doing?" Britt says. "This ain't the deal." George Little glares at him from across the ring, and Britt turns his palms up and shrugs.

The crowd's bellow is unremitting. Near the end of the round Ketchel lands two hard hooks to Johnson's ribs and one to the head, and Johnson grabs him in a clinch, grins over Ketchel's shoulder and rolls his widened eyes, infuriating the crowd all the more with such shucking. They look like man and boy in intimate embrace. But even as Johnson clutches him so close that he cannot punch at his head, Ketchel beats at his backribs and kidneys and feels him flinching. Just as the round ends, Johnson pushes him away like some peskiness, and the arena resonates with a massive jeering. Johnson waves a fist above his head.

While the Goat swabs Ketchel with a sponge and puts a stop to the nosebleed, Britt says, "Tell me, *please* tell me I'm watching the greatest acting job in the world."

"I'm gonna take him, Willie." Ketchel's voice nasal with blood, eyes afire with exhilaration.

Britt rubs his face like a man not fully awake. "Christ, kid, it's supposed to—"

"I'm gonna take him!" Ketchel says.

"Yeah!" the Goat says, and proffers the water bag. Ketchel takes a swig, swishes it, spits it in a bucket.

Across the ring, the veins are standing on George Little's forehead as he bends to Johnson's ear and addresses him in a great agitation about that no-good lowdown double-crosser and the money they're all going to lose for betting on the draw. "I want you to knock that shithead into next week! You got me, Jack?"

"I hear you, man," Johnson says, his smiling gaze fixed on Ketchel across the ring.

In the early going of the next round, Johnson effectively defends against most of Ketchel's punches and consistently scores with the jab. At one point he places the palm of his glove against Ketchel's forehead and laughs as he momentarily holds him at bay in the mocking manner of a large boy staving off a smaller one in a schoolyard scrape. The crowd showers insults on Johnson. A ringsider cries out for him to stop acting like a gorilla and fight like a man.

"Listen at them, Mr. Stanley," Johnson says, smacking him with a jab. "Listen at how they *loves* to hate me."

He stabs Ketchel with another jab and asks when he intends to start fighting. He says he's been in cakewalks rougher than this match. Ketchel rushes in with another flurry but Johnson covers up well and lashes back with a hook to the heart that drives Ketchel back.

They sidle around each other, swapping jabs, Ketchel looking for an opening, cursing himself for his unruly style, telling himself to quit the wild stuff and fight smart, *smart,* goddamnit.

Johnson raps him with a jab and a glancing right and asks what he thinks of the Australian redhead Miss Sheila. "I recollects the way you admired her carnalicious charms."

His japery makes him incautious. Ketchel snakes a cross over Johnson's next jab and rocks him on his heels to an outburst of cheers and then swarms into him with a barrage of punches from every point of the compass, manically seeking his chin, his jaw. The spectators are in mad shriek as Johnson backpedals, shielding with arms and gloves, then sidesteps along the ropes to keep Ketchel moving laterally and unable to punch with full force. Then Ketchel misses with a pair of wild swings, and a Johnson uppercut snaps his head back and the ring tilts under him and he goes down.

The crowd's moan is titanic.

He rolls up onto an elbow, hears referee Welch's cry of "Twoooo!" through the storm of pleading for him to get up, get up. He sees Johnson as a dark blur leaning on the ropes. Britt and the Goat and every man facing him from ringside can see the lack of focus in his eyes.

But at five he is on one knee. Welch counts six. Arrives at seven. At eight Ketchel heaves to his feet and lurches away from Johnson as the crowd howls in jubilation and Johnson bounds after him, backs him into the ropes, hooks him in the ribs, the head, and then Ketchel has him in a clinch and holds on till the bell.

Johnson pats him on the head, and Ketchel swats the hand away.

As Ketchel settles on his stool, Britt bawls, "You took his best shot!" His elation is hardly greater than his astonishment. He has resigned himself to the loss of their wagers. The only concern now is to win the fight. "The dinge ain't got half the punch they say. You can take him, kid, you can. I always said you could take him."

The crowd is strident with thrilled witness of Ketchel's survival of the knockdown, with daring speculations of yet greater possibilities.

Through the third and fourth rounds, Ketchel keeps at a distance from Johnson, stays on the move, circling to the left, sidling to the right, only intermittently engaging in quick toe-to-toe exchanges and each time getting the worst of it. In the fifth, his frustration erupts and he rams a shoulder into Johnson's chest as though trying to break open a door and staggers him into the ropes. Johnson charges back and bowls him off his feet with the sheer mass of his forty-pound advantage and then almost steps on Ketchel's head as he stumbles past him. A reporter notes that it is like a horseman trampling a man underfoot.

Through the sixth and the seventh, the eighth and the ninth, Johnson's longer reach gives him the better of almost every exchange. A grudging consensus has awarded every round to the heavyweight champ.

Ketchel's left cheek now a wedge of blue plum, one ear a wet beet, an eyebrow cut and swollen. The Goat swabs blood from his nose and says, "He's gone scared, Stevie. He knows he can't take you. Now kick the coon's ass!"

"What you think I been trying to do, Goat, borrow money from him?"

In Johnson's corner the seconds work intently at watering and sponging him, tending to a small cut over one eye.

"Goddamnit, I've had enough of you playing with that runt," George Little says. "Quit fucking around and finish him!"

Johnson gives him a look. *"Fucking around?"*

In the early part of the tenth Johnson presses the attack, walloping Ketchel with body punches before Ketchel counters with a ferocious flurry that has the crowd in a wild squall as he drives Johnson into retreat. Ketchel works him into a corner, beats at his belly, his ribs, his chest. Johnson curses and clinches. Then hefts Ketchel off the canvas and heaves him like a medicine ball. Ketchel lights in a tumble and hustles up in a fury. The crowd yowling, objecting of fouls and dirty nigger bastards. Referee Welch warns Johnson against any such further maneuver. Johnson shows his gold teeth and says, "My sincerefulest apologies, Mr. Jack."

Welch gestures for them to resume fighting and Ketchel bulls into Johnson with his head down and butts him under the eye. Johnson grabs him in a clinch and Ketchel punches him low. Johnson curses and locks an arm around his neck and grinds the laces of his other glove into his eye cut. Nearly choking, Ketchel clubs at Johnson's kidney with the heel of his fist. Welch shrilling rebukes. Johnson clouts at Ketchel's battered ear with an elbow. Welch shakes a finger in Johnson's face and as Johnson cuts his eyes at the ref Ketchel hits him with a hook that sprays the sweat off his head. Johnson curses and clinches and they grapple against the ropes, butting, elbowing, oblivious to Welch's commands to break until he bravely wedges between them.

The gong declares a minute's truce.

Ketchel is panting hard when he arrives at his stool. The Goat examines the eye cuts and pronounces them insignificant. So too the cheek welt.

"Keep it up, kid, keep it up," Britt says. "You're whipping him, I swear to God, you're whipping his black ass!"

Ketchel knows better. But he also believes with all his heart and soul that if he can land just *one big punch* he can bring the big bastard down.

In the opposite corner Johnson's seconds minister to the swelling raised under his eye by the head butt as George Little continues to reprove him. "The little bohunk's making you look bad, goddamnit! Don't let him do you like this!"

"I ain't *letting* him do a damn thing," Johnson says.

In the eleventh, Ketchel lands his best punch of the fight thus far, an overhand right that rocks Johnson and raises a thunderous outcry, but even in the instant of landing it Ketchel knows it is not the Big One, it's a little too high on the jaw. Johnson leans backward as he retreats, keeping his jaw out of range, taking punches on the shoulders and arms, fending with his gloves. The crowd baying like a massive wolf pack smelling blood on the air. But again Ketchel's bombardment lacks accuracy and Johnson counters with a straight right that flashes a light in Ketchel's head and almost unhinges his knees and he grabs Johnson in a clinch.

So ends the eleventh.

"Christ sake, Jack," George Little says, "how much longer this gonna go on?"

Johnson works his sore jaw. "I've give him some shots, man. He ain't hardly human." He means the remark as a joke but it does not carry that way to George Little or even entirely so to his own ears.

"He's a goddamn feist dog don't know who he's snapping at, is what he is," George Little says. "And you, goddamnit, are *Jack Johnson*. You're the heavyweight champion of the *world*. Enough's enough. Yank the leash on the son of a bitch. Bust him."

The gong sounds.

Johnson keeps his chin down and hands high to defend his aching jaw, and Ketchel hooks him to the body repeatedly, trying to bring down his guard, expose the chin, make an opening for the One Big Punch.

They jab and close in and clinch, half-wrestle into Johnson's corner, where George Little shouts, "Bust him, goddamnit, *bust him*!" Johnson bangs at the back of Ketchel's neck. Ketchel butts Johnson in the forehead. Welch issues more warnings, orders them to break.

Ketchel backs away and lowers his hands, right fist at his hip, like a gunfighter set to draw. Johnson comes away from the ropes, touches a glove to his forehead where a lump is forming from the headbutt and as he lowers the glove Ketchel springs and hits him with a right cross carrying all of his weight behind it.

Johnson barely manages to avert his chin but the punch bashes into his temple, knocks him into a sideways totter . . . and he drops on his ass.

The arena explodes in a shuddering soar of cheers.

Johnson rolls up onto one hand and tries to rise but is dazed and off balance and falls back again. He braces himself on one arm as the ref starts to count.

Ketchel stares down at him and thinks *Yes, yes, yes*. . . . He barely hears the ref yell, "*Twooooo!*"

Welch swings his arm in a great high sweep with each count, as he cannot be heard above the hysterical din, not even by some at ringside.

"*Threeeeee!*"

Johnson's yellow eyes are glassy and disbelieving.

"*Foourrrr!*"

Ketchel feels the robust pull of his own grin, as aware as everyone in the crowd that he is but seconds away from the heavyweight championship.

"*Fiiiiive!*"

Johnson rolls sideways and pauses with both hands on the canvas.

"*Siiiiix!*"

Johnson now on all fours, pausing. Ketchel thinks, Fall over, fall over, fall over. . . .

"*Seevvvvven!*"

Johnson on one knee. Okay, Ketchel thinks, okay you no-good

lowdown stinking nosebone son of a bitch, *do* it, get up, get up and see what happens, goddamn you.

Eeeiiiight!

Johnson is up.

The referee gestures for them to resume. Johnson's gaze now unglassed. He reads Ketchel's eyes. Shows his gold teeth.

In this moment all Ketchel can think to do is to hit that golden smile with all his might and drop the man for keeps. He leaps headlong, swinging from the hip, letting fly with what is commonly called a haymaker.

It is a rankly reckless move and Johnson has seen it coming. And he beats Ketchel to the punch with a right cross that by his own later admission is one of the hardest blows of his life. It hits oncoming Ketchel squarely in the mouth in a collision of opposing forces not unlike a baseball bat connecting with a fastball. All in a heartbeat Ketchel's forward motion is arrested and reversed and he is aloft and then thumping onto the canvas like a bundle of the latest edition hitting the sidewalk at a newsstand and Johnson's forward momentum carries him into Ketchel's upslung legs and he trips and goes sprawling and immediately scrambles to his feet as the cheers of a moment before transform to a colossal groan.

Ketchel lies supine, spread-eagled, unmoving. As the referee begins the count Johnson leans on the ropes, one hand on his hip, his posture suggesting a workman at rest, a gravedigger, perhaps, who has completed the most arduous part of a job and is watching someone else finish up.

"Ten!" cries Welch. He waves his arms crosswise over Ketchel and then hoists Johnson's hand to a weak chorus of boos, the majority of witnesses still too stunned to do other than stand gaping at the terrible sight of Ketchel flat on his back.

Johnson goes to his corner and says to George Little, "I think I done killed him."

He is not the only one to think so. Not even repeated applications of smelling salts rouse Ketchel to consciousness.

"Let's get to the dressing room while the getting's good," George Little says. Johnson says he wants to see if Ketchel recovers. Little casts nervous glances at the hostile crowd and says they can wait for word in the dressing room. Johnson says he's not leaving the ring until he knows if Ketchel's dead or crippled or what.

Nearly fifteen minutes elapse before Ketchel finally comes around with a moan and is helped to sit up. One of Johnson's seconds chants loudly: "Nine hundred fifty-four, nine hundred fifty-five, nine hundred fif—"

"Cut out that shit," Johnson says. They make their way back to the dressing room in a rain of boos and epithets. And a few minutes later, as he removes Johnson's gloves, George Little says, "Jesus." Embedded in the facing of the right glove are Ketchel's two front teeth.

In the ring, Ketchel is assisted to his feet amid a scattering of relieved cheering and applause. His mouth is a bloody wreck, his balance tentative, his vision indistinct. Britt's face comes into partial focus before him and Ketchel hears him ask, "You okay, champ?" but he is unsure what the question means, and so says nothing.

He is helped into his robe. Helped to step down from the ring. Helped through the crowd, to his dressing room.

IN THE POSTFIGHT interview, Jack Johnson told reporters what he would tell everyone ever after: that the only reason Ketchel came within two seconds of taking the heavyweight title from him was a sneak punch. He said he and Ketchel had agreed the fight would be no more than an exhibition. They would put on a good show for twenty rounds to give the fans their money's worth and both of them would benefit. He would have a hell of a good payday and Ketchel would have the honor of having fought the heavyweight champ to a draw. Everything was going along as agreed until Ketchel double-crossed him with a sneak punch in the twelfth.

"Mr. Stanley ain't so dumb he would imperilize his life by fighting me for real," Johnson said. "But he ain't so honest he wouldn't try and put Poppa Jack down for the count with a sneak punch, neither, get him the heavyweight belt and some big-time glory, know what I mean? Nothing for it after that but to give the little fella what he had coming."

"It sure as hell didn't *look* like an exhibition match, Jack," one reporter remarked. "Not from the start."

There were snickers and elbow nudges among his colleagues, every man of whom was thinking the same thing. Jack Johnson's cavalier attitude toward the truth in matters large and small was already well established.

"Well now, we sure enough made it look good, didn't we?" Johnson's golden grin shone. "Me and Mr. Stanley, we natural-born thespiaters, don't you know?"

ON RETURNING TO his San Francisco hotel after the fight, Ketchel said nothing to anyone. It pained his mouth too much to talk, for one thing, and he in any case did not want to open it and expose the gap in his top teeth. Besides, he had nothing to say.

That evening he lay awake into the depths of the night and behind his closed eyes sporadically saw the same blinding blast of light he saw at the impact of Johnson's punch. He ordered himself not to think about anything and fairly well succeeded. But his heart could not be commanded to cease feeling as it did, and he at last succumbed to weeping. He had a moment of wishing he had been killed. Felt as if, in some way that had nothing to do with breathing, some portion of him had been.

The Hustler

The colonel's telegram congratulated him on a heroic effort and invited him to his estate in Missouri to rest up. His brother John's wire also conveyed admiration, and asked if he would be coming home for a while. Ketchel sent cables to both of them, saying that he had various business matters to tend to and could not get away for now. He told the colonel he hoped to visit him soon, told his brother he longed to go home and spend some time with his family and in his own house, both of which he missed.

The truth of course was that he did not want either the colonel or his mother to see him in his battered state. While the swellings and bruises would dissipate with their customary quickness, his mouth was another matter. On the train trip back to New York he was obliged to nourish chiefly on soups and puddings and beer.

Once back in Manhattan, he underwent extensive oral surgery and was afterward required to wear a wire brace for six weeks.

He spent that time in Atlantic City, accompanied by Jewel Bovine. At her first sight of him on his return she had been moved to tears. They could kiss if they were gentle about it. She had to quit the hatcheck job to be with him, but she was sure she could get another one on her return, and Ketchel gave her enough money to cover her share of the boardinghouse room rent for at least six months. He left a note for Britt and the Goat, informing them he would be away for a time but did not say where. His New York surgeon gave him the name of a colleague in Atlantic City who each week would assess the process of his recovery. They checked into a boardwalk hotel as Mr. and Mrs. Jesse Dalton. Their room was on the top floor overlooking the ocean. They rarely left its confines during the entire time they were there.

When he returned to New York he no longer wore the mouth brace. His new teeth were brilliant, his repaired jaw felt fine. And he learned Willus Britt had been dead two weeks.

The Goat had gone to Britt's room one morning to collect him on the way to breakfast and discovered him on the floor in his bathrobe, blue-faced and half-rigid. The coroner determined a heart attack. There had been a memorial service and Jimmy Britt delivered the eulogy.

Ketchel paid a visit to the grave, found it inundated with the wagonload of flowers he'd ordered for it. He had to dig with his hands through the heap of mums and jonquils and lilies and tulips to expose the white headstone with Willus's engraved name and a simple REST IN PEACE.

My friend, he thought.

It occurred to him how few true friends he had. How few he'd ever had. The reflection brought Kate Morgan to mind, and he sat down in the flowers with his face in his hands.

The cloying fragrances closed around him and he began to feel sick. He raised his face but the sweetness was overpowering and he quite suddenly could not get his breath. He started to rise, slipped on the crushed petals underfoot, and fell into the mound of flowers. He felt he was smothering and nearly screamed in his panic as his feet sought purchase. Then he was upright and running, shedding flowers as he ran. Ran all the way out of the graveyard and for several blocks beyond, his heart banging at his ribs like some crazed thing in a cage.

SHORTLY BEFORE CHRISTMAS he left for a sojourn in Michigan. At the same time, Pete the Goat departed for St. Louis to see an ex-wife with whom he'd remained friends over the years. How many wives had he had, Ketchel asked, en route to the station. "Just about enough," Pete said.

Despite his brother's and Barzoomian's best efforts to keep the details from her, his mother had heard talk of Johnson's devastating knockout of him and had been fraught with worry that her son was somehow maimed. And then he was at the front door and she saw his face as handsome as ever and she hugged him hard and wept with relief.

After two days at his mother's house he went to his own home at Pine Lake and there received a telegram from the colonel asking if he might come to Belmont for a brief visit. Ketchel wired back: ANYTIME OLD MAN STOP MY HOUSE YOUR HOUSE STOP STEVE. Three days later Pete Dickerson was ensconced as his guest.

Every few days, Ketchel took supper at his mother's table, catching up on the latest news of Barzoomian's business, arm wrestling with his brother, dancing with Rebeka. But he chiefly kept company with the colonel. They went fishing on Lake Michigan and damn the gelid winds. They went hunting at his cabin. They drank excellent whiskey and smoked superior cigars. The colonel continued to entreat him to visit his Missouri estate for a while. Ketchel promised he would, and sometime soon. On New Year's Eve they drank to each other's good health and the bright future ahead.

They talked of various topics, including of course the Johnson fight. The colonel felt compelled to remark that Johnson must've hit him with a lucky punch.

"Lucky's the word for it," Ketchel said. "I was lucky it didn't kill me."

Only to the colonel did he ever confess that in the first days after the fight, he'd seriously considered retiring. But in the past few weeks he'd come to realize it would be a mistake. "I'd be quitting for no reason except I got cooled good. That's a yellow reason."

"Christ's sake, son, if there's one thing you'll never be it's yellow. But the thing is, who's left for you to fight? You've beat them all."

"Except for Johnson."

"The boogie don't count, he's a heavyweight."

"And the best there is."

"Only till this summer when Jeffries gets at him."

"Yeah, probably."

"No probably about it," the colonel said. "Tell me, you decided on a new manager?"

In the time he'd been home in Pine Lake, Ketchel had received more than two dozen wires from managers around the country who wanted the job made available by the death of Willus Britt. A dozen of them were from New York. He was leaning toward a man named Mizner. In his cable, Mizner claimed that before coming to New York he had managed boxers in various mining towns out west, and concluded the telegram with: WILD WEST GUYS GOT TO STICK TOGETHER.

HE RETURNED TO Manhattan in late February and met with Wilson Mizner at the man's Broadway office. In his midthirties, Mizner was lean and quick of gesture, bald on the crown but handsome, a dapper dresser, a fast talker of persuasive sincerity. A charming and amusing quipster who would in the years ahead discover his métier as a writer, that enduring profession of skilled liars, authoring Broadway plays and cranking out Hollywood scripts.

He recounted with great animation his days as a prospector in Alaska when he was hardly more than a boy. "I panned for two years and all I got out of it was a total of eighteen dollars in dust, two frostbitten toes, and a no-good partner's bullet through my hat. Oh yeah, and a dose of clap from an Indian squaw."

Mizner himself had fought three boxing matches in his life, all of them in Nome. After winning his first two fights by easy decisions he began to think he might have what it took to be a top pro. Then he fought a fisherman from Juneau and the fight was over in the first round. "He knocked me out on Good Friday and I didn't completely regain my senses till Easter. It was a compelling religious experience and converted me to management."

He was educated in a variety of subjects that Ketchel knew nothing about, but they were familiar with many of the same places. Mizner was from California and, like Ketchel, had enjoyed grand times in San Francisco. He had managed boxers in a number of mining towns Ketchel knew well, though Mizner had been in them a few years before him.

"Now listen, champ, you may have heard it said that I'm something of a hustler," he told Ketchel. "Well, I want you to know that's a base canard. I happen to be something of a *superior* hustler. And why not? The way I see it, God help those who do not help themselves."

Ketchel had known a variety of hustlers, but Mizner seemed in a class of his own, and it was impossible not to like him. He had Ketchel laughing at accounts of shady enterprises he had engineered in partnership with his brother Addison. He readily confessed that the most shameful thing he'd done so far was when he'd first arrived in New York and stolen his brother's girl. That the "girl," one Adelaide Yerkes, was at the time eighty years old was nothing to brag about, either, he admitted, but the shuddering truth of her age was more than offset by the cheerful fact that she was as rich as Midas's widow. In no time at all they were married and then just as swiftly divorced. The whole tawdry episode was played out in the yellow press and made him into something of a roguish celebrity, which in turn and in the naturally perverse nature of things, made him attractive to women who otherwise wouldn't have given him a second glance. The whole tawdry episode also got him a handsome monetary settlement.

"But let me tell you, champ, it wasn't like I didn't have it coming. I mean, you want to even *think* about an eighty-year-old broad with her clothes off? Well, I had to do more than think about it, my good friend. I had to do the deed. I mean, I *earned* that dough."

Ketchel grinned. "I'll say you did."

Mizner had then managed a hotel for a time. "That's hotel as in cathouse," he said. "Rough place. We had a sign on the wall saying guests had to carry out their own dead. If running a cathouse isn't the toughest job in the world I don't know what is. I'd go back to prospecting before running another house."

What he went back to was managing prizefighters. "Back to the Sweet Science, as the great Pierce Egan called it." It was a wise move. He knew the biggest promoters on both coasts and had the negotiating skill to get his fighters top dollar.

"Top dollar's good to hear," Ketchel said. "The thing is, I've also heard you're pretty friendly with some fellas who like to take the risk out of fight bets." He had heard this from the colonel, whose sources had so informed him before Ketchel departed Michigan.

"I won't lie to you, champ, you've heard correctly. My fighters can sometimes earn a little extra by making sure the other fellow wins, the other fella usually being some kid the boys are high on and want to see build a good record."

"The boys?" Ketchel said.

"The gentlemen you referred to, the sort who enjoy making wagers but dislike risk. Sometimes my guy can earn himself even more than a little extra if he sees to it the other fellow wins by a knockout. And *some*times my man can enjoy a very hefty payday indeed if he makes sure the knockout happens in a certain round. But I assure you, champ, those gentlemen will never ask such a favor of you. Christ, kid, with you as champion they do better on their cuts from the promoters over the long run than if you went into the tank. These guys are so crooked they have to screw their shoes on, but they ain't stupid. And even though I've been known to go a little off the vertical myself, I never do it with a friend who wants to play it straight. On that you have my word."

"I've checked around," Ketchel said. "I think you can get me the biggest purses. But I'm telling you right now, mister, I won't lay down, never. Don't even ask."

"Clear as a glass bell, kid."

"Two other things. Pete Stone stays my trainer. And I want a rematch with Johnson. In the next ten minutes wouldn't be soon enough."

"Whatever trainer you want's okay with me. I don't train, I just manage. As for another go at Johnson, I don't blame you. You came *this* close to whipping his ass. I'll talk to his people, but I wouldn't get my hopes up. As I'm sure you know, he's gonna fight Jeffries this summer. The jig stands to make a lot of jack on it, so I sincerely doubt he'll risk losing the belt to anybody else before the match with Jeff. And once he loses to Jeffries . . . hell, why would you bother fighting him again if it ain't for the title? A rematch with a nigger ex-champ won't even draw much of a gate."

"I don't care about the title, or the gate."

Mizner stared at him. "Oh . . . I get it. It's like that."

"It's like that."

"Well, as I said, I'll talk to his people. Meantime, I'll see about lining you up some good-money matches and keep you in the chips."

"Do it. But remember, the minute we can get Johnson, he's next. Any terms he wants, I don't care. And I don't care if we have to bust a contract with somebody else to get him."

"I got the message, champ. Call me Bill."

"I'm Steve."

Mizner checked his pocket watch. "Past the yardarm, Stevie. Let us repair to my other office."

They went to his favorite Forty-second Street saloon, where they ordered a pitcher of Pabst and availed themselves of the free bartop lunch. Their plates held thick slices of ham and bread, chunks of liverwurst and blood sausage, hardboiled eggs, olives and pickles and gobs of mustard. They conversed through the afternoon and into the evening over a steady flow of beers and bumps, enjoying happy reminiscences about the rowdy Western burgs of their former days, their high wild times in Butte. . . .

Evelyn and La Fée Verte

Mizner was even more of a man about town than Britt had been. He introduced Ketchel to the plushest brothel in the city, a place that bore no sign on its handsome brick exterior but was known as the Pleasure Dome. Every one of its girls so lovely that Ketchel could hardly decide which to pick, and finally chose both a Latin girl with skin the color of caramel and a redhead pale as cream.

They afterward had a drink and told each other of the fine time they'd had. "The Dome's got the prettiest girls in New York, no question," Mizner said, "and every one of them with a heart that'll cut glass. Then again, nobody goes to a whorehouse to find a girl like Mom, does he? Not unless he had the sort of mom I'd like to know."

Ketchel admitted he'd had his share of good times with whores, but he preferred to get his loving from women who weren't professionals.

"I'm with you, champ. It's always best when it's from a woman who likes something about you besides your billfold, even if she's no Pleasure Dome girl in looks."

"Like the Widow Yerkes?" Ketchel grinned at him in the backbar mirror.

"Christ, kid, you got a mean streak, you know that?"

Actually, Mizner was on intimate terms with a number of attractive women in the arts and literary worlds, almost all of them given to bohemian attitudes. He knew actresses, singers and dancers, models, copy editors and book illustrators, and over the next few weeks he introduced Ketchel to a number of them. In the company of such women they passed most of their evenings in cafés and night clubs, dancehalls that never closed. The girls were invariably impressed not only by Ketchel's championship but as well by his dancing and singing.

So, too, was Mizner. The first time he heard Ketchel croon was on an evening in a club where they'd gone with a fetching pair of art school models. While the band was taking a break, Ketchel impulsively went up to the bandstand and without preamble or musical accompaniment began crooning "By the Light of the Silvery Moon." When he finished, there was vigorous applause and calls for more. He beamed and said, "You folks like moon songs, do you?" Then sang "On Moonlight Bay" and received an even bigger hand than before. He bowed formally, then shook his hands together above his head.

Back at the table, Mizner clapped him on the shoulder. "I gotta say, champ, you got a real talent. You belong on the stage."

"That's right," said one of the girls. She made a show of checking the wall clock. "I think there's one leaving in about five minutes." She and the other girl giggled drunkenly at this ancient and lamest of jokes.

Mizner stared at them without expression, then said to Ketchel, "The thing about models is, most of them are pretty as a picture but about as intelligent as a turnip."

"Oh *yeah*?" said the other girl. "Well, you're about as intelligent as a . . . as a *rutabaga*." The girls shrilled with laughter.

"As an *eggplant*," the first girl said, and they doubled over the table and hit it with their fists.

"You didn't let me finish," Mizner said. "I was about to say it's a good thing I love the taste of turnips."

"Oh sure," the first girl said.

"I'm not kidding," he said, and leaned over and ran his tongue into her ear.

She hunched her shoulders and giggled. "*Ooooh. . . .*"

Mizner paused and affected to look thoughtful. Then picked up a salt cellar and sprinkled a few grains on the girl's dampened ear, licked it again, and said, "Aaah . . . just right."

DRINKING WITH MIZNER in a Fifth Avenue saloon one evening, Ketchel spied a Gibson Girl poster on the far wall. The one of Evelyn Nesbit as *The Eternal Question*. By way of the newspapers, he had kept abreast of her husband's two trials for the murder of Stanford White and of her testimony on his behalf. The first trial ended with a hung jury, the second in Thaw's incarceration for an indefinite period in the Matteawan Hospital for the Criminally Insane.

Mizner followed Ketchel's gaze to see what held his attention.

"Ah yes, Evelyn," he said, as much in sigh as declaration. "One of God's most sublime creations. Have I told you I know her?" He grinned at the expression on Ketchel's face, then leaned toward him and said in near-whisper, "And I mean *very* damn well."

"Oh brother, tell me another one."

Mizner swore it was true. He'd met her more than a year ago, shortly after her husband got sent to the asylum. They were introduced by a mutual friend, a stage director who also gave acting lessons. Evelyn was one of his students. According to rumor, she was receiving far less financial support from her imprisoned husband than was publicly supposed. Whether that was true or not, she was seeking to make a career as an actress.

"Far be it from me to smooch and tell," Mizner said, "but just between us, I've had some memorable moments with that exquisite lady. I'm not the only one who can make that boast, I admit, but so what? The way I see it, a share of Evelyn is better than none of Evelyn."

Sad to say, he added, she had just a few weeks before fallen in love with a painter in the Village. Her *true* love, as she had described him to Mizner. What Mizner found sad about it was that Evelyn believed in being true to her true love, a concept he found baffling in a woman of her experience, and she had therefore ceased sharing her favors with anyone but the painter. There was, however, reason to hope for a return to sweeter times. Evelyn had twice before in the previous year believed she had fallen in true love, and in both instances she had fallen back out of it within a month.

"Come to think of it," Mizner said, "she's past due to no longer be in true love with that painter. Say now, champ, this may be an opportune time to give her a call."

"I gotta hand it to you, pal," Ketchel said. "You really know how to lay it on. If I didn't know better, I'd almost believe you."

Mizner affected to take umbrage, then went to use the telephone mounted on the rear wall. When he returned to the bar he said, "The lady informs me that the painter became part of her sad past as of last week. *And* she'd love nothing better than to meet the middleweight champion of the world."

"Oh yeah? When?"

"Now."

"If you're pulling my leg, Bill. . . ."

"The only leg I want to get my hand on is Evelyn's. Let's go."

THEY MADE A brief stop at a saloon where Mizner knew the owner and bought a bottle of absinthe from his back room. Although popular with the bohemian set and with artists who praised its inspirational effects, the liqueur was commonly believed to be highly addictive and to cause hallucinations, madness, in some cases death. Its banning in America would precede Prohibition by some eight years and long outlast it.

"Her favorite treat," Mizner said, waggling the bottle. Ketchel admitted that he had never tasted it. "You haven't missed much," Mizner said. "I can hardly stand the stuff, and nothing in the world will give you a worse hangover. But the doll loves it, and I love what it does to her disposition. It bodes immensely well for our visit, mon ami, that she asked if we'd be so kind as to bring a bottle of it."

Evelyn Nesbit's apartment was in an elegant building of brick and dark wood, fronted by a wide sidewalk and trees in new leaf. They were admitted by a doorman who had their names on a list, then took the elevator up to the top floor. Mizner rapped lightly on her door and a moment later it opened and there she was.

"Gentlemen," she said, "I'm so pleased you're here."

Her voice was soft and had a slight rasp. Her eyes shadowed in blue. Her smile small and despite its crimson lipstick somehow shy as a child's. She wore a white shirtwaist and black skirt, her dusky blonde hair loosely bunched at the back of her neck and tied with a black ribbon. Ketchel thought she was even more beautiful than in the first photos he'd seen of her more than three years before.

She ushered them into the foyer and took their hats and gave Mizner a hug. He introduced Ketchel. She offered her hand and said she was thrilled to make his acquaintance. The touch of her fingers deepened his breath.

The parlor was lighted by the low flames of a fireplace and variously colored tapers in tall glass holders. The furnishings were Middle Eastern, the walls hung with darkly colored Persian rugs and but a single painting, a desertscape with a small oasis under a thin crescent moon. There was a faint fragrance of incense. A phonograph, its cabinet doors partially closed to mute the volume, issued music of a sort Ketchel had not heard before, at once lively and mournful. She sensed his curiosity and said, "It's an old gypsy tune called 'The Black Raven.' You like it?"

"Sure do. But why the *black* raven? Ain't . . . aren't all ravens black?"

"Well now, I hadn't thought about that. Maybe the gypsies know something we don't."

"Maybe gypsies don't care a fig about grammatical redundancy," Mizner said. He produced the absinthe and Evelyn brightened. "Why, Wilson, you darling man."

At a small bar against the wall Mizner poured three slim glasses a quarter full each. Ketchel detected a scent reminiscent of licorice.

Evelyn picked up a glass and held it before a candle flame. The liqueur glowed like molten emerald. "La Fée Verte," she said.

Ketchel's stiff face bespoke his ignorance of the phrase.

"The Green Fairy," Evelyn said. "Isn't that a lovely name for it? Oscar Wilde said a glass of absinthe is as poetical as a sunset."

Ketchel figured Oscar Wilde must've been drunk as a coot to imagine a green sunset, but he kept the thought to himself.

Mizner said he himself preferred the "blue ruin," as gin was sometimes called in newspaper editorials and not always in jest. "But in deference to our lovely hostess, I'm willing to risk my so-called sanity on this occasion."

"I have always admired daring," Evelyn said.

She set the glass down. Ketchel watched with keen interest as Mizner placed a sugar cube in a perforated spoon, held the spoon over the glass, and gently decanted ice water a few drops at a time over the sugar.

Evelyn put her lips almost to Ketchel's ear as if she were imparting some deep secret and whispered, "To ease the bitterness." Her breath was warm on his ear and he felt the small hairs stir on his nape. Her eyes gleamed with candlelight. She stood so close he was not sure if he felt the touch of her breast on the back of his arm or only imagined it.

Mizner poured each glass about three-quarters full, the contents now clouded to a milky green. Evelyn raised her glass and regarded the opaque liqueur. "The French say it is now louche," she said. "Such a lovely word for 'indecent.' It actually means cross-eyed, you know."

Ketchel said he hadn't known that. "But I know when it comes to getting cross-eyed most any kind of booze'll do the trick."

Evelyn touched his arm. "You are droll, Mr. Ketchel."

He said to please call him Steve. She said only if he would call her Evelyn. He said they had a deal. Mizner asked if anybody had read any good books lately, but neither of them seemed to have heard him. He cursed himself for a dope for having brought Ketchel.

They sat in the parlor and sipped at their absinthe and talked for a while about her acting classes. She loved the actor's art, she said, the assumption of a character different from oneself. The habitation of an invention, as she had once heard acting described. She now and again rose from her chair to change the record on the phonograph.

Mizner asked Ketchel how he liked the absinthe.

"Tastes like medicine."

"That's what everybody says who's never had it before. Don't worry, pretty soon most of your taste buds will be dead and it won't be so bad."

"It will still taste like medicine," Evelyn said. She sipped from her glass and smiled at Ketchel. "It *is* medicine."

When she played a recording of "Maple Leaf Rag" they paused in the conversation to listen. She was pleased to learn they also liked Scott Joplin's music, and she played several more of his rags, opening the cabinet doors to raise the volume. She finished her drink and asked Mizner for another. Ketchel was only half done with his. The heat it kindled in his belly was different from that of whiskey. He could feel it seep into his bones. The music seemed keener now, the colors of the wall rugs more vibrant, the candle flames brighter. So, too, Evelyn's eyes.

She wanted to know more about him. She'd been familiar with his name for some time and knew of his boxing championship, and she had read about his rugged hobo boyhood and his arduous years in Montana, a place that to her was as distant and foreboding as the moon, yet somehow as romantic too. Ketchel said he wouldn't call Montana romantic as the moon, but it was for sure as cold. She said she had only recently read of his splendid singing voice and wonderful dancing talent. Ketchel said the newspapers tended to exaggerate things. She asked if he might honor her with a song. He was reluctant, thinking how poorly he would compare to the truly great singers she had heard. But she said "Please," and so he said of course. She requested "When You Were Sweet Sixteen." He stood up and sang it to her in a perfect tone of bittersweet melancholy. She applauded heartily and said he was wonderful.

Slumped low in his chair, Mizner flapped his palms together and muttered, "Yeah, real nice, kid."

She asked Mizner for another absinthe. While he prepared it she went to the gramophone and changed the record, re-cranked the handle and set the needle to the spinning groove. The room filled with the strains of an instrumental version of "After the Ball."

"I pray I am not being overly bold," she said to Ketchel, "but may I have the pleasure of this dance?"

He said he admired boldness and the pleasure would be all his. She held her arms out to him and he stepped into her embrace and they danced around the room. Even through the incense he could smell her perfume. The scent of her hair.

Mizner set her fresh drink on the small table beside her chair and watched them for a moment, then said he heard his mother calling and please don't anyone trouble himself to see him to the door. Not until the record played out did they become aware he had gone.

She next played "A Bird in a Gilded Cage" and now they did not so much dance as simply hold each other close and sway in place.

Before the record was finished, they had ceased swaying and held their kiss until the music stopped.

She stepped back and stared at him, her eyes reflecting the firelight. Then unribboned her hair and let it spill in a lustrous cascade over her shoulders.

"Yes," she said.

His fantasies about her proved meager against the reality of the following hour. Her nakedness in the candlelight, the heat and scent of her skin, her tongue at his own, at his chest, at his loins. His face in the lushness of her hair, mouth at her nipples, in the piquant nest of her sex. Now they were face to face, now he was behind her, above, below. Their panting carried through the apartment, their moans, the slappings of their flesh. He felt armed with a club, was astonished at the magnitude of his appetite, his unflagging crave. After a time she led him from the bed to an armless chair and sat him down and mounted him in reverse. The chair faced a cheval mirror and they watched themselves in their rooted writhing. His face behind hers, his hands at her breasts.

"The front row seat," she said. "Stanny taught it to me."

Not until he again spasmed and was done did he realize that she was no longer gasping with pleasure but convulsing with sobs. He thought to ask what was wrong, but then sensed what it was. And knew there was no help for it.

He carried her to the bed and pulled the covers over her, then quickly got dressed. Her face was in a pillow and she was still weeping as he went out the door.

The next day Mizner asked if he'd had a good time, and he said yeah, pretty good.

And neither mentioned her name to the other again.

Reformation

The gym was only a few blocks from the Bartholdi Hotel, where Ketchel and Pete the Goat, who had returned from California, were living. But on days of bad hangover or mid-morning awakenings next to a naked girl, he sometimes didn't train until late afternoon, if he trained that day at all.

He didn't show up in the gym for three days after his tryst with Evelyn, and Pete the Goat was unhappy.

"Boozing. Staying out till the cows come home. Humping yourself juiceless. You're sure enough keeping sharp, ain't you, champ?"

"I already got a mother, Goat, so lay off."

"You're tough as they come, Stevie, but nobody's so tough he can fight good without training."

"Cut it out, man. Soon as we get a fight lined up I'll get ready.

What the hell, I've fought with hangovers and still whipped the mugs."

"I wouldn't want to fight Frank Klaus with a hangover unless he was the one who had it. He ain't no mug."

"Frank Klaus?"

"Next week."

"When this happen?"

"This morning. Mizner phoned. Good money, he says."

It was a six-rounder at the Duquesne Gardens in Pittsburgh, Frank Klaus's hometown. Klaus was an excellent boxer and solid puncher who in two more years would win a share of the middleweight title, and then a year after that win the rest of it from Billy Papke in Paris. He was no mug.

KETCHEL'S TIMING WAS erratic, his footwork clumsy, his punches off target. The crowd booed him. Klaus was cautious through the first two rounds, then grew emboldened by Ketchel's obvious unreadiness and went on the attack. He dominated the next two rounds, scoring repeatedly with head-snapping jabs and crosses, several times jolting Ketchel with speedy combinations. Not until the last minute of round five did Ketchel at last recover his proper rhythm and find Klaus's range. He pounded him into the ropes with body punches, rocked him with hooks to the head. In the final round he landed an overhand that wobbled Klaus and brought the crowd to its feet. But Klaus recovered, and at the final gong they were swapping hard punches in mid-ring. Under Pennsylvania's "no decision" rule, the bout was recorded as "no contest," and most of the newspaper verdicts called it an even match, but a few gave the decision to Klaus.

The next day the Goat handed Ketchel a newspaper he'd folded to a report of the fight. "You *see* this?" he said.

Ketchel scanned it, saw that it called the verdict for Klaus, and flung the paper away in a flutter. "What the hell's a hack know?"

"He knows what he saw," Pete said.

But Ketchel persisted in his cavalier view toward training. He took Jewel Bovine for a weekend at the same Atlantic City hotel they'd patronized before. He caroused into the late nights in Mizner's company. Mizner told reporters that Ketchel was so naturally tough he didn't have to train.

The Goat was beside himself with exasperation.

"Goddamnit, Stevie, Mizner knows how to make a good deal for a match but he don't know shit about boxing or he wouldn't be saloon-hopping with you, he'd be telling you to get in shape."

"What the hell, Pete," Ketchel said, trying to cajole him into a better mood. "Nothing wrong with an evening stein or two. Beer ain't just for breakfast, you know."

"Real damn funny," the Goat said.

FOLLOWING THE KLAUS bout, Mizner signed Ketchel for a big-money six-rounder in Philadelphia against Sam Langford, the "Boston Tar Baby," a short but very powerful Negro widely regarded then and now as among the best boxers of the day. The news put the Goat on edge. One of Langford's losses, he informed Ketchel, had been to none other than Jack Johnson four years earlier.

"Johnson's half a foot taller and couldn't put him away, not in fifteen rounds," the Goat said. "They say Johnson was lucky to get the decision. Do you understand what I'm telling you?"

"Yeah, Johnson ain't nearly as tough as they say," Ketchel said, and laughed. The Goat gave him the two-finger horns.

Once again he was outscored in the early rounds and booed for his slothful performance. Langford was shorter than Ketchel but outweighed him by fifteen pounds, was solid muscle and had almost-freakishly long arms. "Jesus, it's like fighting an ape that knows how to jab," Ketchel said between rounds. But he once again caught fire in the latter part of the bout and had Langford on the defensive at the end. It was another "no decision" match, but every reporter on hand gave the bout to Ketchel.

Yet even as the hacks congratulated him in the dressing room, he knew their verdict was influenced less by the way he'd fought than by the color of Langford's skin. He saw the Goat staring at him from across the room, then turn away and leave.

He stayed under the shower spray for a long while, letting the water beat on his head. He hadn't fought well and he knew it. And knew the reason was his inattention to training. His footwork, reflexes, hand speed, everything, had been less than it should've been.

You're a fine one, all right, he thought. You are really a fine one. It's the only thing that really means anything and you damn well know it. The only thing that's kept your sorry ass off a goddamn farm, out of a goddamn mine. It's the only thing that's made you *somebody*. The only thing that ever could. You're treating it like some cooze you think won't quit you no matter how much you play around on her. Well, it ain't like that, pal, and you know that too. Think you're tough, don't you? Tell you what, tough guy . . . let's see you hang on to it. Let's see you do *that*. We'll see how tough you are.

He knew the Goat's favorite bar was Kelly's by the river, and he found him there, slumped on a stool and moping over a beer.

The Goat spotted him in the cracked backbar mirror and watched him come up beside him at the counter and order a beer.

"Somebody musta give you the wrong directions, pal," the Goat said. "There ain't no models in this joint. There ain't even no hatcheck girls."

Ketchel raised his mug to the Goat in a silent toast.

"What're we drinking to?" the Goat said. "Your lucky stars you didn't get your stupid Polack brains beat out tonight like you deserved?"

"To the billygoats of the world."

"One of these days," the Goat said, "you're gonna know Wilson Mizner is not the best thing ever happened to you. He ain't even your friend. He's just a guy getting fat cuts off you while the getting's good, which, you'll pardon me for saying, won't be much longer, not the way you're going."

"Well, oldtimer, you could be right," Ketchel said. "But as much as I would like to stay here all evening and discuss my sad future with you, as soon as I finish this beer, this *one* small mug of beer, I've got to go hit the hay. Some of us are in training, in case you didn't know."

The Goat flicked his hand dismissively. "Peddle that bullshit somewhere else. I heard enough of it."

"No bullshit. You're right, I been stupid. No more."

The Goat eyed him narrowly. "On the square? Cause if you ain't on the square, Stevie, I'd just as soon—"

"On the square, Pete."

Pete stared at him, reading his face, then smiled widely. "Well hell, like the fella said, I'll drink to that."

LESS THAN THREE weeks after the Langford match and in better shape than he'd been in months, he fought Dan Flynn in Boston. In the third round he had Flynn trapped in a corner and was pounding him with hooks to the head when Flynn's arms suddenly dropped to his sides. Ketchel stopped punching and stepped back but Flynn didn't fall. The man was out on his feet, his eyes closed, but his knees had somehow locked so that he remained rigidly upright and propped against the ring post. Ketchel regarded him a moment, then gave him a light shove on the shoulder and Flynn rolled off the post and fell like a chopped tree. The cheers were almost drowned out by the laughter.

TEN DAYS LATER in New York he walloped the highly regarded Willie Lewis all over the ring through the first round and knocked him out so soundly at the start of the second that Lewis was out cold for more than five minutes. When he came to, he was sitting on his stool and had no recollection of the fight. Ketchel had already left the ring. "When we gonna get started?" Lewis said. "Where's that Ketchel sonofabitch? He chicken out? Christ almighty, I'm getting a headache from all this goddamn waiting."

THIRTEEN DAYS LATER he fought Jim Smith in Manhattan's National Sporting Club. Smith was a crafty fighter with a strong punch, but Ketchel had his measure early and deliberately prolonged the inevitable in order to exercise some new defensive footwork that adapted a few of his dance steps and made him much harder to hit. The footwork was central to a tactic he had conceived to force open Johnson's defenses in their next match. Against Smith the new moves were working well. Smith had landed none of his hardest punches and with each miss was dropping his guard. But it was not until the fifth that Ketchel employed the tactic he was planning for Johnson. Midway through the round, he lowered his fists slightly to expose his chin, as if he were tiring but unaware of it. Seeing such an inviting target, Smith naturally went for it, but his punch hit only air and left him wide open for Ketchel's counter with the old one-two-three-four-five-six. Smith was out before he hit the floor.

Ketchel was laughing as he left the ring, shaking a fist over his head in answer to the crowd's booming chants of "Ketchel! . . . *Ketchel! . . . KETCHEL!*"

A Reckoning in Reno

On the Fourth of July, Jack Johnson and James Jeffries fought for the heavyweight championship of the world under a blazing sun in Reno, Nevada. Hawked as the "Fight of the Century," never mind that the century was but ten years old, it was the most publicized title fight since the great John L. fought Gentleman Jim, both of which luminaries were present on this occasion, Sullivan at ringside, Corbett in Jeffries' corner. The match was scheduled for forty-five rounds and drew a paid attendance of twenty thousand. The promoter of the fight and its referee was George "Tex" Rickard, a natural showman who would in the years ahead promote Jack Dempsey's most memorable and lucrative bouts and make headlines of his own in New York when he was charged with the sexual assault of several underage girls. He'd at various times been a Texas marshal, a Klondike prospector, a faro dealer, and the owner of a saloon. He'd promoted his first fight four years earlier, also in Nevada, and reaped such a handsome profit he knew he'd found his true calling at last. The original venue for the Johnson-Jeffries fight had been San Francisco, where Rickard anticipated an enormous gate, but the growing fear of racial violence that might attach to the event persuaded the governor to refuse permission for the match in California. So Rickard settled on Reno.

KETCHEL'S TRAIN ARRIVED in the late morning on the day of the fight. The Goat had traveled with him from New York but he did not debark in Reno, preferring to go on to San Francisco to visit with his ladyfriend. Ketchel had just checked in at the desk of the Hotel Golden, the promotion center for the fight, when a handsome stocky man strode up and introduced himself as Jack London. He was thrilled to make Ketchel's acquaintance, and Ketchel accepted his invitation to a glass of beer in the hotel bar.

London was reporting the fight for the *San Francisco Chronicle*. He was thirty-four years old and appeared in better health than he actually was. Ketchel knew of him, of course, and apologized for not having read any of his stories.

"Oh hell, that's all right. But come to think of it, I've got something here that might snag your interest." He took a small book out of his briefcase and inscribed the title page, then passed the book to Ketchel. "Here you are, champ. Hope you like it."

It was a copy of *The Road*. The inscription read:

To Stanley Ketchel—
whose fists impart poetic truth more
Potently than any pen.
With immeasurable admiration—
Jack London

Ketchel thanked him. He said his mother was a great reader and was surely familiar with his work. "She's going to be awful proud to know the company I'm keeping."

London said the book was about his experiences as a young hobo. "I understand you rode the rails yourself."

"All over the West. Freest days of my life."

"Weren't they, though! Let me have that book again." He turned to the inscription and under his signature added *One Bo to another,* then slid the volume back across the table.

Ketchel read the addition and said, "I was Steelyard Steve. What handle you use?"

"I had lots of different ones, but my favorite was the Frisco Kid." He produced a flask from his coat and laced his half-finished beer. He raised the flask toward Ketchel and said, "A little bite in those hops?" Ketchel caught the scent of rye and said "Sure," and London poured a dollop in his glass.

London was an aficionado of the prize ring and spoke on the subject with an enthusiastic expertise. He said he'd learned to box when he was a boy and his love of the sport had never abated. He'd spent a good portion of the previous three years sailing in the Pacific with his wife, Charmian, and he'd kept his boxing skill sharp by sparring with her on deck, never throwing a punch at her, of course, only warding off her best efforts to hit him.

"The hell of it is, she developed a pretty swell left, and one day she caught me good with it and I went over the side. She had to bring the boat about to get me before the sharks did. After that I kept a lifeline around my waist when we sparred. She never knocked me into the salt again, but I suspect she was pulling her punches."

Ketchel laughed. "Sounds like a tough cookie."

"You said it." He extracted a photograph from his wallet and passed it to Ketchel. It showed a pretty woman with bobbed dark hair posing in a bathing suit under a seaside palm. Ketchel thought she had fine legs.

"Lucky man, Jack."

"Don't I know it."

London then related his eyewitness account of Johnson's fight with Tommy Burns in Australia and said no match he'd ever seen had caused him greater heartache.

"I wish to God I'd seen your go with Johnson," he said. "I read a dozen different reports of that fight, and every time I got to the part where you knocked him on his rump I thought, 'He's got him, by damn, he's *got* him!' Even though I already knew how the thing turned out. You damn near did it, champ. Jesus, *two more seconds* . . ."

"Shy by an inch or miss by a mile," Ketchel said, "it's still off the mark."

"Yes, of course. But see, reading all those reports of the fight was like . . . like reading a classical tragedy for the umpteenth time. I mean, you already know how the story's going to end, but you can't help getting caught up in it anyhow. You can't help feeling that this time, *this* time, it might turn out differently. You know it won't, but still, you can't help hoping it will. You can't help rooting for the doomed. No offense, champ."

Ketchel flicked a dismissive hand.

"Then again, that's what makes tragedy so grand, isn't it?" London said. "It feeds the heart's rebellion against the tyranny of the inevitable."

"Yeah, well, if you say so, pal. All I can say is there's more than one story, ain't there? Next time there won't be anything *damn near* about it."

London's eyes brightened. "Next time? You mean Johnson? You're going to fight him again?"

"If I have my way. Only thing is, beating him the next time won't be much to crow about after Jeff gets done with him today."

"Oh yes, no question Jeff'll do for him, but it'll still be a hell of a feat if . . . *when* you cool him too. Hell, I was worried the coon wouldn't go through with it with Jeffries. He's got a yellow streak, you know. I'm sure we'll see it today. I say Jeff cools him in less than five."

"Oh, Jeff'll cool him, all right," Ketchel said. "But you can take it from me, bo, Johnson ain't yellow."

"Well . . . We'll see soon enough, won't we?"

THEY SHARED A hack to the arena. On their way there, London took the flask from his coat and tucked it down the front of his pants. "Like to see them search me there," he said. The fight had raised such fear of racial turmoil that police were posted at the entrances to ensure that neither alcohol nor firearms passed through the gates. Ketchel had read the newspaper report about this precaution and left his revolver in the care of the hotel barman. But he'd grown accustomed to carrying the weapon whenever he ventured among strangers and he missed its comforting weight under his coat.

They entered the clamorous arena and shouldered their way through the jammed aisles down to ringside. Looming over one side of the arena was a huge banner, its top line extolling JAMES E. PEPPER WHISKY and the lower proclaiming BORN WITH THE REPUBLIC. They agreed to meet back at the hotel bar after the fight and take supper together, then London went to his seat in the press row and Ketchel to his reserved seat among a variety of other boxing celebrities, all of whom would be presented in the ring before the start of the match. Among these heroes were Bob Fitzsimmons, Tom Sharkey, Tommy Burns, Tom McCarey, and none other than John L. Sullivan.

Sullivan was in the aisle, talking with ring announcer Billy Jordan when Ketchel walked up, and Jordan introduced them to each other. "Ah yes, Ketchel!" Sullivan boomed as he tucked away the flask he'd been nipping from. "The little Polack powerhouse himself! Say, but didn't you land a good one on this big buck in your mill with him! Fucking shame it lacked the weight behind it or he wouldn't be coming out of the woodpile today, now would he!"

Sullivan was nearly six feet tall and carried a belly the size of a sow. Ketchel guessed his weight at above three hundred pounds. Under his golf cap his hair was white, so too his mustaches. His teeth were the color of old dice and his eyes baggy and bloodshot, his bulbous nose netted with veins, his breath fumed with whiskey. Nevertheless, this was the Great John L., champion of champions, and Ketchel was entirely sincere when he put out his hand and said, "I'm honored to meet you, Mr. Sullivan."

John L. pumped Ketchel's hand with his enormous own. "Well of course you are, lad, of course you are!"

Shortly afterward, when the famous fighters were all up in the ring and Billy Jordan introduced each in turn, the greatest cheering was for Sullivan, and John L. clasped his hands above his head and grinned like a merry walrus.

The loudest ovation of the day, however, came when James J. Jeffries entered the ring as a combatant for the first time in five years. He wore light purple trunks and his hair was closely cropped and he was a far sight from the corpulent figure he'd presented when Ketchel had last seen him. A year of intense training had burned more than seventy pounds of fat from his frame and re-sculpted the superb physique of his championship days. He weighed 227 and was the betting favorite at two to one. Johnson was already in his corner and said, "Howdy, Mr. Jeff." At the morning weigh-in Jeffries had told reporters that Johnson had made him work like a dog for almost a year to get in shape for this fight and he intended to give him the licking of his life. Johnson said he hoped Mr. Jeff didn't mean to lick him for real, as he didn't like any tongue to touch him but a woman's. Few of the reporters smiled, and much of what they scribbled in their notebooks could not have been printed in a public newspaper.

Johnson's arrival at the ring had roused an expected deluge of odium and derision. He smiled his golden smile and bowed to the crowd like a ballroom dancer, the mocking gesture raising the volume of insults and curses. His announced weight was 218 pounds, a dozen more than he'd weighed against Ketchel, but he looked to Ketchel as hard and lean as ever. He wore his usual butternut trunks with a colorful rolled bandanna tied to a belt loop. Ketchel did not see George Little among the seconds in Johnson's corner. He asked those sitting nearest him if they knew anything of his absence and was told that Johnson had fired Little, though none knew the reason.

And so the fight.

By the end of the third round it was evident to every man in the place that for all his impressive physical appearance the Boilermaker was not the man who'd retired unbeaten five years before. Though he yet had the muscle, a powerful punch called for more than sinew; it entailed a mysterious body mechanic he no longer possessed. Nor did his fists have the quickness of his championship years. He threw scores of punches in the early rounds but few of them struck where they were meant to and those that did seemed not to hurt Johnson at all. Some who saw the fight and many who did not would later insist that in his prime Jeffries would have destroyed Johnson, but Ketchel knew better. He was in awe of Johnson's art, of the magical way he anticipated Jeffries' every move, caught body blows on his arms rather than the ribs, deflected punches with his gloves, rolled his head from punches so expertly that Jeffries must've felt like he was hitting a hat dangling on a string. Even as the crowd cheered every Jeffries swing, Ketchel knew he was doing no damage, and knew that Jeffries knew it too. In contrast, Johnson's punches consistently breached Jeffries' defense to raise another welt or inflict another cut. By the end of the tenth, Jeffries's aspect was a battered distortion, one eye almost closed and the other fast getting that way, his mouth torn. His ears were crushed plums. Back in his corner, Johnson said to ringsiders, "I sees Mr. Jeff's plan now. He gonna get me all tired from hitting him and then he just gonna push me over and let Mr. Tex count me out." The ringsiders roared with invective. Ketchel could see that Johnson was protracting Jeffries' punishment for his own amusement as well as to torment every white soul in the place. He easily dodged Jeff's desperate swings and landed ripping counterpunches that sent Jeffries stumbling rearward. Jeffries more and more took to clinching and holding on till Rickard separated them. Johnson at one point reacted by holding Jeffries as if he were a dance partner and swayed like they were waltzing, prompting the crowd to scream for Jeff to kill him, kill him. With Jeffries clinching him repeatedly in the fourteenth round, Jack Johnson bawled, "Oh, Mr. Jeff, don't *love* me so!" and rolled his eyes over Jeffries' shoulder. The crowd's rage was exceeded only by its swelling pity for Jeffries, who was enduring on sheer will. In the fifteenth Jeffries clinched again, but before referee Rickard could step in, Johnson wrenched free and landed a perfect hook to the jaw that dropped Jim Jeffries to the canvas for the first time in his life. But the man never lacked for courage, and he was back on his feet by the count of nine, swaying like a drunk. Bloody sweat jumped off his head from a Johnson overhand and down he went again, rolling to the edge of the ring. An agonized chorus of voices now pleading with him to stay down, his own cornermen beseeching him. Jeffries strained to rise as Rickard began the count. Johnson stood ready. It seemed Jeffries might make it. Rickard looked to Jeff's corner even as he counted. And then a bloodstained white towel fluttered out over the ring and fell like failed wings.

SLUMPED ON HIS stool with an ice pack being held to his eye when Johnson came over to shake his hand and tell him he'd fought a square fight and no hard feelings, James Jeffries said: "I ought have got you."

Johnson shrugged and left for his dressing room.

And then, enrobed and about to depart the ring, James Jeffries said: "Six years ago it might've been another story, but I sure didn't have it today."

And then, stripped naked and shuffling toward the shower room, James Jeffries said: "Christ, I couldn't hit him. I couldn't have hit him in a thousand years. I couldn't have beat the bastard on my best day. How I let myself get talked into this jackpot I'll never know. Damn the money and God save me from my friends. Now maybe everyone will leave me the hell alone."

In the *San Francisco Chronicle* Jack London would write:

> Johnson has sent down to defeat the chosen representative of the white race, and this time the greatest of them all . . . From the opening to the closing round he never ceased his witty sallies, his exchange of repartee with his opponent's seconds and with the spectators . . . The golden smile was as much in evidence as ever . . . The greatest battle of the century was a monologue delivered to twenty thousand spectators by a smiling Negro who was never in doubt. . . . No blow Jeff ever landed hurt his dusky opponent. . . . Jeff today disposed of one question. He could not come back. Johnson, in turn, answered another question. He has not the yellow streak . . . let it be said here and beyond the shadow of any doubt. Not for a second did he show the flicker of fear at the Goliath against him. . . .

Headlines around the country wailing of Johnson's victory would be followed by headlines of racial violence in more than a dozen cities, the worst of the rioting incited by the motion picture of the fight.

Pair of Jacks

He went to Jeffries' dressing room and pushed through the clamoring pack of reporters to get up close to him. He leaned down to Jeffries' raw ear so he would not be overheard and told him he'd fought bravely and had not a damn thing to apologize for to anybody. Jeffries nodded but said nothing.

Ketchel then went to see Johnson. The police guards at the dressing room door recognized him and let him pass.

Johnson was knotting his tie in a mirror. His cornermen, one white and two Negroes, were there too.

"Well now, lookee here," Johnson said, smiling at Ketchel in the mirror. "My, my, what a splendiferous surprise to see you, Mr. Stanley. Say, now, that's a fine-looking set of teeth."

"Came to say congratulations."

"Well thank you, sir. Some of them reporters was here a minute ago but I don't recollect anybody telling me no congratulations. Just want to know do I *respect* Mr. Jeffries. Do I believe I coulda beat him when he was champ. Ask me would I give him a *re*match. I say that be fine with me but I ain't so sure about Mr. Jeff. He big but he not dumb. I say, 'Do he *look* like he want a rematch?' "

The seconds chuckled.

"He's not the man he used to be," Ketchel said.

Johnson finished with the knot and carefully attached a gold stick pin to the tie. Then cut his eyes at Ketchel in the mirror and said, "Ain't nobody is."

He turned and gestured at the seconds. "This here's my crew. The buckra's Eddie Joe and them two shiftless coons're Red and Pogo. I guess you boys know who this fella is."

The cornermen and Ketchel exchanged nods.

Ketchel asked about George Little, and Johnson said he'd fired him for trying to steal his woman. "He musta figured since they both white she just naturally gonna drop me for him. Man don't know diddly about women, specially about Etta."

"I thought her name was Sheila," Ketchel said.

"Oh man, Sheila long gone. This one Etta. *Fine* woman. High society. She ingesticates tea. Like this." He demonstrated Etta's tea-drinking technique, pinky finger high.

"Where's she at?"

"Waiting on me in Frisco. But look here what she did." He indicated a vase of geraniums on a table. "Sent a wire to the hotel and had them deliver these while I was entertaining with Mister Jeff. Didn't want me to see them till the fight all done." He broke off a flower and inserted it in his lapel, then checked himself in the mirror. "Say now, ain't that fine."

There was not a mark on him but for a slight cut on his lower lip. He noted Ketchel's glance at it. "Got that in training a coupla days ago. Mr. Jeff accidentally bumped it with his head or he wouldn'ta got no blood from me noways."

"He couldn't hit you, that's for sure."

"Man didn't stand no chance, did he?"

"Didn't look like it to me."

"You know, I believe *you* mighta taken Mr. Jeffries today. What you think?"

Ketchel did believe that. "I don't know. All I know is he couldn't hit you."

"Not many can. But you did, huh?"

"Not hard enough."

"And you like to try it again. That's why you here." Johnson turned to his seconds. "I believe this little man wanna ask for a *re*-match, what yall think?"

Ketchel was the only one in the room not smiling. He had not expected Johnson to beat him to the point. "That's right," he said.

"Do tell," Johnson said. "Well now, I must say you got some sizable testicular baggage, Mr. Stanley, seeing how we had us an arrangement and you tried to sucker me. Now here you is, wanting Papa Jack to do you a good turn."

"But I didn't sucker you, did I?"

"Not cause you didn't try." Johnson's grin widened, Ketchel's smile small and wry, his ears warm.

"I want another go, Johnson."

"Man, another fight with you wouldn't draw flies, not after how I done you already."

"To hell with the gate."

"Easy for you to say, little mister, kinda jack you make. Not so easy for us niggerboys got to hustle to make a dime."

"Goddamnit, you're the greatest fighter I ever saw. What you did today—"

"And you wants to be the greatest fighter you ever saw. Therefore and henceforth, you gots to beat *me.* You can't never do it but you got to try on account of it eating you up, ain't it, Mr. Stanley? Ain't that the lowdown truth?"

Ketchel's ears burned. "Look you . . . I don't give a damn what you think, all I want's—"

"Don't bullshit a bullshitter, man. I *know* what all you want. Think I don't know how it is?"

"Goddamnit, give me a rematch."

Johnson cocked his head and smirked. "I sure hope you ain't gonna demeanify yourself and say pretty please."

The seconds sniggered.

"Go fuck yourself."

Johnson and his seconds whooped. "*That's*-a-way, Mr. Stanley!" he said. "Don't be taking no shit."

"Come on, man, give me a—"

"No," Johnson said, pointing a finger at him.

". . . rematch," Ketchel said. And smiled.

Johnson sighed and looked at his seconds. "I believe somebody gonna have to shoot this fucker to make him quit."

"Woooooo," the Pogo one said, "it getting too damn *in*-tense round here. We heading on, Jack."

"Awright. I see you boys in Frisco and I don't wanta hafta bail nobody out, yall hear?"

Jostling each other as they made for the door, the seconds waved so long and left.

Johnson consulted his pocket watch. Then gave Ketchel a look he couldn't read. Then said: "Look here, little man, I been told there's a niggertown down the road got a place with pretty good barbecue and a loud piano and some fine high yella gals. Calls itself a roadhouse but it's a cathouse with a kitchen, what it is. What say we go have us a mess of ribs and a drink or two, do some high-kicking with them yellas?"

"Niggertown?"

"What's the matter, Stanbo? Never heard of the place?"

The idea of sporting in a Negro whorehouse struck Ketchel's fancy. He'd never had a colored girl but had always wanted to.

"Yeah, all right," he said. "But I'm supposed to meet a fella back at the hotel, so I better stop by and—"

"Who that?"

"Man named London. Jack London."

"The writer fella? I know him. Met him in Australia after I put down Tommy Burns. Man looked about to cry, he was so sorry to see a nigger champ. Tell you what, ask him to come along. Dollar to a doughnut he says no. He's scared of niggers."

JOHNSON DROVE A yellow Packard touring model with the convertible top down. He and his crew had come from San Francisco by train, but on his first night in Reno he'd finagled his way into a crap game in a back room of the Hotel Golden and won the car from the lieutenant governor of Oklahoma or Arkansas or Kansas, he couldn't remember which.

"Man was down to his last dollar after I made about seven passes in a row," Johnson told Ketchel, "so he wagers this here car against five hundred dollars. And damn if I don't roll a seven. Real sore loser, that fella, the sorta man shouldn't never gamble, know the kind I mean? Couldn't stop cussing me. Said after Jeffries got done beating the shit outta me there wouldn't be nothing left but my gold teeth. I ask you, that any way for a lieutenant governor to talk? Say, what the hell a *lieutenant* governor do, anyhow?"

Because the car was known to almost everyone in Reno, he thought it wise to approach the hotel by way of backstreets. "Some drunk peckerwoods spot this car, they're like to be all over it like flies on a picnic basket," Johnson said. "I might have to bust me some heads and maybe get all sweaty, muss up my new clothes. Ruther stay neat and allurifying for them gals." He waited in the alley with the motor running while Ketchel went in to see London.

He found him at the far end of the bar and told him of Johnson's invitation.

"Niggertown?" London said.

"He said you won't come. Says you're scared of niggers."

"He did, did he?" London tossed off the rest of his drink. "Let's go."

Ketchel gestured to the bartender, who brought him his revolver wrapped in newspaper. Ketchel held the package down low and slipped the gun out of the paper and under his coat.

"Good idea," London said. "A safeguard for the white-race contingent."

Johnson grinned when London came out with Ketchel. "Why, Mr. Jack, I'm jubilated to beat the band you're joining us. I have heard you got a liking for the colored girls."

London got in the back seat. "My favorite color in women is the same as yours, Johnson."

"What color's that, Mr. Jack?"

"Pretty."

Johnson laughed and gunned the motor and they roared away. He wore a driving duster and goggles and gauntlets, his cap visor pulled low. He had long fancied himself a driver of professional racing talent, and whenever he got behind the wheel he drove as though bent for a finish line. He often bragged that he'd gotten more speeding tickets than any man in America, even though he more often outran the police than not.

Yelling to be heard over the rumble of the motor and the rush of air, he said the Packard was fun, but couldn't compare to any of his racing cars, especially his ninety-horsepower Thomas Flyer, which he was going to race against the one and only Barney Oldfield at Sheepshead Bay, New York, in late October.

"Man said didn't want to race against no *Ethiopian.* So I bet him five thousand dollars and he quick say it's a deal. Ain't no paint in the world as white as money."

They sped over a winding, uneven road, the Packard pitching and yawing, raising great clouds of dust behind them. Ketchel with a tight grip on the door as they slued through curves. Johnson shouted a complaint about the lack of a sufficiently long straightway where he could get the car up to its top speed. He hollered that he wished driving fast didn't make him so happy. "My teeth gets all muddy!" He let out a wolf howl with such gusto that Ketchel joined in, even as he held to the door for dear life. In the back seat, London covered his head with his coat and sipped from his flask and coughed in the swirl of dust.

THE NEGRO QUARTER was a small settlement east of town between the river and the railroad tracks. Raul's Riverfront Drink and Dance Emporium was the largest building in the hamlet and the only one of two stories. The sun had set and the rolled-down shade of every upstairs window was yellow with interior light against the twilit evening.

Johnson parked the Packard between two horse wagons almost directly in front of the building. From its confines came the clamor of ragtime piano, raucous laughter, loud voices. They alit from the car and Johnson took off his driving outfit and brushed the dust from his bowler and set it at a rakish angle on his head, then checked the lay of his boutonnière and took up his walking stick and they went inside.

The crowded room was cast in a dim amber light. The laughter and loud talk fell off and the two couples on the floor stopped dancing. Every eye fixed on the three of them. The skinny piano man continued playing but not as loudly nor as fast.

None of the patrons had ever before seen Johnson in the flesh, but most of them recognized him on sight and in low voices informed those who did not. Some were obviously thrilled by his presence but some were as clearly displeased by the company he'd brought with him. Ketchel and London were the only whites in the room, and there were mutterings and glowers. Even through the pall of smoke and the odors of whiskey and sweat and the reek of urine from the piss trough behind the wooden partition at the rear of the room, Ketchel detected another smell, too, one he had come upon many times before in many other places. A smell of rank carnal pleasures and blood in high heat.

A large man in a red-and-black pinstriped suit rose from a table and hurried over to them. His complexion as pale as Ketchel's but his features distinctly Negroid. He introduced himself as Raul, the owner and manager. He congratulated Johnson on his victory that afternoon and said he was honored to have him in his establishment.

"Well I don't see nothing to be so goddamned *honored* about," said a tall man at the bar. He wore a pink shirt with black garters and had a white scar on his chin. "You in the wrong place, Little

Arthur." It was a nickname that had trailed Johnson all the way from Galveston. "Ain't no whitemeat chicken here."

"You hush your head, Louis," Raul said.

"That's all right, Mr. Raul, the man just flapping his big African lips," Johnson said, prompting sniggers through the room. He pointed his walking stick at the Louis fellow. "Not that it's any your damn business, Sambo, but I come here to get me a rest from all that whitemeat chicken chasing after me. It ain't the kinda problem *you* ever gonna have."

Hoots and cackles. The Louis fellow glared but held mute.

"Reason I come *here*," Johnson said, "is I was told this place got the prettiest gals in Nevada." He made a show of slowly scanning the room, then smiled big and rolled his eyes. "And I'll tell yall one damn thing. They wasn't lying."

Laughter and a cry of "*That's* right!" Flirty smiles and winks from the girls.

"You welcome here, man," somebody called out, "but what you doing with them ofays?"

"They *my* guests, huckleberry, and this my party. If I'm welcome, they welcome."

"That fella there's Stanley Ketchel, ain't it?" somebody else said. "He the hunky boy knock you on your black ass!"

A hum of impressed remarking rippled through the room. Ketchel heard a woman say, "*That* the boy knock Jack down?"

"This the very fella," Johnson said. "Stan the Man. Anybody fight good as him, least I can do is buy him a drink and a barbecue rib. Howsomever, looks like some yall don't like it he's here. Well, tell you what . . . any you mammyjammers wanta throw his white ass out, you welcome to try."

A low roll of laughter, a few men goading each other, one nudging and whispering to the Louis fellow, who cursed low and shoved the man away.

"Now this here other fella," Johnson said, nodding at London, "this Mr. Stanley's big brother. Name Jack, too. He the one taught Mr. Stanley how to fight and he the only white man can kick his ass. Any you coons try giving *him* the boot, you be twice the fool."

More laughter. London stood with hands in pockets and his feet apart, his aspect one of easy confidence in the prowess Johnson claimed for him. In fact he was simply drunk.

"Now yall looka here," Johnson said. "You mighta heard I had me a significant discussion with Mr. James Jeffries this afternoon." He smiled all around at the laughter, and somebody yelled, "He sure enough heard what you had to signify, too!"

"I believe he did," Johnson said. "And all that sweaty signifying with Mr. Jeff has done give me a elephantous thirst and a gargantuate hunger. Now if we done with all the bullshit, we'd like to sit down and have some of Mr. Raul's famous ribs and about three four pitchers of cold beer and a bottle or two of the best rum in the house."

"Right this way, gentlemens!" Mr. Raul said, and led them to a table.

And the piano man resumed banging at the keys with brio.

THEIR COATS AND ties came off—Ketchel furtively pulling out his shirttails under the table to hide the revolver snugly tucked into his waistband. They rolled their sleeves. They gorged on pork ribs, London and Ketchel agreeing they were the best they'd ever put tooth to. Johnson said it was okay barbecue but he knew a dozen places in Texas where he could get better. Each man of them had his own pitcher of beer and drank directly from it rather than use a glass. Johnson had uncorked the bottle of rum and they now and then passed it among the three of them. London was also sipping rye from his flask. It seemed as if every few minutes he was compelled to visit the piss trough, and Johnson kidded him about having a bladder the size of a goober shell.

Johnson produced three Cuban coronas and each man lit up. London commended him on his fine taste in cigars. Even before he'd finished eating, Johnson had been entreated by various girls to dance with them, and now he and Ketchel let themselves be led onto the floor, London begging off with a sore foot. Johnson was smooth and flashy but Ketchel was a dynamo, and he and his partner were soon engirt by a crowd of spectators whooping and yelling about the white boy's natural rhythm. When he demonstrated his expertise at dancing with two girls at once, there was howling admiration and piercing whistles.

"Christ damn, Stanbo," Johnson said, "where you learn to dance thataway?"

"It's an old Indian way of dancing," Ketchel said. "I ever tell you I used to live with the Indians?"

"That so? Which ones? The Heap Big Bullshit tribe?"

"You'd been in that tribe, they'da made you chief."

They were joined at their table by a half-dozen girls. There weren't enough chairs for them all, so each man had a girl on his lap. The one perched upon London took the skimmer off his head and put it on her own, cocking it over one eye. She said he had a nice head of hair and mussed it with her fingers. Her dress was cut low and the bare tops of her breasts were almost in his face and to the vast amusement of the table he was staring at them like a man entranced. He was very drunk.

"You just gonna *look,* baby," the girl said, "or you gonna *do* something?"

Whereupon London ran his tongue along her cleavage and the table roared.

The night progressed in a growing haze, in a din of ragtime piano and high hilarity, the sporadic crashings of glass followed by happy female shrieks.

At some point London asked Johnson if he chased around with white women simply to provoke white society.

"Oh man, hell no," Johnson said. "What I care what white *society* think?"

"It's on accounta he can't boss us like he do them narrow-ass whiteys," one of the girls said.

"Say girl, ain't nobody rattle your cage," Johnson said. "The real and actual reason, Mr. Jack, is that every colored girl I ever took up with done two-timed me, and I mean every single one. No pink-toes gal ever did."

"Poor lil Arthur," the girl on his lap said, petting his smooth pate. "Us nigger bitches *so* bad to him."

"Damn right," Johnson said, showing his gold teeth, running his hand over her flank.

Ketchel wanted to know if it was true that some woman once ran out on him and took his clothes with her and then met up with a jockey and had the clothes cut down to fit him.

"You talking about Queenie," Johnson said. He shook his head and sighed. "I so crazy for that gal I went and married her. Back in Texas when I was a pup. Coupla months later she flew the coop. Then I come to hear she was shacked up in K. C. with this jockey call himself Kid somebody-or-other. So I go there and find the place but wasn't nobody home. I bust open the door and take a look around and there's a closet fulla clothes about the size for a boy, and then I see it's *my* goddamn clothes all cut down. Right about then the jockey come running 'cause somebody gone to the barroom and told him his place was being robbed. I say where Queenie at and he say she long gone. Say for me to get out his house before he kick my ass. Little nigger four feet high, maybe ninety pounds. Didn't know if I wanted to laugh or toss him out the window or what. I felt awful bad about Queenie, but there was nothing for it but go on back to Texas. You shoulda seen what she done to them clothes, though. Looked like something from a store for fancy midgets."

The girl on Johnson's lap said, "That's a real sad story, baby."

"It the kinda story I always have with you Negro womens."

"Yes, well, be all that as it may," London said in a slight slur, "the fact is, Johnson, here you are, two-timing that woman you were telling me about, the one waiting for you in Frisco in saintly Caucasian forbearance while you're sporting in this blackamoor den of iniquity, the woman you say you *looovves* so much. If you're so keen on fidelity, sir, what are you doing here?"

Johnson cut his eyes at Ketchel, "You hearing this drunk fool?" Then said to London: "Say man, I ain't married to Etta, leastways not yet. You the one that's married, Mr. Scribbles. What the hell *you* doing here?"

"Me? Well . . . as I happen to be a writer, my good fellow, I am . . . doing investigative research, you see."

Ketchel and Johnson hooted and pounded the table with their fists and upset several drinks.

"Oh honey," the girl on London's lap said, squirming her buttocks on his lap, "your research pokin its nose in my business real nice."

London's face reddened but he joined in the laughter.

At some still later point in the evening, London clambered up on a table, brandished a fist at the ceiling, and bellowed, "I would rather be ashes than dirt! Do you hear! Rather ashes than dirt!"

Then lost his balance and fell onto a girl in a chair and they both crashed to the floor. She got up, cursing and kicking at him, but London was passed out. "Damn fool wanna be ashes," she said, "I'll put a match to his drunk ass."

"You do that and I'll fry your ass in the fire," Johnson said. He dragged London over beside the piano and told the player to keep an eye on him.

None of them knew of London's profound grief for his third daughter, who had died only two weeks before at the age of thirty-six hours. He and Charmian had named her Joy.

The next time Ketchel came off the dance floor to quench his thirst, the girl he'd been dancing with sat on his lap and felt something hard nudge her hip. She said, "Is that a gun in your pants, sugar, or you just got a good idea?" She pulled up his shirttail. "Oh lordy."

Johnson caught a glimpse of the revolver as Ketchel yanked the shirttail back over it. "Goddamn, Stanbo. You come all set for us spearchuckers. Tell me something, and no *bull*-shit. You ever shoot anybody?"

"Just shoot, or shoot dead?"

"Hell man, it ain't serious shooting if ain't nobody dead."

Ketchel cut his eyes at the girls sitting with them, then back at Johnson, his aspect gone shrewd.

Johnson leaned over the table and said in low cajole: "Aw, come on, man, let's hear it. These gals ain't gonna rat you to no po-lice."

"Your secret safe with us, baby," the girl on Ketchel's lap whispered in his ear, stroking his nape.

Ketchel looked sidelong to right and left. He leaned across the girl and held his fist toward Johnson and slowly opened one finger and then another, and wiggled them.

"And I mean deader'n yesterday."

Johnson tilted back in his chair and showed his gold teeth. "Just *two*?"

HE DID NOT remember having gone upstairs but found himself in a large room with two beds, himself and a girl in one, Johnson and a girl in the other, everybody naked and going at it like wrestlers, the bedsprings screeching, frames scraping the floor, thumping the walls. The girls were lovely octoroons with skin the color of honey and nipples dark as chocolate. His was named Rubella.

They were paused in their sporting when Johnson decanted a dollop of rum into his girl's navel and invited Ketchel to come on over and have a drink. Ketchel knelt beside the bed and lapped at the little amber pool and the girl's belly nudged at his nose as she giggled. Johnson poured more rum and it ran in a rivulet into her private hair and Ketchel lapped after it. The girl squealed and clamped her thighs on his ears.

Until now none of them had noticed his tattoo, but positioned as he was, it could hardly be overlooked. The Rubella girl whooped and pointed, and Johnson said, "My, my, Mr. Stan, if that ain't a real exotical memento you got there."

Ketchel sat up, feeling himself blush. "*That* damn thing," he said.

The other girl wanted to know what they were talking about, so Ketchel stood up and showed her. They insisted on knowing how he came by it, and he told them about the Arapaho Sisters.

"Whoo-eee, honey," the Rubella girl said, "you farmer boys go to a city and you just turn into some kinda *wild* things!"

She fetched a lipstick from the dresser and made Ketchel lie on his stomach so she could draw a similar if much less artfully rendered heart on his other buttock. She wrote "Rubella" above the arrow, though the name carried well outside the boundary of the heart and was mostly illegible, and below the arrow wrote "Maxine." She gave Ketchel a small hand mirror so he could have a look. Who was Maxine, he asked.

"Me, sugar," the other girl said.

Ketchel said he wasn't sure it was legal to have the name of a girl on your ass if you hadn't done anything more with her than drink rum from her belly. Maxine said he'd drunk rum from more places than her belly but she knew what he meant, and she pulled him down onto the bed, saying they better make sure her name was on that ass all nice and legal. Johnson and the Rubella girl repaired to the other bed.

Sometime after midnight they were all hungry again, and the girls put on robes and went downstairs to fetch something to eat. Johnson and Ketchel sat on the edge of the bed, passing the last of the rum between them. Ketchel got the final swallow and set the empty bottle on the floor.

"Don't know about you, Stanbo, but I've had a time or two worse than this."

"It's always best right after you win."

"You oughta know, many as you won."

"Except it ain't true and you know it. The best is in the doing. That's always the best, the *doing*. All the rest of it's just . . . I don't know . . . waiting. Waiting to go back in and do it again."

Johnson smiled and regarded him sidelong. "Ain't good to talk it too much."

"Yeah, I know. Give me a rematch, Jack."

Johnson's smile faded. He sighed and rubbed his face. "Oh man, I thought we done settle that."

"We didn't. Give me another go."

"Forget it."

"Look, you *gotta* give me another shot."

"Man, I ain't *gotta* do a goddamn thing but be a nigger all the way to the grave."

"Jack, I'm asking you."

Johnson stared at the floor. Then at the paneled wood wall. Then got up and went to it and tapped it with his knuckles.

"Come here check this out."

"What?"

"Just come do it."

Ketchel went over and rapped the wall with his knuckles. It was made of some kind of dense wood. The panels were about six inches wide and joined in tongue-and-groove fashion.

"Look here," Johnson said. "I want you to punch it hard as you can. Right in the middle there. I mean give it your sweetest lick."

"How come?"

"Just do it. Your hardest lick. Go on." Johnson stepped back to give him room.

"You think I won't?"

"Quit talking and do it."

Ketchel set himself. Then lunged and hit the wall with a straight right that had everything in it. The impact sounded like a hammer blow and he felt the wood crack and knew he'd hit it just right. The indentation was almost an inch deep where the knuckles had struck, and it tapered out to the diameter of his fist.

"Hell of a punch, little man. Lemme see you hand."

The middle knuckle was disjointed and the hand swelling fast. It hurt like hell but he could wiggle the middle finger and knew the knuckle wasn't broken but only jammed.

"What in the *world* . . . ?" The girls were at the door, each bearing a tray with plates of ribs and bottles of beer.

"Yall be still," Johnson said. He faced the paneling and drew a deep breath. Then struck the wall with such sudden force the Maxine girl flinched and a bottle of beer fell off her tray and shattered to foamy shards.

The panel was buckled two inches deep. The wood cracked and splintered almost all the way through. The full indentation half again as large as the one made by Ketchel.

"Lord Jesus," the Rubella girl said.

Johnson held up his right hand for Ketchel to see. Three of the knuckles were skinned but none jammed.

"Think about this, little man."

"Ah hell, Jack, this doesn't—"

"You think on it good. And then live with it."

"I don't want to think about it, goddamnit, I want—"

"I *know* what you wants, fucker! You can't have it. You *can not* beat me. Not today, not tomorrow, not never. You can't, man. I know it's just *killing* you you can't and I know you willing to die trying to make it be different. But see . . . I ain't looking to have to kill you just 'cause you willing."

They held glares for a moment. And then Johnson feinted with the left and grazed him above the ear with an open right hand as Ketchel drew back with his fists up.

Johnson smiled at him and turned up his palms. Then turned to the girls and said, "Yall gonna stand there gawking at our peckers for the rest of the night or you gonna bring that chow on in here before we starve to damn death?"

• • •

When he woke in the morning he was the only one in the room. He was hungover and his hand hurt, the knuckles swollen tight and blue, but he could still work the fingers. The shade was up and pale yellow light slanted through the window.

His revolver was on the washbasin table and had a lipstick jammed in the muzzle. He checked his pants and his money was still there, then put them on and went to the bathroom at the end of the hall. Behind one of the doors a saxophone played a soft melancholy tune he didn't recognize.

After dressing he went downstairs and found the two Jacks having coffee in the kitchen and a fat Negro woman frying ham and eggs at the stove. Johnson grinned and winked at him, seeming utterly refreshed. London was in a wretched state. His features blurred and complexion waxy, his eyes weighted with dark bags. Ketchel sat down and accepted coffee from the woman and saw that she was missing parts of the last two fingers of one hand.

"Our man London here look like he wearing the thorny hat this morning, don't he?" Johnson said. "Look about near to being the ashes he all the time talking about."

"Go to hell," London said, his voice cracking.

After breakfast Johnson drove them back to town, he and Ketchel harmonizing on "Frankie and Johnny" and "In the House of Too Much Trouble" as they barreled down the dusty road. London sat slumped in the rear seat and said nothing until they arrived in the alley behind the hotel, then shook Johnson's hand and said he was a hell of a fighter and would probably be champion for a long time.

Ketchel waited till London went inside. "Listen, Jack—"

"You listen. I hear tell that Papke fella saying *he* the middleweight champ because you been fighting over the limit ever since you went against me. Now what you got to do, Stanbo, is set the man straight. *You* the middleweight champ. Be what you *is*."

"Jack—"

"*Be* it, man," Johnson said. Then flashed his gold smile and raised his fist in farewell, gunned the Packard down the alley, turned the corner, and was gone.

Ambush Country

He spent the next two weeks by himself in San Francisco. He went to the wharves before sunrise every day and watched the fishing boats set out, went back in the late afternoon to see them return, riding lower in the water with their catch. He ran in the park before breakfast. He exercised in the children's playground, chinning himself on the crossbeam of the swing set as kids swung on either side of him and kept loud count of his repetitions. He straddled a seesaw and worked it up and down by shifting his weight from one leg to the other. He attended stage shows. He dined on seafood every evening. He walked the hilly streets and explored those areas of the city he was unfamiliar with. He went to the apartment house where the Arapaho Sisters had lived, hoping they'd changed their minds about marrying the rich brothers and stayed put, but when he rapped on the door he found that a young Russian family was now living there.

One day he went to the zoo. When he arrived at the panther cage, the black beast within was pacing back and forth from one stone wall to the other, observed by a dozen spectators lined at a rail some three feet from the bars. Then the cat caught sight of Ketchel and came up to the bars and held him in an unblinking yellow gaze. A boy hissed and clucked his tongue to try to attract the cat's attention, but its eyes would not leave Ketchel. When Ketchel started to walk toward the next cage the cat moved with him. He stopped and the cat stopped. "What the hell, Mac," a man said, "you got a trout in your pocket?" Ketchel stepped to one side and the cat moved too. He sidled the other way and so did the cat. The panther paced with him to the end of the cage and then Ketchel whirled and sprinted in the other direction and the cat sprang with him and reached the wall in three strides and went halfway up and came down heavily on its feet as spectators shrilled and scampered away from the rail. Ketchel walked back slowly and the cat kept pace. The onlooking crowd now larger, its amazement louder. Some among them tossed peanuts and pretzels and chunks of ice at the cat to try to attract its attention, but the cat was oblivious to it all, even when a piece of ice hit it in an eye and made it blink rapidly for a moment. Ketchel told them to stop, but they paid him no mind, and there were too many to force them all to cease. So he said hell with it and walked away, following a long curving pathway until it passed out of sight of the panther cage, and then his blood jumped at the cat's piercing scream. There were shrieks and laughter. He had a moment of wishing the beast might break free of its bars and tear into the bastards fang and claw. He dreamt that night of unblinking yellow eyes with pupils like black pits.

ALL THE WHILE he was in San Francisco, he thought about Jack Johnson. And the more he thought about him, the more certain he was he would beat him the next time.

You'll fight smarter next time, he told himself. You'll wait for the right opening, just like before, but next time you'll stay in control. When you drop him next time and he's ready for the kill, you'll finish him, but you'll do it right. No wild and wooly.

No leading with your chin like some barroom chump.

You'll nail *him* on the chin. You'll make damn sure of the chin.

Christ, if only you'd nailed him on the chin. The jaw, at least.

That wall business doesn't mean a damn thing.

A chin's not a goddamn wall. Neither's a jaw.

He's going to New York at the end of October for a car race. You'll go to New York then, too. And put it to him straight.

Face to face. Man to man. You'll tell him you thought about it like he said. And you want it.

What if he says no?

You won't take no for an answer.

What if he still says no?

Seventy-thirty split his way, eighty-twenty, winner take all, whatever he wants.

What if he still says no?

What the hell, he can have every nickel, win or lose. You'll fight him for nothing. He can't turn *that* down.

What if he still says no?

You'll call him a coward. You'll call him a goddamn yellow coward sonofabitch in every newspaper in the country.

What if he still . . .

He *won't*! He's got to say yes!

Man, I ain't got do a damn thing but be a nigger all the way to the grave . . .

He telephoned Wilson Mizner in New York and told him he wanted no fight but with Johnson. Mizner sighed and said he had just seen the film of the Johnson-Jeffries match. "Jeffries is a monster, kid, and the jig played with him like—"

"I was there, Bill, I know how it went. Look, I'm just telling you don't waste your time setting up a fight for me with anybody else."

"You sure, kid? Billy Papke's people have been at me for another fight. Bastard's claiming he's the champ now but he's willing to fight you again to settle it once and for all. Christ, we could make—"

"Piss on Billy Papke! I can whip Billy Papke once a week. It's Johnson I want."

Another sigh. "The thing is, champ, and no offense, but after what he did to you last time, and considering what he did to Jeffries since then, well, I mean, I don't see much of a gate for a rematch."

You don't see much of a payday for yourself is what you don't see, Ketchel thought.

"Are you listening to me, Bill? I *will not* fight anybody else, only Johnson. On any terms he wants, I don't care. You get me?"

The biggest sigh yet. "I hear you, kid."

That settled, Ketchel departed San Francisco for Pine Lake to wait for October.

A WIRE WAS waiting from the colonel:

NO JOY IN MUDVILLE RE JEFFRIES STOP BUSY WITH BIZ BUT SEE YOU SEPT STOP TELL ME MICHIGAN OR NY STOP RPD.

Ketchel wired back that he would still be in Michigan in September and was looking forward to seeing him.

The remaining summer passed pleasantly. He hired a cook and had his family over to dinner several times a week. His mother seemed happier and healthier than ever. Barzoomian's business throve. John and Rebeka were content with their life on the farm, and Julie Bug, soon to be five years old, was already reading better than children twice her age.

He ran ten miles every day before sunrise. He shadowboxed for an hour, constantly on his toes, now gliding like a dancer, now darting like a cat, his fists moving so fast you could hear them whipping through the air. He pounded the heavy bag with punches that popped like gunshots. He worked the speed bag with a steady racketing rhythm, his fists pumping like pistons. In the afternoons he did calisthenics and rowed on the river and took long walks in the woods. He ate well and slept soundly.

And he thought about Jack Johnson.

The colonel arrived, and they went fishing on Lake Michigan in his boat. They went to the cabin in the Manistee and hunted, never mind that it wasn't legal season. They had long talks over campfires and across the cabin table. Ketchel drank sparingly and the colonel commended him for it. He said drink was beginning to make him melancholy in his advancing years, that lately he'd found himself wishing he were young enough to go down to Mexico where a hell of a revolution was about to break loose. He'd heard the rebels were already passing out flyers in El Paso to try to recruit American dynamiters and machine gunners. All that hullabaloo down there reminded him of his time with Teddy in Cuba and how it had been the most fun he'd ever had in his life.

"It goes by too fast, son," the colonel said. "You got no idea, not at your age. You wake up one day and wonder where it all went."

Ketchel agreed it was high time he paid Missouri a visit. In the second week of September Dickerson wired his ranch foreman that he would be home soon and was bringing with him his dearest friend and world middleweight champion, Stanley Ketchel.

THEY STOPPED for two days in Jefferson City, the capital, where the State Democratic Convention was being held. Dickerson had numerous friends in politics and had a standing invitation to the celebration party that closed each year's convention.

"All those bigwigs will want to shake your hand," the colonel said. "Hope you don't mind me showing you off some."

Ketchel said of course not.

The party began that afternoon on the enormous lawn behind the biggest hotel in town, its privacy protected by high brick walls and shaded by lofty elms. Some seven hundred people were in attendance. The weather was fine and bright. Every guest was given a silk tag with his name on it to pin to his lapel. There were a half-dozen open-sided, red-white-and-blue-striped tents set up on the lawn, each with its own bar and bandstand. The air was dense with the ragtime tunes of Negro ensembles, with laughter and loud talk, with the smells of roasting meats and charcoal fires. The colonel steered Ketchel from tent to tent and one political luminary to another, every man of them proud to make the champion's acquaintance and welcome him to Missouri, many of them remarking on how close he had come to knocking out Johnson. Ketchel smiled and nodded and shook countless hands, retaining few of the names they belonged to.

Then they were at the bar of another tent and Dickerson was

embracing and slapping the back of still another senator whose name Ketchel didn't catch, a lean and weathered man who was descended from a family of "damn jayhawkers," according to Dickerson, before they finally had the good sense to move to Missouri. Dickerson addressed the senator as "Sarge," for such had been the man's rank when they soldiered together in Cuba. Alongside the senator was a man in a black suit and cowboy boots, a pale, wide-brimmed Western hat tilted forward to shadow his eyes. He held a drink in one hand and the thumb of the other was loosely hooked on the front of his belt, his posture somehow suggesting both ease and readiness for quick movement. His name tag was folded and stuffed in his breast pocket. After shaking Ketchel's hand, the senator turned to the man in the Western hat, saying, "I'd like you fellas to meet my special guest at this shindig. This here's the one and only Emmett Dalton, the last of the old-time badmen."

Dalton gave the senator an unsmiling sidewise glance and shook the colonel's hand, saying, "Colonel," then shook Ketchel's. "Pleasure, champ."

Ketchel's heart was hopping with a kind of excitement he'd not felt since boyhood.

A young man appeared at the senator's side and whispered into his ear. "Oh, all right, I'll talk to him," the senator said, and turned to Dickerson. "You might want to be in on this, Pete. It's to do with the timber bill for next session."

The colonel told Ketchel to have fun, he would search him out later, then left with the senator.

Dalton signaled a barman for another drink. He looked at Ketchel and said, "Bourbon?" Ketchel nodded and Dalton held up two fingers to the barman.

They stood leaning against the bar and sipped from their

drinks without conversation for a minute before Ketchel said, "It's my pleasure to know you, too, Mr. Dalton." And immediately felt stupid.

Dalton raised his glass toward him in a silent toast.

Another half-minute passed before Ketchel said, "It's none of my business, but . . . well . . . I thought they put you in prison for life."

"They did," Dalton said. "Felt like it, too, for fifteen years."

"You got a pardon?"

"Three years ago."

"What do you do now? For a living, I mean."

"Lawman."

He said it with an absolutely straight face, and for a moment Ketchel simply stared. Then Dalton smiled. "Ain't it a hell of a note? Tulsa police officer. And been married two whole years. I'm a regular upright citizen."

"How you like Oklahoma?" Ketchel said.

"To tell the truth, I about had my fill of it," Dalton said. "Believe Julia and I'll head to California, see if there's any gold still to be struck."

"You'll like California," Ketchel said. He was intensely aware that he might never have a chance to talk to this man or any such again. "I wonder something, Mr. Dalton."

"What's that, Mr. Ketchel?"

"I've read an awful lot about the Coffeyville scrape. There's a few things different the way some stories tell it from the way others do, but they mostly all tell it the same. They say you fellas wanted to rob two banks in the same town on the same day because it had never been done before and you wanted to outdo the James and Younger boys. What I wonder is, is that true?"

Dalton considered the question a moment as though for the first time. "Bob always was dead set on beating the best." Dalton's older brothers Bob and Grat had been killed at Coffeyville. So had the other two members of the gang.

Ketchel knew the story well. When the gang came out of the banks to make its getaway, nearly every man in town opened fire on them. Citizens were blasting at them with rifles and revolvers and shotguns from the rooftops and windows, were lined up in the alleyway like firing squads. Bullets came at the gang from everywhere. Only Emmett made it to his mount. He was in the clear and galloping away when he looked back and saw that his brothers were fallen. So he turned around and rode back for them. The citizens could hardly believe it. They shotgunned him off his horse and then shot him some more when he was down. Every story Ketchel ever read about the Coffeyville slaughter agreed it was God's own wonder Emmett Dalton survived it.

"Some say you were shot a dozen times, some say more," Ketchel said. "At Coffeyville, I mean." He could not bring himself to ask the man outright how many times it was.

Dalton did not offer to say. He smiled and took a sip of his drink. Then said: "What *I'd* like to know, Mr. Ketchel, is what sorta pistola you got tucked in your belt there?"

Ketchel looked down to see if the weapon was showing, but it was not. "What makes you think I'm carrying a gun?"

Dalton smiled.

Ketchel looked around and then opened his coat so Dalton could see the revolver.

Dalton nodded, and drew his coat aside to give Ketchel a glimpse of the same model Colt in the holster under his jacket. "Frontier's a honey, ain't it?"

Ketchel grinned.

"I wonder something else," Dalton said.

Ketchel raised his brow.

"Will you be fighting Johnson again?"

Ketchel took a swallow of bourbon. Then said: "Got to. If it's the last damn thing I do."

"Yeah," Emmett Dalton said. "That's exactly how Bob felt about going for two banks at once."

FOR THE LAST half hour of the trip he could not take his gaze from the coach window. "Sweet Christ, I've been around and seen a lot of pretty country, but this is . . . special."

"Must be something in our blood the Ozarks calls to," the colonel said. "I felt the same as you the first time I saw it. So did my daddy before me."

"Captain Jerry." Ketchel liked to say the name. "Grandpa."

"He woulda loved hearing you call him that."

They got off the train in Conway, some thirty-five miles from Springfield. The colonel's ranch lay about seven miles distant. He had sent word ahead to the Conway livery where he kept a team and carriage, and the vehicle was ready to go when they got there.

They drove out of town and followed a narrow road that went winding through groves of oak and hickory, stands of pine, over plank bridges crossing streams and gullies. Except for their own voices, the only sounds were of the horses' hooves and the carriage rattles, the thin cries of high-wheeling hawks.

"Most folks around here will tell you that the prettiest parts of the Ozarks are farther south," the colonel said, "and I'd have to agree. You got the mountains down there, though people like yourself who seen the Rockies might laugh at what Missouri considers mountains. Hunched up, choppy hills more like it, all cut up with ravines and gullies, all full of caves. Hollows so deep and thick with trees the ground never sees a spot of sunshine. Fogged up as often as not. It's pretty, all right, but you play hell trying to grow much of anything in all that rock. Around here, I can raise me a little wheat, a little corn."

The only thing Ketchel had known about the Ozarks was that during the Civil War it had been part of the region ruled by fearsome Confederate guerrillas the like of William Clarke Quantrill and Bloody Bill Anderson, both of whose daring exploits he had read about many a time. He could see why the guerrillas had fared so well. This was country made for ambush.

He'd heard that former members of Quantrill's Raiders or allied bunches had been having an annual reunion somewhere in Missouri ever since the end of the war. There wasn't a man among them under the age of sixty anymore, and some were into their seventies, but there were at least two dozen or so of the rascals yet walking the earth and they got together every year. The colonel said he'd heard about the bushwhacker reunions, too, but didn't know where they were held. They'd have to find out and attend one. Could be fun listening to those old killers telling their war tales.

Dickerson wasn't surprised there were so many bushwhackers left. "Missourians are a rough folk in general," he said, "but these Ozarkers are the roughest of the lot. Take my word for it, son, they're not a people to chivvy with."

THE ESTATE WAS as beautiful as the colonel had claimed. It was bordered by a river from which a dozen streams branched and went meandering over the property. There were stands of hardwoods, grassy meadows, a field of wheat and a larger one of corn. Late afternoon sunlight lay in a golden mist on the grass, glowed softly green through the trees.

"Most of the creeks on the place are spring-fed," the colonel said. "Clear as glass and cold as ice all year round. Some good-size trout in them."

As they drew near to the ranch house they passed by one of the several tenant houses scattered over the property. A man and his wife and child were out in the yard and waved as they went by.

The colonel yelled, "Howdy, Luther! Howdy Miz Brazeale, Sally Jean. This here's Stevie!" Ketchel and the family waved to each other.

The ranch house stood at the edge of a dense hollow. It was a large two-story structure with gabled dormers and fronted by a screened porch. A stout man in work clothes and a woman who might have passed for his twin in female dress came out to greet them and help unload the baggage. Behind them stood a young girl in an apron. The colonel introduced them as the ranch foreman, Mr. Bailey, and his missus. The girl was Hilda, Mrs. Bailey's helper.

The colonel told Ketchel that Bailey had recently tendered his resignation, effective the middle of next month. He and his wife were moving back to Kentucky to help Bailey's sickly bachelor brother manage his farm.

"You're leaving me high and dry and you know it, you damned hillbilly," the colonel said to Bailey. "Where am I going to get somebody able as you and your missus to run this place?"

"Oh really, Mr. Dickerson," Mrs. Bailey said, "you've been saying the same thing for weeks now."

"Well hell, it's been true for weeks. You're running out on me."

"Gee whiz, Colonel, you're gonna have us all blubbering in a minute," Bailey said.

"Whoever I get to take your place might not be as good," the colonel said, "but for damn sure he'll have a more respectful tongue in his head." He leaned toward Ketchel and said in lower voice, "Hell, he's not going anywhere. He's just holding out for more jack. Soon as I make the right offer he'll stay."

"I heard that," Bailey said. "And you're wrong. I keep telling you."

"Oh sure I am," the colonel said, and winked at Ketchel.

The colonel's quarters were on the second floor. The main floor comprised three rooms: a bedroom on one side of the house, a dining room with fireplace on the other side, and a parlor between them. The dining room also served as the Baileys' quarters. There was a kitchen off the rear of the house, and the Hilda girl slept there on a cot in a corner. The colonel told Ketchel the downstairs bedroom was his for as long as he wanted it. "It's your house, son."

As they were settling in, the sky abruptly clouded and a wind kicked up and minutes behind it came whipping sheets of thunderless rain, a hard storm that rattled the windows for a quarter hour and then was gone. After a supper of chicken stew and biscuits they retired for the night. Ketchel positioned his bed directly under an open window, and after extinguishing his lamp he lay awake and let his senses acquaint themselves with the Ozark evening. The sky had cleared but the moon was not yet risen, and the night's only light was in massive clusters of stars. A soft chill breeze came through the window. A tree branch gently scraped the side of the house. He heard an owl hoot. Was surprised by the wail of a coyote. He breathed deeply of the crisp air and its moist aromas of sweetly rich earth and unfamiliar vegetation. He thought he might have found a home.

DURING THEIR FIRST few days on the ranch the colonel took him on hikes over various sections of the property, through shadowy hollows, along the banks of rippling creeks, across meadows of yellow grass to their thighs. The more of the place Ketchel saw, the more he was taken with its beauty. One afternoon they reeled in a half-dozen trout from one of the streams and that evening fried the fillets in butter and seasoned them with coarse black pepper and a touch of lemon. Another day they brought down several fat quail with the colonel's shotguns, and Mrs. Bailey roasted them to perfection.

Within view of the house was a newly constructed barn with one wall yet unpainted, and a few feet from it stood a high mound of excavated dirt and scrub brush that Ketchel used as a backstop for target practice with his guns. It pleased the colonel to hear him at his daily shooting, to peer out the window and see him making short work of bottles and tin cans. Sometimes he went out and joined in with a gun of his own.

Ketchel had been there a week when he told the colonel he believed the Ozarks was the place to settle down. He would let his brother have the Pine Lake home for whatever price he could afford to pay. The colonel was delighted by his decision. It happened that a large parcel of property adjoining his own was for sale, a nice place to build a house and fertile enough to be farmed if he took a notion. Ketchel liked it, and when he asked if Dickerson could suggest something to invest in, the colonel drove him out to view a dense section of timberland on which he had an option but was willing to let Ketchel buy in his stead. Ketchel bought both properties and for the first time he felt as if he were truly putting down roots.

And yet. . . . He could not stop thinking of Johnson. Or, for that matter, of Wilson Mizner. The more he thought of his telephone talk with Mizner, the more he had come to see that Pete the Goat was right, Mizner was no true friend of his, only a business partner whose sole concern was the size of his own cut. But so what? That was the man's job, after all, it was how he made his living. No, what truly grated him about Mizner was the man's apparent certainty that he could not beat Johnson. You don't know me, pal, Ketchel thought. You don't know me worth a damn. Still, Bill Mizner was a hard man not to like, and he'd had a hell of a lot of fun in his company. He saw no reason to end things on a sour note.

He wrote Mizner a letter saying he was resettling in the Ozarks, that he had bought timberland and farm acreage and was going into business in both. He was quitting the fight game. He wished him well and said maybe they could have a drink together if he was ever again in New York. As he sealed the letter in an envelope, he thought, You'll find out how wrong you were when you read it in the papers, old pard.

He then wrote to Pete the Goat in California to tell him he was settling in Missouri but would be seeing Jack Johnson in New York next month to try to get a rematch. He told Pete about his letter to Mizner and said he would be acting as his own manager in dealing with Johnson. He wanted Pete to be ready to come out to the Ozarks and set up a training camp as soon as the rematch was all set.

OVER THE NEXT two weeks they made frequent trips to Springfield, where the colonel took him around to meet every man of importance in town, from the mayor to the chief of police to the editors of the local newspapers. He took him to a meeting of the Elks Club and introduced him personally to every member. A few nights afterward, Ketchel was initiated into the lodge by special decree. The formal rite was accompanied by a rendition of Chopin's "Funeral March," which the colonel knew to be Ketchel's favorite musical composition. After the ceremony the "carefree, boisterous crowd," as the local newspaper characterized the company, celebrated late into the night.

Some days later Dickerson booked a showing of the Jeffries-Johnson fight film at the Landers Theater, and Ketchel was the evening's special guest. When he entered the theater and went down the aisle to his reserved seat, the applause shuddered the walls. Ketchel waved in recognition of the tribute.

"You haven't been here a month and already you're a hometown hero," the colonel said. "You picked the right place to make a home, son."

"Feels like home," Ketchel said.

THEY WERE A week into October now and despite his persistent blandishments and tenders of an increase in salary Dickerson could not persuade Bailey to stay on.

"Goddamn it, man, I already offered you more than I ever intended," the colonel said. "It's one thing to hold out for a raise, but I won't be robbed."

"I've told you and told you, Colonel, I'm going. It's nary to do with money."

"What the hell is it? What you got against me, anyway? I thought we liked each other."

Bailey sighed and turned to his wife and shrugged.

"Well, by God, I won't stand for this insolence," the colonel said. "You're fired. This fella here"—he pointed at Ketchel—"can run this place good enough."

"You can't fire me, I already resigned," Bailey said. "But I said I'd stick till next Saturday and I will, unless you say leave right now."

The colonel ran a hand through his sparse hair. He was his father's son and not used to being put over a barrel.

"I don't doubt Mr. Ketchel can manage the place," Bailey said, "but he can't run it by himself and you know it. You best get him another working man and a housekeeper unless you're fixing to do the plowing and cooking."

"Goddamn it," the colonel said.

"I'll stay till next Saturday like I promised, but it's only another week. You best get to hiring somebody."

"I know, I *know,*" the colonel said.

That afternoon he and Ketchel went to Springfield to spend a few days. The colonel had some business to attend to and also wanted to help Ketchel arrange for timber contracts on his new property. But the first thing he did was go to an employment office managed by a friend of his named Spears. He told Spears he needed a field hand and a housekeeper who could cook, preferably a married couple. He needed them right away but he didn't want any slackers or drinkers or complainers. If any likely applicants should come around, Spears was to send them to him lickety-split.

The following Monday afternoon a young couple presented themselves at the colonel's office and said they had been referred by Mr. Spears.

After a brief interview, Dickerson hired them.

Goldie and Walt

Goldie Smith had for a few years used her stepfather's last name of Bright. She had at different times of her life also been Goldie Woods, Goldie Knight, and Goldie Osborne. She was a pretty woman, blonde and gray-eyed and well proportioned, and on the day Dickerson hired her she was twenty-two years old.

An Ozarks native, she had been a sexually precocious girl who enthusiastically parted with her virginity at the age of thirteen. She knew several lovers in the following year and was not yet fifteen when she eloped with a dapper and darkly handsome man named Woods. He was a gambler by trade and a procurer by inclination, and Goldie earned a fair share of their keep as they traveled about Missouri. They avoided K. C. and St. Louis, where Woods said the competition was too stiff and the cops too rough with those who didn't pay off. She did not object to the life. Indeed, she considered herself lucky in comparison to women such as her mother, farm wives who worked like plow animals and were old and swaybacked before they reached forty. She did, however, object to her husband's infidelities, and she registered her objections in the tantrum fashion of the child she in some ways yet was. But Woods had low tolerance for shrill antic and each time responded by slapping her silly. It would not occur to her until much later that she was not his first whore-wife.

They had been married a year and were living in Jefferson City when Woods informed her they were now divorced. He gave her a copy of the decree and a five-dollar bill and said so long. She watched from the window as he got behind the steering wheel of a little runabout in which a woman in a feathered hat had been waiting and then drove out of her life forever.

All she could think to do was return to the Ozarks, where her mother and stepfather were living on the outskirts of Chadwick, about thirty-five miles from Springfield. It was not a warm reunion, as both her mother and Mr. Bright had long before given her up for bad. But she promised to make herself helpful and mind her behavior, and so they took her in.

Inside of six months she was again desperate to be free of the farm. Deliverance presented itself in the form of R. W. Knight, a station agent for the Frisco line who was posted at the Chadwick depot. She had just turned sixteen when they wed. Nine months later she bore a baby girl. Knight was delighted. Goldie loved the infant, too, and yet shortly after her initiation to motherhood she began waking in the night in a gasping terror that she would soon be an old woman and soon thereafter die. To counter these fears, she reverted to sexual adventure, to sporting with passing drummers, tinkers, the occasional hobo just off a freight and in search of a handout. Time passed and suspicions slowly sprouted among the neighbors. Rumors made the rounds and eventually reached her husband's ear. He confronted her and she made heated denials. But the rumors did not abate, and he began to uncover evidence of their truth: a crushed cigar butt at the bottom of the kitchen steps, a faint trace of whiskey in a sink-side cup, a sooty hand towel balled behind the wash basin. One morning he reached under the bed for his shoes and found a man's shirt collar, and the game was up. She could not muster the words to explain the fears that drove her to it. And so a little more than two years after they married they were divorced. Knight readily agreed to pay support for the child, then transferred to a station in Arkansas.

For a time she made ends meet by dint of Knight's support money and by taking in seamstress work. But she was lonelier than ever and continued to engage in liaisons. She read of Evelyn Nesbit and her adventurous life in New York, of the red velvet swing and the rich men who vied for her, killed for her. She wept with the want of such glamorous excitement in her own life.

Word of her indiscretions again made its way to her former husband Knight, albeit it had farther to go this time and took longer to reach him. Two years after leaving her, Knight returned to Missouri long enough to gain legal custody of their daughter, a simple matter in light of the copious neighborhood testimony regarding Goldie's iniquitous conduct. On conclusion of the legalities, he told Goldie to stay out of their lives forever and took the little girl off to Arkansas.

She told herself then and would tell others later that the loss of her child unmoored her from all sense of purpose and worth and was likely the reason that some months later she married a man she hardly knew and moved with him to Kansas. In truth, she could not then or later have named a clear motive for this marriage. The man's name was Osborne. He was a traveling salesman, a drummer, and for reasons as murky as everything else about their time together, they divorced in Cherryvale after being married only four months. She stayed in that town and worked as a waitress for a time, and now and then turned a trick. From what she heard about Coffeyville, which lay a little farther to the south, she thought the pickings might be better, so she moved there. And despite her young years was soon managing what she called a boardinghouse for women but which the local sheriff correctly suspected was a different sort of house. He raided the place, confiscated all of her money, dispersed the other girls, and gave her one day to get clear of the county or, as he put it, he would have her ass on the women's work farm.

Thus, in September of 1910, she began making her way back to Missouri, hoping her mother and stepfather would once more give her shelter while she considered how she might best confront the future looming so bleakly before her.

On a sunny Sunday morning, after a change of trains in Springfield, she at last arrived at Chadwick, the end of the line. To get to her mother's, she would have to hire a rig. She had a cup of coffee at the station, then went to the livery. And there ran into Walter Dipley.

WALTER DIPLEY HAD also been born in the Ozarks, in Webb City, where he grew up. He was twenty-three years old and strikingly handsome, short but well muscled, having labored in the lead mines of Jasper County through most of his teenage years.

His widowed sister lived in Blue Creek, a hamlet just south of

Chadwick. She was a kind woman who supported herself with an insurance settlement and she had always doted on Walter. In his boyhood he spent every summer with her, and at a barn dance in his fourteenth summer he met the thirteen-year-old hellion Goldie Bright. Soon afterward they happily fumbled through the first coitus for both of them, and they were ardent lovers through the rest of that summer. But when he came back to Blue Creek the following year he learned she had run off to be married, and so he forgot about her.

In February of 1908 he enlisted in the navy in order to see more of the world, and see more of it he did. He was assigned to a transport ship that made ports of call in Hawaii and countless islands of the South Pacific, in the Philippines, in Hong Kong. He had adventures of sundry sorts and acquired a vast sexual education. He also acquired a razor scar on his neck from a fight over a Manila whore. And a welter of outlandish tattoos. His chest and back came to be covered with dragons, flaming swords, esoteric emblems of wizardry, willowy naked women. Each of his pectorals was emblazoned with a circle of yin and yang, a symbol he thought beautiful although he had difficulty grasping its concept. One arm was entirely entwined with a fearsome long-fanged snake, the other bore the words HONG KONG, CHINA down the outer bicep, and, on the inner side of the forearm, a bleeding heart impaled by a poniard.

He liked everything about the navy except its premium on regimentation and ranked authority. He was frequently punished for insubordination. He spent a large part of the return voyage to the States in the brig. The day after the ship docked in Oakland, he deserted.

For months he drifted through the West. He used a different

name in every town. He worked odd jobs, including an entire day in a copper mine of Butte, Montana, which, on applying for the job, he had thought couldn't be as bad as the lead mines of Jasper County. But the experience made him promise himself to jump in front of a train before ever again stepping into a copper mine. He baled hay, cut wheat, laid track, he hewed timber, he graded roads. He broke a wrangler's arm in a South Dakota bar fight over a half-breed girl. And in the late summer of 1910 he headed back to Missouri.

When he got to Webb City, he learned from his parents that a navy investigator had been to their house twice, the second time only two weeks before. The investigator had talked to the neighbors as well, to some of the people in town. Dipley agreed that it was unsafe for him to stay there, and so he decided to go to his sister's.

He caught the evening train to Springfield. The following morning, a brilliantly sunny Sunday, he took the flyer to the end of the line in Chadwick, then went to the livery to hire a carriage. And there ran into Goldie Smith.

WHEN SHE ASKED the stableman about a conveyance to her mother's house, he told her a fellow had just hired a rig to take him to Blue Creek, which was in the same area. He suggested she see if the man was willing to split the cost with her. "He's around the side where my boy's getting the rig set."

She knew him the instant she saw him. He was watching the boy harness the horse and wasn't aware of her until she stepped up beside him and said, "Pardon me, but aren't you Walter Dipley?"

He did not know her at first, this shapely blonde with bold gray eyes whom he had not seen in the nine years since she was thirteen.

She saw his lack of recognition and made a face of mock injury.

"I must say, I'm deeply hurt. Do you suppose Captain Ajax has forgotten me as well?"

Captain Ajax was the name she had given to his penis in the course of their lickerish summer those years before.

His face warmed at the sudden recollection, and he cut a look at the stable boy, who was paying them no mind. "My God," he said, "is it Goldie Bright?"

"The same," she said, "though the name's Smith. It's the one I was born with." Her eyes danced over his reddened face, which seemed to her even handsomer than when he was a boy.

"We're all set, mister," the boy said, leading the horse and rig to them.

She said she was going to her mother's, which was on his way, and asked if she might share the carriage with him.

Well, of course.

THE DISTANCE TO her mother's house was only some five miles, and the horse moved at a brisk trot. From the moment of their meeting, however, they'd felt the same carnal draw of their passionate childhood romance, and they did not need much time to arrive at an understanding.

The rig had barely cleared sight of Chadwick when she pressed closer to him and said in low voice, "Do you remember when we—" And then his mouth was on hers. The kiss lasted a few fast heartbeats before they glanced at the boy in the driver's seat to ensure his attention was on the road ahead, and then they kissed again, this time touching tongues before pulling apart. The boy at the reins seemed engrossed in his own thoughts.

She slid her hand over his thigh and clasped him, her eyes bright. "Captain Ajax seems in happy disposition," she said. And whipped her hand away as the boy said over his shoulder that they'd be at the turn-off road to the Bright place in another quarter mile.

Dipley talked low and fast. She could come with him to his sister's house. They could tell her they were married, that they'd eloped a few days ago and intended to live in Springfield, but the house they would be renting wouldn't be available for a while yet and they needed a place to stay in the meantime. His sister would be happy about his marriage and welcome them for as long as they wished. There was an extra room where he always stayed, and they would have their privacy.

Given her circumstance, what deliberation was called for? She kissed him quickly and squeezed his thigh. He told the boy to forget the turn-off and go on to the Widow Dipley's place in Blue Creek.

THEY WERE AT his sister's for almost three weeks, and from the first it was as if the nine years had been a mere nine days, so familiarly did they tend each other's flesh, the sole difference between then and now being in the greater expertise each brought to their lovemaking. He'd been her first ever, and now was the first in a long time to show her anything in the sexual arts she didn't already know. She relished the flex and feel of his muscles, was enthralled by his tattoos. They made love deep into the nights. His sister heard them and smiled in recollection of her own honeymoon ardor of so many years ago. They did it in the barn, deep in the woods in the shade of the trees, under the sun in the high grass of the riverbank while a flock of cackling crows wheeled overhead.

If Walt Dipley had a time or two in the past mistaken lust for love, he was sure that this time it was the real thing. Even after she had confessed most of her mistakes of the past nine years, just as he had confided to her most of his own, he was no less certain that she was the one, the woman with whom he could finally settle down. He told her he loved her and wanted to marry her. He would work hard and save some money and somehow finance the purchase of a small farm. They would have lots of children. He wasn't worried about the navy. They wouldn't hunt for him forever. If he took a different name and stayed well away from Jasper County, they'd never track him down.

She had to think fast. She dearly enjoyed herself in bed with Walt Dipley, but marriage was another matter. She'd come to believe she wasn't truly meant for it, for sure not with gamblers, station agents, or drummers. And not, she knew, with Walter Dipley, whose idea of a better life was not at all hers. Her early dislike of farming had now grown to abhorrence. And though she would never admit it to anyone, she no longer missed her daughter. She had come to accept that she was no more meant to be a mother than she was a wife. She was not sure *what* she was meant for, but believed she would know it when she met it. Still, what was she to do? If she were not with Dipley, where else might she be? None of the available alternatives owned the least allure. What she needed was time. Time for another possibility to present itself.

And so she told Dipley that nothing would make her happier than to be married to him, but there might be a slight problem. She had earlier told him she'd run away from her third husband, Osborne, because he beat her once too often, but, she now clarified, they were not yet divorced when she fled. She had assumed Osborne would file for divorce on grounds of abandonment, but what if he hadn't? Bigamy was a serious crime. She could write to him and ask if they were divorced, but he was a vindictive man and couldn't be trusted to tell her the truth. She would have to write to the court clerk in Coffeyville to find out if a divorce decree was on record. If Osborne had not filed, she would have to do so herself.

"It might all take a while, darling," she said, "but it will be worth it, so we can be married without any doubt over our head."

He was not pleased by this turn but knew she was right. They had to ensure she was lawfully free to remarry. It was important to steer clear of any legal complication that might help the navy to find him.

All right, he said, for now they would just *say* they were husband and wife. They would be Walter and Goldie . . . Hurtz. He'd known a fellow in the navy by that name. Luckiest dice roller he'd ever seen. Besides, living together was sort of like being married too, wasn't it? Married by the common law. Only not so it was bigamy.

How very true, she said, that was the way to look at it.

The thing to do now, he said, was for both of them to get some kind of jobs and put aside some money. As soon as they could afford it they would go to Coffeyville and talk to the court clerk and see for themselves what was what with her divorce.

She patted his arm and said it was a fine plan. She said it was a comfort to be with a man who knew how to get things done.

"Stick with me, girl," he said, "and you'll go places."

ON MONDAY AFTERNOON a few days later, they presented themselves as man and wife in a Springfield employment office and interviewed with a Mr. Spears. In answer to the man's questions, Walter Hurtz assured him that he was an able ranch hand with plenty of experience working in the fields, and Goldie Hurtz assured him she was indeed a good cook, if she did say so herself, and a first-rate housekeeper.

Spears excused himself and went into a glass-walled rear office and they saw him make a telephone call. Then he came back out and gave them directions to get to R. P. Dickerson's office.

The interview with Dickerson was brief. He was pleased they were natives and therefore familiar with the region. He made clear the sort of help he was looking for on the ranch. He asked to see Walter Hurtz's palms and seemed satisfied with their calluses. He asked Goldie Hurtz her recipe for fried chicken and she was but half-finished telling it to him when he flicked his hand dismissively and said, "Good enough, girl, good enough. Can't wait to taste it. The job pays thirty a month plus room and board. You folks want it?"

"Sure do," Walter said.

"Then it's yours. We'll go out to the ranch morning after tomorrow. Meet me at the depot. Train leaves at ten-forty-five sharp."

"We'll be there, Mr. Dickerson."

"Call me colonel."

Three Ranch Days

Dickerson was waiting for them when they got to the depot. He gave them their coach tickets and said he was riding in a different car. When the train reached Conway they were all to meet at the baggage carrier. He then went off to the smoking car, where Ketchel was already ensconced.

It was nearly noon when they pulled into Conway. Ketchel and Dickerson stepped down to the platform and the colonel pointed. "There they are."

The couple was making their way toward them, the young man holding a valise in each hand, the woman carrying a smaller valise and a handbag.

"Fella seems fit enough," the colonel said. "Got a good grip on him. I always test that the first time I shake a man's hand. I think he'll do all right. Who in hell needs Bailey anyway?"

Ketchel's attention was entirely on the woman. She wore no hat, her yellow hair knotted in a bun atop her head. As she came nearer he saw that she was pretty, her eyes gray.

The colonel introduced Walt and Goldie, and beamed as he told them, "And this fella here is none other than Stanley Ketchel, middleweight boxing champ of the world. He'll be your boss."

Dipley put down a valise and put out his hand. "Heard of you," he said. Ketchel's once-over and handshake were perfunctory.

Goldie had not heard of him, but she was entirely familiar with the way he looked at her. "A champion!" she said. "I've never met a champion before."

"Let me help you with that," Ketchel said, taking the valise.

"Why, thank you, kind sir."

He told himself she could not possibly be the girl who'd smiled at him from a passing streetcar in San Francisco two summers ago, the girl whose face had come to him in the night so many times since. But she could have been her twin.

On the ride to the ranch he sat up front with the colonel, who drove and did most of the talking, and the girl and Hurtz sat in the rear seat. Ketchel intermittently glanced back at her as casually as he could, and she every time smiled at him.

During a pause in the colonel's monologue, she asked, "Does your wife live on the ranch as well, Colonel Dickerson? Or at your home in Springfield?"

"Not married," the colonel said. "Never had the good fortune to find the right woman like your man Hurtz here."

"What about you, Mr. Ketchel?" she said. "Have you had such good fortune?"

He had a fleeting vision of Kate Morgan's lovely face.

"Sorry to say I haven't," he said. And returned her smile.

When the carriage reined up in front of the house, the Baileys came out to meet the new couple. Dickerson and Ketchel took down their bags, and then Bailey drove Walt and Goldie to a cabin just the other side of the hollow, where they would be staying for the next two days until the Baileys had moved out of the ranch house and they could move in.

Ketchel did not see her again that day.

THE CABIN HAD been stocked with canned goods and baking supplies. That evening, over a supper of beans and beef stew and biscuits, Goldie said they'd been lucky to get jobs at such a fine place.

Walt said the place was all right. There was no ignoring the pique in his voice, so she asked if something was bothering him. Was there was something about Colonel Dickerson he didn't like?

"The colonel's all right," he said. "It's just, well, that damn boxer sure thinks he's something, don't he? The way he looks at everybody like he's so much better. So what he's a champion? Just means he's got a harder head than everybody else is all."

She laughed as though he'd made a good joke, then leaned across the table to stroke his arm. "I bet he could crack walnuts on that hard head, huh? I bet he could use it for an anvil."

"I bet," Walt said. "But say, I wish you wouldn't, well . . . be so damn *friendly* with him. I think he's a wolf."

She made a wry face and said, "Oh now, honey, I don't think he is, but don't worry, I know how to handle wolves. Besides, he *is* our boss. I think we ought to try and get along with him, don't you?" She squeezed his arm. "Listen, every time we think of something that hard head might be good for, we'll save it up to tell each other when we're alone."

"Hell, we'll be laughing to beat the band every night."

She came around the table and took him by the hand and over to the bed and began to undress him. And took his mind off Mr. Stanley Ketchel.

Afterward, lying under the covers against the cool night, Walt snoring lightly beside her, she thought: You best play it mighty careful, girl.

But oh, did he give you the eye, this famous champion. This surely prosperous and famous champion.

Play your cards right and, well . . . who knows?

SOMETIME IN THE night she was jostled awake in darkness when Walt leaned over her to get at the lamp.

"What is it?" she said.

He struck a match and the walls quavered in the sudden flare of light.

"Jesus!" he yelled.

Hunched over the supper dishes she'd left on the table was a huge yellow rat. Its eyes flamed at them and then it streaked to the floor and vanished through a crack in the boards she wouldn't have believed it could fit through.

THE COLONEL SPENT the following morning attending to paperwork up in his quarters. He had pressing business in Springfield and would be departing for the Conway depot that afternoon, taking Mrs. Bailey and Hilda in the carriage with him. He would check the women into a Springfield hotel for the next two nights. Bailey would arrive in Springfield on Saturday and they would leave for Kentucky on that evening's train.

After putting Walt to work at finishing the paint job on the barn, Bailey packed his and his wife's clothing and smaller belongings and put the bags in the carriage. The Hilda girl's goods all fit into a single small suitcase. The bed and wardrobe in the dining room, both of which Bailey had crafted himself and which his wife meant to have in Kentucky, he would dismantle and take by wagon to Conway for shipment Saturday morning.

Mrs. Bailey kept Goldie occupied in the kitchen all morning, showing her where everything was stored, instructing her in the mealtime routines and the colonel's favorite recipes, each of which was written on a small card and kept in a file box in the pantry. She lectured Goldie on the vagaries of the ice box and of the man who delivered the ice for it. She wrote down her usual shopping schedule in Conway and what supplies could be procured there, which things she could get only in Springfield.

The noon meal was a hectic affair, the colonel giving Ketchel last-minute instructions about things that had to be done in his absence, Bailey chiming in with any particulars that Dickerson left out and reminding him that a carpenter named Noland was coming from Conway on Saturday morning to finish a few interior details on the new barn. Also, another sharecropper family would be arriving in a few days, a little earlier than previously expected, and the house they would be living in was still in need of a cleanup and some minor repairs. If Ketchel lent him a hand, Bailey said, they could have the place ready by tomorrow afternoon. Ketchel said sure thing. As for Walt, he would be working with Brazeale for the next week or two. Brazeale had agreed to plow an extra field in exchange for a better share of the next crop, but he needed help, and Dickerson had promised him Walt Hurtz. The colonel told Ketchel to just make sure Walt tended to the horses in the barn first thing every morning before going to Brazeale's.

While the men ate and talked in the dining room, Ketchel caught glimpses of Goldie moving about in the kitchen as she worked with Mrs. Bailey. Only once did she look out the kitchen door just as he looked toward it. She smiled brightly and waggled her fingers. Then Mrs. Bailey was beside her and scowled from one of them to the other before drawing the girl out of his view.

AFTER DINNER, KETCHEL went out to the shooting range beside the barn for his daily session, pushing a wheelbarrow full of empty bottles. The Colt was tucked in his waistband and the Remington .22 rifle the colonel had given him in Michigan was slung across his back. A week earlier he'd accidentally knocked the little rifle to the floor after giving it a cleaning and he had been intending to test the sights to be sure they had not been jarred out of alignment.

Walt was high on a ladder, brushing paint along the top of the barn wall, his paint bucket hung on a ladder hook. He paused in his work to watch as Ketchel wheeled the barrow up to the mound only a few yards from the foot of the ladder and transferred the bottles to the dirt slope, spacing them at various heights. His boots crunched on the broken glass of previous practice sessions.

"If you're fixing to do some shooting," Walt said, "hold on till I get out of the way."

Ketchel looked up at him. "You wouldn't be in the way unless you sat right in front of what I was shooting at." He took up the barrow handles and started away from the mound.

Walt watched him a moment and then carefully set his brush across the mouth of the paint can and started down the rungs. About forty feet away Ketchel unslung the rifle and set it against the barrow, then faced the mound and drew the Colt.

"Wait a minute!" Walt called out. He was not halfway down the ladder.

Ketchel raised the Colt. Walt pressed himself tightly against the ladder and tried to make himself small as Ketchel fired six shots in steady succession, each one shattering glass.

In the kitchen Goldie's heart heaved. "What's that!"

"Mr. Ketchel killing bottles," Mrs. Bailey said. "Kills him a bunch every day. Murders a whole lot of tin cans too. Now pay attention here, girl, to this pecan pie recipe. It's nothing in the world the colonel likes better for dessert than pecan pie, but there's a tricky part to this and you best get it right."

Ketchel slipped the empty revolver back into his pants. Walt exhaled a long breath and swore softly, his heart shoving against his ribs.

Now Ketchel had the Remington to his shoulder. Walt again hugged the ladder hard and the first riflecrack sent a tin can flipping through the air. Ketchel continued shooting, whanging away one can after another. With one bullet left in the magazine, he worked the bolt and aimed up toward the barn roof.

Walt cringed and felt a great urge to urinate. "Oh, Jesus!"

Ketchel squeezed off the shot and the bullet rang on the weathercock atop the barn roof and set its arms spinning.

The Remington's sights were fine.

While Ketchel reloaded the Colt, Walt scooted down the ladder and hastened to a spot well behind the firing line. Ketchel did not even look his way. After shooting up several more loads of .45 cartridges, he called it a day.

"You're a pretty fair hand with that thing," Walt said.

Ketchel's glance seemed surprised, as if he'd forgotten Walt was there. He put the Colt in his waistband and slung the rifle over his shoulder and started rolling the wheelbarrow back to the shed behind the house.

Walt hurried up alongside him. "Say, Mr. Ketchel, could I borrow that rifle, you reckon?"

"Say what?"

Walt told him about the rat. "I figure with that rifle I might could pop him good if he shows again tonight."

"Nothing nastier than a damn rat," Ketchel said. "You know how to clean a rifle?"

"Sure I do."

Ketchel handed him the Remington and Walt followed him back to the house, where he was left waiting at the kitchen door while Ketchel retrieved a handful of bullets and a cleaning kit.

AS THE COLONEL settled himself in the driver's seat and took up the reins, all set to leave for Conway with Mrs. Bailey and Hilda, Ketchel told him not to worry, he could take care of things.

"Hell, son, if there's anybody can take care of things, it's you. I'm not worried."

He hupped the team into motion and Mrs. Bailey once more waved so long. Bailey called out that he'd see her the day after tomorrow and he'd better not find her drunk and dancing on a saloon table, by God, and everybody laughed.

Goldie worked in the kitchen the remainder of the day, preparing supper for Ketchel and Bailey while they loaded the dismantled bed and wardrobe on a mule-drawn dray and took it down the road to Brazeale's house, where Bailey would spend his last two nights on the ranch.

Just before sundown, Walt finished the final brushstrokes on the barn. The plan had been for him and Goldie to move their things into the ranch house late that afternoon, including the cabin bed to replace the Baileys' bed, but everything had fallen behind schedule and Ketchel said the move could wait until the next day. Walt said that would be a problem, since he would be in the field with Brazeale until almost dark. Ketchel said that was all right, he would help Mrs. Hurtz move their things to the house as soon as he was done helping Bailey clean up the tenant house.

Bad Saturday

They were finished with the tenant house by midafternoon and headed back to Brazeale's house, Ketchel at the reins of the wagon. They didn't talk much. Bailey kept looking around as if trying to memorize every shrub and tree. He said he was going to miss this place. Ketchel said he believed him.

When they came to Brazeale's house, Bailey hopped off the moving dray and said good night and that he'd be sure to say so long before he left in the morning.

When Ketchel got to the main house, she was ready to go get the things at the cabin. She had prepared his supper, a rabbit stew whose wonderful aroma wafted from the kitchen, and had put it in the warmer to be ready when they returned. As they drove to the cabin, Ketchel asked how she liked the ranch, and she said she liked it fine, but of course she'd spent most of her life in this neck of the woods and so it wasn't anything all that different for her. She guessed he'd seen an awful lot of different places, though, hadn't he? Had he ever been to New York?

He talked about New York all the way to the cabin and she continued asking questions about it even as she gathered Walt's and her belongings and he dismantled the bed. She helped him load the frame sections on the cart. He said she seemed pretty strong. She flexed her arms like a circus strongman and said, "Ozark girl, mister. Tough as that mule there."

She was already back on the dray and he was about to shut the cabin door behind him when he spotted the Remington .22 propped in a corner and went back in and got it. He asked if Walt had shot the rat. She said they'd left a plate with some leftover greasy potatoes on the table, then lain awake for a long time, just listening. She struck a match every so often while he held the rifle ready to shoot, but after almost two hours the rat hadn't shown so much as a whisker. So they went to sleep.

"This morning the plate was so clean it was like the rat washed it after he was done eating."

Ketchel laughed along with her.

They got back to the house and unloaded the cart. They set the baggage and the rifle by the fireplace in the dining room, then lugged in the bed frame sections and she helped him to reassemble them and then they pushed the bed up against the back wall, a few feet from the kitchen door. They were both sheened with sweat. She poured two cups of water from a pitcher and handed him one. They stood close and drank and studied each other's eyes.

He's got it for you, girl, she thought. He might could be the one, the ride out. Her heart sped.

"You ever been in San Francisco?" he said.

"Me? I've never been farther west than Coffeyville, Kansas."

"Coffeyville? That's where it went bad for the Daltons."

"Well, I don't know anybody named Dalton, but it wasn't a real happy place for me, either."

And just like that, in the altered timbre of her voice and the change in her eyes as she remembered her time in Coffeyville, he knew who she was. Her mien of that moment made utterly familiar to him in countless whorehouses across the country.

All in that instant he felt profoundly foolish, sad in ways he couldn't have explained even to himself, outraged that she should have the face and smile of the girl on the trolley.

Whoever that girl had been, this one could never be her.

And for the first time allowed himself the thought that whoever that girl had been, she could never have been Kate.

He felt heat in his eyes, an ache deep in his throat.

"Penny for your thoughts," she said.

He checked the impulse to say something rude, was about to bid her good night and walk away, when she smiled that smile. And slightly shifted her stance so that her breasts stood higher.

He knew it for a whore trick. Well hell, he thought. And pulled her to him.

In less than a minute they were naked and in bed. She was nicely put together and awfully good at the deed, he had to give her that, and maybe all her show of enjoyment was fake and maybe not, it of course did not matter at all. All that mattered was the carnal balm of the moment. He thrust into her as if he would impale her to the bed, suckled at her breasts so hard she cried out even as she clutched him tighter, buried his face in her neck.

When they were done, she cuddled to him. Stroked his hair.

They were sweating and her skin was sticky on his. He got up and began dressing.

"Oh God, you're right," she said, gazing toward the window. "He'll be here pretty quick now, it's so close to dark." She smiled the smile. "I guess we're just a pair of reckless fools for love, huh? Taking such a chance."

Then stopped smiling when she saw his face as he buckled his belt. He stood over the bed and stared down at her. Then pulled a thick roll of currency from his pocket and peeled off a twenty-dollar bill and dropped it on her bare stomach.

"It's the smallest I got. I figure you owe me eighteen dollars change."

She could not speak.

"I don't know if that fool's your pimp or your stooge or what the hell he is, and I don't give a damn. Tell him whatever you want. If either of you care to stay on, you can, the place can use you both. But if you want to go, go."

He went to his bedroom and put on his woods jacket and slipped the Colt into his waistband in front of his hip. Then went out and got in the wagon and drove to Conway to have a drink or two.

Feeling the way one does on learning of the distant death of someone dear.

WHEN WALT ENTERED the house it was already full dark outside. The only light was in the dining room and the kitchen, where he found her stirring the pot of rabbit stew. He at once saw in her face that something was wrong and asked what it was. She said it was just a bad feeling she'd had all day. She couldn't explain it, but she thought they'd made a mistake coming here. She wanted to go. They could get work somewhere else.

"*Go?* But you . . . I thought you liked the place. You said you did."

"I thought I did too, but I was wrong. I hate it, I want to go."

He sensed there was more to it and kept asking what it was. She kept saying there wasn't anything else, she just wanted to leave.

"Well, all right, honey, if that's what you want," he said. "It's just, I thought . . ."

"Let's not talk about it anymore. Let's just go, let's go tomorrow, okay? Can we?"

"Sure, honey, sure."

"We can ride with Bailey when he goes to Conway. Go ask him if we can. Please. Go over to Brazeale's and ask him right now."

He did. And Bailey said of course they could go with him, just be ready to leave around nine o'clock. He asked what was wrong, if something had happened. Irritated by his own perplexity, Walt gestured impatiently and said, "We're just quitting, that's all. We had enough of this place. We'll be ready when you come by."

When he got back to the house, he ate supper and wanted to discuss the matter further, but she would have none of it. As soon as he was done eating, she latched the parlor door and they went to bed. He held her close, first in comfort, then gradually with other intentions. It was the last thing she was in the mood for, but she indulged him, if only to pacify him and get him to sleep all the sooner.

Walt was snoring deeply but she still lay awake when she heard the wagon's low rumble and its creaking halt. She heard the front door open and close. Heard Ketchel's boots on the parlor floor. Heard his bedroom door open and shut.

THE ROOM WAS gray with dawn light when he shook her awake with a start.

"*What?* What is it?"

"You tell me, goddamnit," he said through his teeth. "What *is* it?" He had her hand mirror ready and held it in front of her face. She saw her own large and fearful eyes, and then, even in the weak gray light, saw the livid little splotches on her neck.

Oh, you son of a bitch, she thought. And you *dope*, she told herself. Why the hell didn't you check?

"While the cat's away, huh?" Walt said.

"No baby, *no!* Listen, listen. He . . . he . . ." She stifled her sobs with the sheet.

"He *what?* . . . Oh, Jesus Christ . . . Did that bastard? . . . Goddamnit, I'll kill him!"

He started to get up but she caught his arm and held tight and whispered: "No, baby, no, he didn't, he didn't. I mean, he wanted to . . . I mean, he wanted to kiss me, see, but I said no, and he held me against the wall and he's so strong and wanted to kiss me, that's all he wanted to do was kiss me he said and he . . . he was kinda drunk, see, and I kept turning my head away and saying no, and so he . . . he was kissing my neck and such and. . . . He doesn't even know he did this, I bet, I know he doesn't even know. He was drunk, baby, he was drunk is all, but he didn't do anything, not really, he didn't *do* anything, he probably won't even remember anything about it. . . . Please, Walt, don't say anything to him, don't. . . . He's got that gun, baby, he's got. . . . Let's just leave, okay? Can we just leave? Say we'll just leave . . . *please*."

He drew a deep breath and looked up at the ceiling, exhaling slowly.

"You pack us up and I'll make breakfast," she said. "Let's do everything just like normal, all right? Just like normal. You won't say anything to him and—"

"I ain't afraid of him."

"I know, baby, I know you're not, but let's not start any trouble, please. Everybody around here's for him and nobody's for us, so let's just do everything like usual and then we'll go away with Bailey. All right? Okay, baby?"

Walt shrugged and sighed. "Yeah, okay. If that's what you want, honey, then that's what we'll do."

HE WOKE HAPPY from the Johnson dream. The one where his punch landed on Johnson's chin and felt just perfect. And Johnson started down. . . .

Next time, oh man, *next time.*

Then remembered the night before. He was sure she would want to leave and would talk hubby into it, give him some horseshit reason.

Then remembered the love nips he'd put on her neck and how the mug was bound to see them. Brother, was she in for it.

What if he braces you about it?

Him? The mug nearly pisses his pants whenever I look at him. He may be dumb but he ain't totally stupid.

Yeah well. You shouldn't have done it. Not the nips.

What the hell, the whore had it coming. Thinking she could play me.

She can't help it she's a whore. And she couldn't have played you in a hundred years.

She *thought* she could.

Who cares what *she* thought? It was mean and you did it for the lowest reason there is.

And what's that?

You felt sorry for yourself.

About *what?* That she wasn't the trolley girl? Hell, I knew that.

You're sorry she wasn't Kate. You're sorry the trolley girl wasn't Kate. You're sorry none of them is ever—

Cut it out.

If you say so.

Oh, *man* . . .

Tell her you're sorry. Tell her and square it.

She doesn't rate it.

Square it for *you*, man. It wasn't jake and you know it.

All right, all right, enough of this bullshit.

He took the Colt out from under his pillow, where he tucked it every night, then got out of bed and laid the gun beside the washbasin on the dresser.

He washed and got dressed. He was about to go out when he caught sight of himself in the mirror. He took a fighting stance in front of it and began throwing punches, his fists moving in a blur and his head bobbing as he at once tried to hit himself and evade his own attack. He kept at it for several minutes before finally dropping his hands, his chest heaving. Then snaked one more punch at the fellow in the mirror who struck back in the same instant and neither of them flinched and both grinned bigger.

"Call it a draw?" They traded winks.

HE WENT OUT and across the parlor and into the dining room. There was a plate with leftover flapjacks and syrup at one of the places at the table, a mug with a little coffee still in it, a wadded napkin. Another place at the table was set with silverware and a cup and a fresh and folded napkin.

Goldie came out from the kitchen and looked at him without meeting his eyes. "Ready for breakfast?"

"You bet. I see hubby already had his. He tended to the horses?"

"He's doing it now. I'll get your breakfast."

He sat down at the set place, his back to the kitchen door. She returned with a plate of flapjacks and sausage and a mug of smoky coffee. She still would not look at him directly.

"Awful shy this morning."

"I'll get you more butter."

"Wait a minute, listen." He turned in his chair, and she paused at the kitchen door and looked at him without expression.

"Ah . . . about last night, I just want to say I'm—"

"Don't! Please. Let's don't talk about it, not ever." She disappeared into the kitchen.

Well hell. If that's the way she wanted it.

He'd eaten only a few bites when he heard the rear door of the kitchen open and close and the woman say, "Oh God, no."

He looked over his shoulder to see Walt Hurtz standing in the kitchen door, holding the little Remington at the hip and pointed at him.

"Tell her you're sorry, goddamn you," Walt said.

"What?"

"Walt, please—" Goldie said. She stepped up beside him, her eyes frantic.

"*No*, he's gonna tell you he's sorry! Go on, tell her!"

"Sorry?" Ketchel said. "For what?"

"You know goddamn good and well for what, you son of a bitch! Now tell her! Say you're sorry!"

Ketchel stood up and faced him. Walt backed up a step and raised the rifle to chest level. Ketchel gauged the distance between himself and the muzzle.

"Tell her, I said!"

"Quit yelling or you're gonna get me sore." He turned toward Goldie, shifting his weight and setting himself. "What'd you tell this moron?"

Walt cut his eyes at her and Ketchel lunged and snatched the rifle aside, Walt's finger slipping off the trigger. He shouldered Walt hard against the door jamb and wrested the gun from him, then slapped him, dislodging his cap.

Walt gaped at him, his eyes wide and watering and his nose abruptly running. Ketchel's handprint bright red on his cheek.

"You sorry little puke," Ketchel said. He held the rifle like a pistol and jabbed Walt in the chest with the muzzle. "Real killer, huh?"

Walt cringed at the touch of the muzzle. His mouth twitched.

"Take some advice, moron. You want to kill a man, use a real gun, not a toy like this." He waggled the barrel in Walt's face and laughed. "You'da shot me with this, I'da said *ouch* and then took it from you and rammed it so far up your ass it woulda come out your nose."

He looked at Goldie, who stood paralyzed with her fists to her mouth, her eyes huge.

"This stupid hillbilly's exactly what you deserve," Ketchel told her. He tossed the rifle on the bed. "Get out of here, both of you. You're fired."

He turned and sat down to resume his breakfast and was raising the fork to his mouth when Goldie cried, "*No!*"

He was halfway out of his chair when the rifleshot shook the room and he was punched hard on the back and lurched forward and jarred the table and then fell to his knees and folded to the floor. He couldn't catch his breath. He saw the fine grain of the floor planks under his face and felt sick to his stomach and thought he might throw up and then closed his eyes and felt slightly better. He heard the woman saying Oh God oh God and Hurtz saying He had it coming goddamnit he did and then their voices incomprehensibly fast and urgent and then she was saying No listen *listen* here's what happened and then again he couldn't understand their words and then heard heavy fast steps going out of the room and he felt something on his cheek and he knew it was the woman's hand and he wanted to open his eyes but couldn't and he sensed her face near his and heard her ask in a whisper if he was alive and heard himself groan and her hand left him and again heavy running steps and Hurtz saying I got it I got it and he felt hands at his pockets and heard steps hurrying into the kitchen and the screech of the rear door and voices outside and a shout of I shot the son of a bitch!

HE KNEW HE'D been unconscious but sensed that it hadn't been long. He was not breathing well, as if something sharply rigid were wedged high under his ribs near the base of his throat. He could not overcome his astonishment at being floored by a .22 round. He made it to hands and knees but when he tried to stand up the floor swayed and he fell over. He was able to get back to all fours, then moved ahead ponderously, each forward placement of hand and knee a grunting effort, the floor seeming to give to right and left with each shifting of his weight as if it were a thin raft afloat. His improbable notion was to get to his gun and go after Hurtz. He traversed the dining room and made the parlor, blood dripping from his chin, smearing on the planks under his knees. He several times collapsed and then was crawling again. Now he was in his room and paused to rest. Now at the dresser and pausing again, thinking It was only a goddamn .22 for Christ's sake, you only had the wind knocked out of you, that's all, you're all right, you're all right. Now *get up*. Onnnne. . . . Twoooo. . . . Groaning, gasping, using the dresser knobs to help pull himself up to his knees. Threeee. . . . Foooour. . . . Up on one knee now. Fiiiive. . . . Siiiix. . . . Grabbing the top of the dresser and bringing down the wash basin on its doily with a clanging splash. Sevvvven. . . . Eiiight. . . . Get up, man, get up! . . . Niiinne. . . . He was up. And saw the Colt was gone. The room undulated. He reeled to his bed and fell.

WHEN NEXT HE opened his eyes, he was lying on his side, his breath coming harder.

A stranger sat in a chair close beside the bed. He said, "I'm Noland, the carpenter. Bailey phoned the doctor in Conway. The constable, too. And the colonel over in Springfield. The colonel's coming on a special train. Help's coming, mister."

"Thirsty," Ketchel said. He started to roll onto his back but Noland grabbed him and said, "Don't do that. You been shot in the back. Stay on your side."

Noland fetched a glass of water and sat on the edge of the bed and held Ketchel's head as he put the glass to his lips.

Ketchel took a few sips. "There's blood in the water. I taste it."

"Hang on, mister. They'll be here soon."

"I guess they got me, huh?"

Noland nodded sadly, wondering who this man was and who it was that had got him.

THE CONWAY CONSTABLE arrived, accompanied by a doctor. Ketchel was only partly conscious as they got his shirt off and the doctor examined the wound. He heard the doctor speaking low like a priest in the confessional, felt the constable gently searching his pockets, heard him curse and say he'd likely been robbed. And then he was out again. . . .

And then again awake, though he could not muster the strength to open his eyes. He heard talk. . . . Walt Hurtz on the lam. . . . The woman under arrest. . . .

And then again awake to feel a hand stroking his hair, and opened his eyes. Saw it was the colonel, his gaze tearful.

"You're going to be all right, son, you are. You are. Tell me, *was* it Walter Hurtz? Was it him, son?"

"Yes." He tasted blood.

The colonel stroked Ketchel's face and said they were taking him to the hospital, where surgeons would be waiting to fix him up good as new. "I'll be right back, son. And I'll be with you all the way." He left the room and then Ketchel heard him say, "No-good lowdown bitch!" and the sound of what could only be a slap, and a woman yelped and someone said, "Enough! Enough now!" Then the colonel shouting, "*Five thousand dollars* to the man who brings me that son of a bitch dead. *Dead,* you hear! Not a nickel for him alive! Put the word out! Five thousand for the bastard's head! Bring me his head!"

Daddy. . . .

THEY CARRIED HIM out lying sidewise on the mattress and laid it in a wagon and drove him to the train, the colonel and two doctors at his side. He heard one say something about a kind of cavity filling up, about drowning, and he wondered who it was that had drowned and where. At the depot they carried him into a coach and laid him on a waiting cot. He heard somebody say all scheduled runs had been shunted onto sidings so the colonel's train could speed straight through to Springfield. And it seemed as though the train rumbled under him for bare minutes before they were carrying him off and under a bright cold sun to a motor truck and placing him on the mattress in its bed and the truck was moving and the colonel was saying, "Almost there, son, almost there," and he could hear his father sobbing and cursing the driver, ordering him to go faster, goddamnit, and then they had him on a gurney and were wheeling him down various corridors and into a room with overhead lights so bright he could see them through his closed eyelids and all the while his breathing became more labored and the taste of blood was stronger and he felt himself quivering as if he were still on the rumbling train and. . . .

. . . he's riding the rails on a boxcar roof under a starry night sky and laughing at some joke by the hobo called Steamer and seeing the one called Eight Ball dangling from the rods and ripping to pieces and remembering Butte's bonecracking winter cold and its summer stinks and its lack of color and no birds and Kate Morgan's eloquent eyes and marvelous ass and happy laughter and expert instruction in shooting a revolver and he loves her more than he'll ever love anyone else on earth and the blue fog of San Francisco like a dream and pretty Molly on that New Year's Eve so happy and then so scared and fighting Joe Thomas in a nighttime thunderstorm and laughing with the wonderful Arapaho Sisters and the three of them dancing together and them talking him into the tattoo and all the fine days in all the good training camps and playing poker with Joe O'Connor and the Goat and getting caught cheating in the bunkhouse and the train trips across the amazing beauty of the country and Billy Papke's heartbreak on his bloody face after their last fight and the redhead with Jack Johnson and her peachy tits and wondering evermore if they were freckled and seeing big black Jack on the canvas looking up in disbelief and laughing with those gold teeth as he hit Jeffries again and waving so long as he gunned away in the yellow Packard and Jack London's grand inscription and swaying on the tabletop in Raul's yelling of ashes and dust and all the grand times in New York with Willie Britt and the smothering flowers of his grave and Jewel reading his behind and Evelyn showing him the front-row seat and sobbing into her pillow and his mother playing the piano and he and John singing and Killer Kid Tracy saying where you want the body sent and . . .

. . . he laughed through the blood and. . . .

From the *New York Times* edition of October 16, 1910:

> SPRINGFIELD, Mo., Oct. 15—Stanley Ketchel, champion middleweight pugilist of the world, died here tonight at 7:03 o'clock as a result of being shot through the right lung early to-day. . . .

From the *Springfield Leader* edition of October 16; 1910:

> **GRIM REAPER CONQUERS KETCHEL IN LAST GREAT FIGHT OF HIS CAREER**
>
> *Pugilist Dies Shortly After His Arrival At Springfield Hospital*
>
> Though fighting with the same dogged grit and vitality that have marked his career in the ring, Stanley Ketchel, the pugilist, went down to defeat in his last battle, fought against the one foe before whom all must fall. . . .

VERY LATE THAT night Wilson Mizner was in a Manhattan saloon rolling dice with the bartender for the round when a sportswriter came in and announced that Stanley Ketchel had been shot dead in Missouri by the jealous husband of a tootsie who was making Ketchel's breakfast.

There was excited murmuring along the bar. Mizner stared at the hack a moment, then rolled the dice. Boxcars.

He swore softly and paid off the bartender, then headed for the door. He was almost to it when he stopped and turned and shouted at the room: "Bullshit! They couldn't kill that kid with a cannon. Tell them to start counting to ten over him and he'll get up. They'll see! They'll see!"

Finales

The day after the shooting, Walter Hurtz, soon revealed to be Walter Dipley, was captured at a nearby farm, identified by the tattoos on his arms, and charged with the murder of Stanley Ketchel. Goldie Hurtz, soon revealed to be Goldie Smith, was charged as his accomplice.

Goldie cried rape. And Dipley claimed he killed Ketchel in self-defense when he confronted him about the attack on his wife and Ketchel threatened to shoot him.

At first, the couple received a measure of public sympathy due to the "unwritten law" that justified a husband's killing of his wife's violator, but when it became known that Walt and Goldie were in fact not married but living in sin, the sympathy largely waned. And as still other unsavory details about the defendants were brought to light in the newspapers, public opinion almost entirely turned against them.

Stanley Ketchel's body was buried in the Polish cemetery in Grand Rapids, Michigan, on October 20, 1910. Three months later Walter Dipley and Goldie Smith stood trial in the hamlet of Marshfield, seat of Webster County, Missouri.

ACCORDING TO THE defendants, Ketchel raped Goldie on the night of October 14, and later that evening she told Dipley about it. The following morning, Ketchel was seated at breakfast and had his revolver in his waistband when Dipley accused him of the assault. He looked at Dipley over his shoulder and threatened to kill him, saying: "God damn you, if you start anything I will shoot you in two." Dipley grabbed up a .22 rifle leaning against the foot of the dining room bed and told Ketchel to put up his hands. Ketchel said he would not, then started to stand and reach for his gun. Fearing for his life, Dipley shot him. He took the revolver from the fallen Ketchel in case he yet had the strength to use it. He and Goldie then left the house and ran into Bailey and Brazeale and told them what happened. Bailey advised that he turn himself in to the Conway constable. But Dipley knew that R. P. Dickerson had many friends in the region, including the constable, and he feared what they might do to him in the Conway jail. He intended to give himself up to the sheriff in Marshfield, in whose jail he believed he would be safer. But he was captured before he got there.

Assisted by a talented attorney hired by R. P. Dickerson, the prosecution derided Dipley's claim of self-defense and emphasized the defendants' criminal pasts and low reputations. As a navy deserter, Dipley had been a fugitive from justice even before taking flight after murdering Mr. Ketchel, and the Smith woman was on judicial record as an unfit mother and was widely known to have led a sordid personal life. The sheriff of Coffeyville himself testified to her immoral livelihood in Kansas. In contrast, the state presented Stanley Ketchel as a person of exemplary character and called forth a series of respectable witnesses to so testify, though it seemed odd to some observers that R. P. Dickerson was not put on the stand, he who had been Ketchel's closest friend.

The state offered at least two possible motives for the murder. The most likely was robbery. Mr. Ketchel was known to carry as much as a thousand dollars on his person at all times, but when he was found mortally wounded in the house his pockets were empty. Although no cash had been found on Dipley when he was arrested, neither had he been in possession of Mr. Ketchel's pistol, having hidden it in a corn crib, as he later confessed, and where it was recovered. Who could say where he might have hidden the money in hope of recovering it later? Perhaps the defendants had intended simply to rob Mr. Ketchel and make their escape before he could notify police, but of course Mr. Ketchel would have resisted, and he was shot from behind when some distraction, most likely the Smith woman, caused him to turn his back to Dipley. The couple had then hastily fabricated their account of rape and mortal threat. Another possibility, considering her nature and personal history, was that the Smith woman attempted to seduce Mr. Ketchel and, given his upright character, was certainly rebuffed. Her pride injured and her relation with Dipley at risk should Mr. Ketchel inform him of her overture, she lied to Dipley about being raped, enraging him to homicide.

Whatever the killers' true motive, the prosecution concluded, all that mattered were the facts. And the plainest and most irrefutable fact of the case was that Stanley Ketchel, the middleweight champion of the world and a man revered by millions, a man who in the short time he'd lived in the region had become a highly respected member of the Springfield community, had been shot in the back. *In the back,* gentlemen of the jury. What could be more deliberate than a back shooting? What could be more cowardly? What could be more manifestly murderous?

Other than hold fast to the contention of self-defense, Dipley's lawyers could do little except to claim prejudicial motive by the prosecution. The persistent disparagement of the defendants through R. P. Dickerson's friends in the press and the denigration of their characters by Dickerson's crony lawyer in the hire of the state were motivated expressly by Dickerson's misguided desire for revenge. And the reason R. P. Dickerson was so vehemently bent on vengeance was that he was in fact the sire of Stanley Ketchel.

The assertion raised eyebrows across the country. What basis the defense had for making the claim was never revealed, nor what evidence, if any, it possessed to substantiate it. Nevertheless, defense lawyers asked various witnesses if they were aware that R. P. Dickerson was Stanley Ketchel's father. In every instance, the state immediately objected and the judge each time sustained.

Dickerson publicly refuted the allegation. He said he wished it were true he was Stanley's father, for he was the sort of young man anyone would be proud to call son, but in fact he and the young champion had simply been the best of friends. He admitted that he had been schoolmates with Ketchel's mother in Michigan, but that was the extent of his relationship with her. He said the defense attorneys should be horsewhipped for causing such malicious and unwarranted embarrassment to Mrs. Ketchel with their falsehoods, especially in this time of her immeasurable grief.

Sought out by reporters for comment, Julia Ketchel said the

matter was embarrassing, and was quoted as stating: "If necessary to convict the slayer of my son, I will go to the witness stand and tell the whole world of my relations with R. P. Dickerson."

The colonel hastened to explain that the brave woman simply meant she was not only willing to come all the way to Missouri to undergo the terrible humiliation of denying the outlandish accusation in an open courtroom, but was willing as well to suffer at even closer hand the publicity attendant upon her son's murder, not to mention the ordeal of having to look upon the faces of his assassins.

As it happened, there was no need of Julia Ketchel's appearance in the courtroom. The judge ruled that since R. P. Dickerson had not been obliged to take the witness stand, the question of his relationship to the victim was immaterial.

On January 24, 1911, Walter Dipley and Goldie Smith were found guilty of the first-degree murder of Stanley Ketchel. The only point of debate among the jurors during their seventeen hours of deliberation pertained to the matter of sentencing. All of them were in favor of Dipley's execution, but some argued that since both defendants were equally guilty they should receive equal punishment, and not a man of them was willing to send a woman to the gallows. Thus did Goldie save Walt from the noose. They were both sentenced to life imprisonment.

Their conviction was appealed to the state supreme court, which determined that, since she had taken no part in the shooting and there had been no proof of conspiracy, Goldie was guiltless. She had served seventeen months when she was set free.

Walter Dipley's conviction was upheld. He would be paroled in 1934 and die in Utah of kidney disease in 1956.

• • •

GOLDIE SMITH HAD hoped for celebrity on her release from prison, envisioning herself portrayed in national magazines as the Evelyn Nesbit of the Ozarks. She was bitterly disappointed by the universal lack of interest in her story. She would move back to Springfield and manage a café for a time before taking her fourth husband, "Gentleman Jim" Hooper, a silver-haired gambler of bright personal charm whose luck at the tables went suddenly dark. He would finally turn to barbering in order to make a living, then one day settle into the shop chair for his usual noontime nap and never wake up. Goldie would grieve briefly. By then a corpulent dowd, she would not marry again, and would spend her final years as a seller of gimcrackery from the porch of her house.

ROLLIN P. DICKERSON paid five thousand dollars for a Vermont marble monument more than twelve feet tall to stand over Ketchel's grave. He refused, however, to pay the five thousand dollar reward to the men who'd captured Dipley. The reward, the colonel argued, was specifically for bringing in Dipley dead, not alive. The case went to court and the judge ruled that Dickerson's stipulation was unlawful in that it amounted to solicitation of homicide. The colonel was ordered to pay the reward.

Age would neither dull the color of Dickerson's character nor curb his eccentric leanings. On America's entry in the Great War, he would propose to create and command a volunteer regiment of "Rough Riders" to confront the Hun, and the United States government would politely decline his offer. So he would instead establish the world's largest mule ranch in order to ensure that the U. S. Army met with no shortage of good mules. Following the armistice, he would press his political friends in Jefferson City to pass legislation granting surplus military armament, including machine guns and hand grenades, to police departments around the state, the better to arm them against the red troublemakers that continued to plague the republic. He would be instrumental in the formation of a loyalty league whose purpose was to foster patriotism in all corners of the country and maintain vigilance against subversive groups. He would keep wild animals as pets, including a pair of African lions, one of whom he named Stanley. He would permit them to roam freely over the estate and would quip that he had no problem with trespassers.

He would make a sort of shrine of Ketchel's ranch house bedroom. Would hang its walls with posters advertising his fights against Joe Thomas, Billy Papke, Philadelphia Jack O'Brien, and Jack Johnson. With framed photographs of Ketchel in the ring and on the town in New York, at work on the ranch, puffing a cigar on the porch, dandling his young niece on his knee. With a photo of Ketchel standing alongside Emmett Dalton at the Democratic convention in Jeff City and both of them staring narrow-eyed at the camera, and with one of Ketchel and the colonel himself, each with an arm around the other's shoulders, both of them laughing hard at some joke the colonel had ever since tried to recall but could not. Every year, on the fifteenth of October, Dickerson would go into that special room with several bottles of whiskey and a box of cigars and shut himself inside and not emerge until two or three or four days later, haggard and red-eyed with drink and with weeping. An annual ritual he would maintain until his death in 1938.

THE NEWS OF Ketchel's killing nearly broke Billy Papke's heart. Now he could never prove to the world he was the better of that son of a bitch.

Born just three days after Stanley Ketchel, Billy Papke would outlive him by twenty-six years. Yet it would be difficult to argue that his extra quarter century of life constituted any kind of victory over his nemesis.

Even after Ketchel's death, Papke's claim to the middleweight title would not be universally recognized. The lack of full recognition would rankle him for the next three years and then he would lose his portion of the championship to Frank Klaus in Paris by disqualification for persistent fouling. He would not fight for more than two years, and then barely manage a draw in Brooklyn against a palooka. Almost four years would pass before his next and final fight, a four-round loss in San Francisco.

He would then work as a referee for a time. He would serve as host for a posh Los Angeles nightclub and regale patrons with recounts of his fights, the most often requested being those of his contests with Ketchel. He would invest heavily in California real estate and prosper hugely. He would drink to excess. He would fall in love with and marry a woman of a nature as mercurial as his own. They would have tempestuous quarrels and she would eventually file for divorce on grounds of extreme cruelty. On Thanksgiving Day of 1936, he would present himself quite drunk at her house and attempt to have sex with her. She would threaten to call the police. He would plead. She would laugh at him. He would break things and she would curse him. He would hit her. She would say she wished she could have met Stanley Ketchel and fucked him till she fainted.

Whereupon he would produce a pistol and shoot her through the heart.

And then put the gun to his own head.

• • •

When he heard of Ketchel's fatal shooting, Emmett Dalton mused upon the irony by which he himself could absorb a number of large-caliber bullets and two loads of buckshot squarely in the back and still be walking the earth eighteen years afterward, albeit with a permanent limp, while the middleweight champ was done for by a single .22 round.

He would go to California and write Western movies and even star in one of them, would appear on moviehouse stages in a desperado getup, sign autographs for wide-eyed boys. He would gain entry to Hollywood social circles. He would write books, one of which was called *When the Daltons Rode* and was adapted into a popular motion picture, as well. He would become a building contractor and real estate broker and grow richer in those enterprises than he and his brothers could have dreamed of becoming by way of robbing banks. He would take up golf, join a Moose Lodge, become a Rotarian. He would regularly attend church with his wife. At age sixty-six he would die in his sleep. With, according to some, a discernible smile.

Evelyn Nesbit read Ketchel's obituary in the *New York Times.* The report roused a vague memory of their evening together, but then she pushed it out of her mind and hurried off to that morning's rehearsal. It was a stage comedy in which she portrayed the part of a beautiful girl torn between the true love of a poor but goodhearted farm boy and the lickerish attentions of a rich and randy old man. Over the following years she would have other small parts in other trivial theater works and then play minor roles in insignificant motion pictures. Then be an old and lonely woman for a long time before dying in a Hollywood nursing home in 1967.

• • •

JACK LONDON HAD just finished his day's writing when he got word of Ketchel's murder. He poured a full tumbler of rye and raised it to his eastward window. "Here's to you, champ. Ashes, I say, *ashes*!" Then drained the entire glass in a single breath and coughed until his eyes were pouring tears and his lips were flecked with blood.

Even as he continued to travel about the world and write his daily quota of a thousand words, London's health would degenerate apace and his luck run poorly. Within the next six years he would be plagued by a worsening insomnia, his wife would miscarry and thenceforth be unable to conceive, his beloved Wolf House would be razed by fire, he would have an appendectomy, he would contract dysentery and pleurisy, he would suffer from acute rheumatism and a severe and chronic nephritis. He would die in bed on the 22nd of November, 1916. The cause of death officially recorded as "uraemia following renal colic," though in truth it might have been a stroke. Or, as some would have it, an ultimate failure of the heart.

JACK JOHNSON WAS at Sheepshead Bay to race against Barney Oldfield when he was told the news in all its particulars. He did not respond immediately but looked off to seaward and the muscular white clouds rising off the horizon. Then showed his golden smile and said: "Dollar to a doughnut Mr. Stanley was starting to turn around to try and catch that bullet with his *teeth* . . ."

The following year, Johnson would marry Etta Duryea, who some months later would kill herself, by some accounts because of Johnson's relentless philandering. He would own a popular café in Chicago. He would continue his public dalliances with white women and would be charged with violation of the Mann Act, a federal law enacted to combat the white slave trade but also quite useful for the prosecution of bothersome persons who had broken no other law. At the time of his conviction in 1913, he would be married to Lucille Cameron, another white woman. While his case was under appeal he would flee the country and spend the next seven years in vagabond exile. He would wander through Europe and Latin America, live for a time in France, in Germany, Spain, Mexico. He would have great difficulty contracting for matches of much worth. In a span of almost five years after the Jeffries fight, he would be able to arrange but four defenses of his title. The last of them would be on April 5, 1915, in Havana, Cuba, against gigantic Jess Willard, who would batter him terribly and knock him out in the twenty-sixth round. Johnson would afterward claim the fight had been fixed, that he had taken a bribe to lose, that part of the deal was a government promise to drop the charges against him but he was double-crossed. To everyone who was there, however, it was obvious that Willard outfought him. In 1920 he would at last surrender to American authorities. He would be sentenced to a year in Leavenworth penitentiary and be released before the full term of the sentence. He would divorce Lucille and marry yet again. His last ring victory would be a third-round knockout when he was fifty-four years old. He would continue to box exhibition matches into the mid-1940s, the last of them at age sixty-seven.

On June 10, 1946, on a highway near Raleigh, North Carolina, he would be killed in a car crash. The cause of which, according to reports, was excessive speed.

WITHDRAWN
BY
WILLIAMSBURG REGIONAL LIBRARY

Acknowledgments

For their kind and valuable assistance I am grateful to:

Robin Urban and Richard I. Gibson of the World Museum of Mining in Butte, Montana;

Sharol Higgins Neely of the Springfield–Greene County Library in Springfield, Missouri;

The Tucson–Pima County Library in Tucson, Arizona.